THE FORGOTTEN WORLDS
BOOK 2

THE NAVEL
OF THE WORLD

P.J. HOOVER

CHILDREN'S BRAINS ARE YUMMY BOOKS
AUSTIN, TEXAS

The Navel of the World
The Forgotten Worlds
Book 2

Text Copyright © 2009 by P.J. Hoover

Jacket Art © iStockphoto.com/cvoogt

For more information, write:
CBAY Books
PO Box 92411
Austin, TX 78709

First Edition 2009
ISBN(10): 1-933767-14-6
ISBN (13): 978-1-933767-14-7
CIP data available.

Children's Brains are Yummy Books
Austin, Texas
www.cbaybooks.com

For Zachary, my original Nogical

TABLE OF CONTENTS

CHAPTER 1

THE INCONVENIENT GIANT SQUID

As soon as the elevator passed by, Benjamin Holt jumped; and then he started falling—straight down the shaft. Sure, he'd planned to levitate himself, but seeing as how he was out of practice, he dropped a good two hundred floors before he finally got the whole levitation thing under control. Outside the world looked like thick black soup, with glowing sea creatures hitting up against the elevator shaft, staring in at Benjamin. Half of them looked like they'd survived the fall of the dinosaurs and never planned to chance extinction again. He reached out toward them, and they flitted away, back to wherever they'd lived for the last million years. So Benjamin turned back around. And here the day had started out so boring.

At first Benjamin thought working in his dad's office over spring break would be cool—spending the week hanging out in Wondersky City with Andy Grow. And to be honest, at first it had been—being back in Lemuria; skyscrapers so tall they poked out of the top of the underwater dome and into the ocean above. But things had gone downhill—fast.

For starters, the last person in the world he'd wanted to see had shown up—Ryan Jordan. Apparently Ryan's parents thought working in an office all vacation was a good idea, too. Then when Nathan Nyx, their boss for the week, had shown them the Records Room, the real torture began:

 1

hours upon hours of mind-numbingly torturous, pointless filing. The problem with the records was that they never stopped. Before one could be filed, five more pumped in through the feed.

Ryan had been the smart one. He left the room a nano-second after Nathan teleported away and only came back during breaks. And it hadn't taken Andy long either. He decided spying around the office was way more fun than filing records, so he left, too. Some best friend. Which left Benjamin alone most of the time playing mental games to keep himself from going crazy.

But Wednesday mid-morning when Benjamin found the record with his name on it, everything changed. It must've come through the chute months ago. Maybe even years. It only caught Benjamin's eye when, by sheer luck, one of the stacks toppled over and almost killed him.

"Look at this." Benjamin handed the record over to Andy when he walked into the room. It looked like all the others: thinner than a piece of paper; stripes on the side to distinguish which boring category to put it in; yellow graphical screen with data crammed everywhere. After looking at millions and billions of records, Benjamin needed a second opinion. The words and pictures on them shifted each time he read one; by now, his eyes hurt so bad, he'd started filing with them closed—which resulted in sometimes the records going in the right places, some-times not. Benjamin didn't really care.

"What?" Andy reached out and took it. "Another re-cord on garbage disposal in Lemuria?"

Benjamin shook his head. "I don't think so."

"But it has the funny purple stripes on it." Andy pointed

at the colored stripes running up the left side which labeled it as waste management.

"I know," Benjamin said. "But I don't think it's about getting rid of trash. Read it."

Andy looked down at the page. "I can't."

Benjamin shrugged. Okay, so he couldn't read it either. Most of it looked like it was written in Ancient Lemurian—the language of the hidden continent at the bottom of the Pacific Ocean—which Benjamin hadn't bothered to learn.

"We'll have to get Gary to translate it. But what can you read?"

Andy looked again, then met Benjamin's gaze. "Your name."

Benjamin nodded.

"And what's this weird symbol at the top of the page?" Andy asked.

Benjamin shook his head. "I don't know. I've seen it before, but I can't remember where."

Actually, Benjamin remembered exactly where he'd seen the three intertwined hearts. He'd seen then above the door to the secret chamber where he'd left the three keys of Shambhala. The three keys he'd spent all last summer looking for.

Andy handed it back over. "Maybe Gary will recognize it." Which might actually be possible. Their friend Gary Goodweather recognized constellations in other galaxies. And if he ran into something he didn't know, he went to the library to find out.

Before Benjamin could reach out and take it back, the door opened, and Ryan Jordan walked in. Benjamin caught the flash in Ryan's mind before his mind block went

 3

up. He'd been eavesdropping. Ryan took one look at them, reached out and grabbed the record, and ran.

Which explained the elevator shaft thing—kind of. Benjamin took off after Ryan, bumping into the boss man Nathan Nyx as soon as he ran out of the room. Nathan flew backwards and landed flat on his butt.

"What's the rush?" Nathan stood up and rubbed his back side.

Benjamin saw Ryan run for the elevators and enter something on the keypad. He forced himself to take a deep breath and look at Nathan.

"No rush," Benjamin said.

Just then Andy ran out of the horrible record room and stopped.

Nathan laughed. "Are you guys having too much fun filing?"

Benjamin cringed. Nathan gave him the willies. It wasn't that Nathan looked gross or creepy or anything. It was just that after three days of taking orders from the over-energetic brown-noser, Benjamin couldn't stand the sight of him—not to mention the sound of his voice. What his dad saw in this guy was nothing short of a mystery.

"Yeah," Andy said. "We're having way too much fun."

"Which is why we need to get some fresh air," Benjamin said. And then he started walking for the elevator. Whatever the record had said, Benjamin needed to get it back. With both his name and the strange heart symbol on it, it was probably the closest thing he'd found to a lead since the end of last summer—back when everything had changed, back when Helios Deimos, one of the rulers of Lemuria, had told him he was actually one of triplets, separated at birth and hidden away. And that Benjamin's most important task in life was to find his two missing brothers.

Yeah, and that was all Helios had said. No other hints. Or clues. Or anything that might give Benjamin some idea where his brothers might be. For all the luck Benjamin had finding them so far, they may as well have teleported to Saturn.

Nathan Nyx stepped out of the way, letting Benjamin and Andy pass. "Just don't be gone long; we have lots of records to file."

If by 'we' he meant Benjamin, then Nathan was right.

"And the elevator on the left is only going up," Nathan added. "Giant squid stuck on the lower floors again."

Great. As long as these elevators took, it would take another hour before he could follow Ryan. An hour Benjamin did not plan to wait. So when the elevator on the left lifted, Benjamin looked down the shaft, took a deep breath, and jumped.

It's not that Benjamin couldn't levitate himself. After all he was a telegen—not a human, and if anything, he was one of the better students in telekinesis. Once he got the fall under control, he slowed at each floor and peeked out. No Ryan so far. Sure, the giant squid hanging on the outside of the shaft was pretty cool. But after three days of having elevator delays because of tentacles wrapped around the lifting components, he kind of wished squid-rights activists didn't care so much, and that the squids could just be zapped or something.

Around floor 314, Benjamin finally spotted Ryan. He slowed his descent, jumped from the elevator shaft, and chased Ryan down a hallway. But then Ryan ran into a room and slid the door closed behind him. It was only once Andy managed to join Benjamin that they were able to pry the door open. Ryan stood there amid ten record copying machines, holding the purple striped record in his hand and smiling.

"Oh, was this yours?" Ryan held up the record with his thumb and two fingers.

Benjamin reached out to grab it. "Seriously, why are you such a pain?" But before he could get the record, Ryan yanked it away.

"Me?" Ryan feigned a pathetic innocent look. "I'm only filing things."

"Just hand it over," Andy said, and Benjamin noticed the record come loose from Ryan's fingers. Andy was using telekinesis to get it. So Benjamin joined in. After all, two of them working against Ryan would be a sure win.

But Ryan grabbed it back. "It's a trash record. Nothing else." And before Benjamin or Andy could do anything, Ryan flung it across the room with telekinesis and pitched it in the record recycler. Then he smirked at Benjamin and walked out of the room.

Benjamin ran over to the recycler even though he knew it would be useless. He'd recycled enough records this week to know there was no coming back. Once a record had gone to the great big graveyard under the ocean, it was gone. And with it so was any clue as to the location of Benjamin's brothers.

"What now?" Andy walked over to join him.

Benjamin turned around. "Now we kill Ryan Jordan?"

Andy laughed. "Fine with me, but Nathan Nyx may

have a problem. He'd have to tell Ryan's parents."

"They'd probably thank us," Benjamin said. "When we get back to summer school, I swear I'm going to teleport Ryan's teeth out of his mouth."

"You guys have a problem?"

Benjamin and Andy turned at the sound of the voice.

"Joey!" Sure, Benjamin had known Joey Duncan worked with his dad, but it was already Wednesday, and they hadn't seen him yet.

"What are you doing here?" Andy asked.

Joey laughed. "Shouldn't I be asking you that? You guys work two hundred stories up."

"There's a squid on the shaft," Benjamin said. "We can't get back up."

Joey smiled. "You'd think with all the technology this place has, they'd be able to figure out how to solve the squid problem." He narrowed his eyes. "What are you guys doing down here anyway? This is a restricted area."

Benjamin thought fast, glad he'd been working on his mind blocks. He could keep his parents out. He could keep Joey Duncan out. And he could definitely keep Andy out. Probably the only person he'd never be able to keep out of his mind was Heidi Dylan, but then, when it came to telepathy, she was nothing short of an enigma.

"We were trying to make a copy of a record, but then it accidentally got recycled," Benjamin said. Which wasn't all together untrue.

Joey walked over to the nearest machine. "So you made the copy then?"

"No," Benjamin said.

Joey pushed a couple holographic buttons. "But the

machine says it just made a copy."

Benjamin looked at Andy. "*Ryan*," he said to Andy telepathically. "*He copied the record.*"

Andy's eyes lit up. "Can it make us another copy?" he asked Joey. "We must've recycled the other one."

So the good news was at least they now had a copy of the record. The bad news was Ryan Jordan almost certainly did, too. And the even worse news was that once Joey took them back up to the five hundred and whatever-eth floor, they had to explain to Nathan Nyx why they'd been down there anyway.

Luckily, Joey was way cool and covered their butts. "We were just hanging out watching the squid intervention team," he said.

Nathan narrowed his eyes. "Mr. Holt won't be happy. He wanted Benjamin and Andy to work over spring break. Not watch the sea life."

Like Benjamin's dad would really care. Benjamin had hardly seen his dad all week aside from the commute.

Joey smiled. "I'll talk to Mr. Holt myself."

Nathan frowned, but given that he was really nothing more than a glorified mail boy, and Joey was...well, Benjamin wasn't really sure what Joey was, but then again he wasn't sure what his own dad did either, Nathan didn't say anything. All he knew was neither Joey nor his dad were responsible for spring break interns, and Nathan Nyx was, which had to say something about the pecking order.

Nathan placed a hand each on Benjamin and Andy's shoulders. "Time for more filing."

CHAPTER 2

JACK IS BACK

Benjamin and Andy bolted for the door when Benjamin's dad finally showed up at lunchtime, leaving Ryan alone amidst the remaining untouched towers of records. Seriously, Benjamin had about reached the point of just shoving them all in the record recycler. Okay, so he had shoved a few hundred in; who would ever miss them anyway?

"Isn't Ryan joining you guys for lunch?" Benjamin's dad asked while they waited for the elevator. Thankfully, an hour ago whoever was in charge of building maintenance had decided it was acceptable to shock the squid to remove it, so now both elevators were in service.

"Ryan's a jerk," Benjamin said.

Andy nodded. "Yeah, talk about having to work with your arch enemy all week. It sucks."

"Not to mention the records," Benjamin added. "I swear, Dad, if you ever make me work here again, I'll run away from home."

Benjamin's dad laughed. "And go where?"

Benjamin scowled. "Anywhere that doesn't involve staring at tiny letters that keep changing around on a screen." His mind flew to the copy of the record with his name on it. Not that he could read the thing, but at least the information stored on it seemed to stay constant.

By the time they reached the atrium, Benjamin felt the first bits of freedom seep into him. No more records. No more Nathan Nyx—at least for a few hours. They had an extra long lunch and were planning to use a public teleporter to meet Heidi, Gary, and Iva back in the capital city of Mu.

But when he rounded the corner, Benjamin slammed to a halt, just barely stopping in time to avoid running his face into the tiny green man hovering in the air.

"Jack! Where've you been?"

The Nogical laughed and squinted up his yellow eyes. "Not filing records in Wondersky City."

Benjamin shuddered, trying to put the records out of his mind. "Weren't you supposed to visit or something?"

"You know a Nogical?" Benjamin's dad asked.

Benjamin turned to look at his dad. "Oh, I guess I forgot to mention it. Dad, this is Jack. Jack, this is Dad."

"It's a pleasure to meet you," Jack said and pointed to his blue hair. "And as you can see we don't all have orange hair."

"So that rumor is false," Benjamin's dad said, then turned back to Benjamin. "Do you know how rare Nogicals are?"

"Proteus Ajax mentioned that last year, but I guess I never really thought about it," Benjamin said. Sure, they were illegal genetically engineered creatures and all, but Benjamin had met Jack the first day of school last summer, and they'd been friends ever since. "Really, Jack, what gives? I didn't hear from you all year. I thought you were gonna come visit."

"I was," Jack said, "but I didn't want to teleport outside the dome."

Andy narrowed his eyes. "Why? I thought you were a master of teleportation."

"Skill has nothing to do with it." Jack put his small hands on his hips and stood every bit of his six inches tall.

"Jack's right," Benjamin's dad said.

Benjamin and Andy looked at him.

"There've been reports of telegens teleporting outside the dome—both naturally and with machines—and then not being able to teleport back," Benjamin's dad explained.

Jack crossed his arms and nodded. "Exactly."

"Why?" Benjamin asked. "What stops teleportation?"

"Well, you know how the power shield around Atlantis is failing?" Benjamin's dad said. The sunken continent of Atlantis had a protective shield around it just like Lemuria did. Except, unlike Lemuria, in the case of Atlantis, the shield was supposed to keep people in.

"Sure." Benjamin had learned all about the shields encasing the two hidden continents last summer. Heck, he'd seen the scales in the Ruling Hall showing how the Atlantis shield was failing.

Benjamin's dad nodded. "The theory is that since the overall shield generating output has to be increased for Atlantis, it's actually causing high changes in the flux of the output for the shield around Lemuria."

Andy's eyes went vacant. "You lost me there."

"Our own shield isn't as stable because of the work being done on the Atlantis shield," Jack translated.

"Exactly!" Benjamin's dad said. "I couldn't have said it better myself."

"I know," Jack said.

 11

"Oh," Benjamin said.

"So that's why I didn't come visit," Jack said.

"Couldn't you have called on the telecom or something?" Benjamin asked.

"Sure, if I wanted my conversation monitored," Jack said.

"Monitored?"

"Of course. You don't think all that exchange of information just gets lost do you? Our security operations have all sorts of agents assigned to listening in on Lemurian and Atlantian conversations all day long." He looked directly at Benjamin's dad. "Right?"

Benjamin's dad flushed and looked down to straighten his shirt collar. "Well, I guess that's somewhat accurate."

Benjamin crossed his arms. "You could have tried telepathy, right?"

"Are you kidding?" Jack said. "You could try listening. Of course I tried telepathy. But after a couple months, I gave up."

"Maybe you were doing it wrong," Benjamin said.

Jack didn't acknowledge the implication. "Of course, I was able to talk with Heidi, but she has an exceptional telepathic mind. Which, I might add, you do not."

"Speaking of which, we really should get going," Benjamin's dad said. "You boys don't want to miss your lunch date."

Benjamin groaned. "It's just lunch, Dad."

"Yeah, not a date," Andy added, though Benjamin was pretty sure Andy wished it was.

Benjamin's dad laughed. "Fine. You don't want to miss your lunch appointment. Let's go."

CHAPTER 3

TELEGNOSTICS ARE LIKE BLOODHOUNDS

Heidi, Iva, and Gary stood outside the Deimos Diner waiting. When Heidi spotted them, she ran over and gave Benjamin a hug. Which was a little weird. Sure, he'd missed her and all, but he'd missed Gary, too, and it's not like he would have hugged Gary. Iva maybe. Or maybe not. Iva Marinina was just so pretty, it made Benjamin's lungs feel like collapsing to even look at her sometimes.

But apparently the pretty thing didn't seem to bother Andy. Benjamin looked over just in time to see Andy lean into a hug with Iva. It lasted a few seconds too long, which Heidi noticed also. She grinned at Benjamin but kept her mouth shut.

"We were wondering if you'd be able to get away." Gary extended his hand to shake both Benjamin's and Andy's. Jack slapped Gary a very small high five before settling back down on Benjamin's shoulder.

Andy laughed. "It was pretty touch and go there at the end, but luckily Benjamin's dad cleared things up with Nathan."

"Who's Nathan?" Iva asked as they headed into the diner and found a table.

"This guy who works for my dad," Benjamin said. "Apparently we work for him this week."

"Really, really boring work." Andy shuddered.

"But at least Ryan Jordan has been suffering with us." Benjamin grabbed a menu and flipped it over. It lit up and started to talk, but before it got a full word out, he flipped it back over.

"Ryan is working there, too?" Iva flipped her own menu over and switched it to the vegetarian options. "In Virginia?"

Andy looked up when Iva asked about Ryan. Benjamin felt jealousy pound through the Alliance bond. Like Iva would ever be interested in Ryan Jordan. Or would she? Sometimes girls were just so hard to understand. Actually, they were always hard to understand.

"It turns out my dad works in Wondersky City." Benjamin watched how Iva silenced her menu, and then he flipped his back over and did the same. At least now he could order.

"Really?" Heidi asked. "What does he do there?"

Of course Heidi would ask.

"I don't know," Benjamin said.

"You've worked there three days, and you don't even know what he does?" Heidi asked.

"Two and a half days," Benjamin said. "And we haven't seen him that much."

"I think he works for an information security company," Andy said.

Benjamin narrowed his eyes. How had Andy come up with something like that? "You do?"

"Did you notice how uncomfortable he got when Jack asked him about monitored conversations?" Andy asked.

Benjamin thought for a moment. "That's true." He

turned to his shoulder where Jack had appeared. "What kind of work, besides filing stacks and stacks of boring records, goes on in Wondersky City?"

"Are you kidding? Did you happen to notice how big the place was?" Jack put up his arms to elaborate which wasn't saying much since they were only a few inches long. "Everything goes on there."

"So you guys have been spending the week filing?" Heidi ordered dessert, and her menu disappeared.

"There's this awful room full of records that need to be sorted," Andy said.

"Actually, there are four rooms. We've only gotten to the first one so far." And then Benjamin remembered it. The record. "There's something you guys need to see, though." And he pulled out the record and handed it over to Gary.

Gary studied it for under a second. "Ancient Lemurian."

Andy laughed. "Yeah, even Benjamin and I figured out that much. But what does it say?"

"Besides my name," Benjamin said.

"Your name's on here?" Iva grabbed the plastic sheet from Gary's hand.

Gary stared at her while she looked at the record. "You plan on translating it?" he asked.

Iva handed it back to Gary. "Maybe."

"Yeah," Andy said. "Once you learn Ancient Lemurian." Iva shot him a glare.

"So what's it say?" Heidi pointed to it. "And what's this weird symbol at the top?"

Gary shrugged. "I don't know about the symbol—it just looks like a few hearts twisted into a paradoxical pattern. But the writing isn't all that old."

 15

"So it's not Ancient Lemurian?" Benjamin asked.

Gary shook his head. "It is. But the sentence structure and grammar look pretty modern as opposed to the ten thousand year old wording I would have expected."

"Whatever." Benjamin shifted in his seat. "Can you read it?"

Jack floated over. "I could have read it. You didn't ask me."

True. Of course Jack knew the forgotten language. "I didn't want to say anything about it in front of my dad."

"Why?" Heidi said. "Didn't you ask him about all the stuff Helios told you last summer?"

"Sure," Benjamin said. "I mean I told him part of it."

Heidi eyed him. There she went reading his mind again.

"Fine," he said. "I didn't tell him anything. I asked him about my birth and all, and he and my mom told me about the whole adoption thing. But they didn't know anything about my birth parents or any triplets or anything like that."

"So you've found out nothing in the last year," Iva said.

"Nothing?" Benjamin pointed to the record. "I found this, didn't I?" Now seemed like a good time to divert the conversation. "Anyway...?" He motioned at Gary and the record.

Gary squinted and frowned.

"What?" Heidi said.

"Well, it's talking about a hidden object," Gary said. "But none of these names or places sounds familiar." He moved his hand over the record and pressed on it. A holographic map appeared in the air above it.

Andy's eyes grew huge. "Whoa."

They crowded closer to Gary. "Whoa is right," Heidi said. "It's a map of Lemuria."

Gary nodded. "Yeah, but where's Mu?" He pointed to some strange letter that looked nothing short of an eyeball on its side. "And here it talks about Geros, the old capital city, and its Ruling Hall, but the capital of Lemuria hasn't been there in millennia."

"Not to mention the ruins of the old ruling hall there were torn down a thousand years ago," Jack added. He floated over and took a giant sip from Benjamin's drink, leaving only about an inch at the bottom.

Benjamin grabbed it away and finished the rest, shooting Jack a dirty look.

"So what about the hidden object?" Iva asked. "I can find it if we go there." Which was true. Iva was so good at telegnosis, she could pick out which hallway Benjamin had walked down three week earlier just by sensing the vibes. Not to mention she could see into the future. So finding random objects never posed a problem.

"It says here to travel to the Ruling Hall in the capital city of Geros," Gary said. "Sixteen floors underground, in a hidden chamber, we'll find the object we need to continue our search."

"More like start my search," Benjamin muttered.

"Fine," Iva said. "So we just go to this Geros place, look in the ruins, and get the object. Right?" She looked around.

Jack settled onto the table and burped. "Geros is a long way away."

"So we use a teleporter," Andy said.

But Jack shook his head. "Nope. There's a problem. Geros is off limits."

"Figures," Andy said.

"And actually there's another problem," Benjamin said.

Heidi's mouth dropped open.

He scowled at her. "Would you stop reading my mind?"

She shut her mouth. "Sorry. It's just with you guys all around, the Alliance bond is a bit overwhelming."

Which was true. The bond the Emerald Tablet had formed last year between the five of them seemed to have intensified five times over since last summer.

"What's the problem?" Gary asked. "We just figure a way to get access and go."

Benjamin sighed. "The problem is Ryan has a copy of this record, too."

Andy laughed. "It's not like he'll be able to read it."

"Ryan's not an idiot," Iva said. "He could get it translated."

Andy's face fell. "I guess that's true. But why would he care?"

But Iva's frown only increased. "What if he doesn't care, but he gives it to someone who does?"

"Like who?" Andy said. "Mr. Burton's dead. And I don't see anyone else trying to kidnap Benjamin and get him to use the keys of Shambhala for their own diabolical purposes."

"Except my birth dad." Benjamin had been trying not to mention it, hoping maybe it would magically go away. But whether he liked it or not, his birth dad was still out there somewhere, trying to find Benjamin.

 18

"He doesn't know who you are," Heidi said.

"But I don't know who he is either," Benjamin said. "And if he's looking for me, then he's bound to be looking for my two birth brothers also."

"Which would explain why Ryan Jordan would care about copying the record," Benjamin said.

Gary stood up. "Ryan may be a worm, but you really think he's working for the enemy?"

Jack shrugged. "Someone always has to be."

"You know, there's one thing I've been thinking about," Iva said. "Something to help find your brothers."

"What?" A weight lifted off Benjamin. Good thing she'd been thinking about ideas, because aside from the record, he had nothing.

Benjamin felt a solid mind block go up around all of them. He looked to his shoulder at Jack, and Jack smiled in return.

"*We can talk without being overheard.*" Jack directed his thoughts to them.

Iva smiled. "*I was talking with Kyri last week on the telecom and she mentioned something.*"

Andy glanced sideways at her. "*You were talking to a teacher during break?*"

Iva ignored him. "*She mentioned some telegnostics can imprint samples of DNA in their minds and then search the earth looking for that specific DNA sequence.*"

"*You mean like bloodhounds?*" At the mere mention of DNA, Gary's eyes had bugged wide open.

Iva nodded her head. "*She told me there are secret organizations that employ telegnostics for just this purpose.*"

"*Our teacher told you about secret organizations?*"

Andy's mouth fell open.

It was pretty amazing. But then Iva was their telegnostic teacher's pet.

"*They employ telegnostics to find people?*" Heidi twisted up her mouth. "*Why?*"

"*All sorts of reasons,*" Jack said. "*Maybe they're criminals, or spies working for Atlantis, or anything.*"

"*Even people looking for long lost relatives,*" Benjamin said. "*But there's one big difference.*"

"*What?*" Iva asked.

"*You said they needed a sample of the DNA to imprint on their minds.*" He blew out the breath he'd been holding. "*We don't have a sample of my brothers' DNA.*"

"*No, we don't.*" Iva smiled. "*But we have you.*"

"*I get it,*" Gary said. "*You're willing to bet that Benjamin's DNA is close enough to his brothers' that we can use it to track them around the Earth.*"

"*Exactly!*" Iva said. "*Even if they aren't identical, they are triplets.*"

Benjamin couldn't help being a little skeptical. "*So, even if my DNA could be used to match up to the DNA we're looking for, what do we do then? March up to the door of one of these secret organizations and ask them to help us locate my long lost brothers?*"

"No, that's not what I'm suggesting!" Iva shouted aloud, forgetting where she was. Telegens at some of the closer tables turned to look, but Iva ignored them. "*If you'd let me finish, maybe you'll understand.*"

Benjamin sighed. Iva was just trying to help. "*Go on.*"

Iva crossed her arms and leaned on her elbows. "*Some telegnostics can do this on their own. But for those*"

who can't, there's a telemagnifier that can boost power."

Gary snapped his fingers. *"So you could use this tele-magnifier and track the DNA signature?"*

Iva nodded. *"That's what I'm hoping."*

"So what is it?" Andy asked. *"And where do we get it?"*

Iva smiled. *"It's called Peridot, and I'm thinking we need to pay Morpheus Midas a visit."*

CHAPTER 4

THE RETURN OF THE CHESS SET

They walked down Mu Way until they found the three dimensional sign with the floating silver cube. The door to the Silver Touch chimed when they walked in—which didn't happen every time. The entry chime was about as reliable as the giant squid in Wondersky City. Sometimes they let go. Sometimes they didn't.

Gary walked over to the center of the store and stopped dead in his tracks. "It's back." His eyes were the size of golf balls, and he almost drooled.

"What's back?" Andy asked, already looking elsewhere.

"The chess set. The Ammolite chess set," Gary said.

Iva ran over to join him. "Oh, it's so beautiful." Her hand went to the pendant she wore around her neck—an oval piece of Ammolite on a leather strap.

Benjamin walked over to join Iva and Gary. "I thought it got sold last year."

"It did," a voice said from the back of the store. "But the new owner decided it could stay here as long as we played a game once a week."

They turned at the voice.

"Morpheus!" Heidi said.

Benjamin turned to see Gary staring in the direction

of Morpheus' voice with his mouth wide open. And then he saw what Gary was staring at. Actually who Gary was staring at.

"*It's him!*" Gary said telepathically. "*It's the guy from the Bangkok Chess Open.*"

"*You're right!*" Iva said. "*And also Fortune City.*"

"Sheer coincidences I assure you," the man standing next to Morpheus Midas replied, obviously reading their thoughts.

But based on all those coincidences, if anyone had asked Benjamin last year who he thought the person searching for the keys of Shambhala had been, this man would have been first on the list—way ahead of Mr. Burton, the real perpetrator.

"What are you doing here?" Gary looked like he was about to have a convulsion. "What's he doing here?" he asked Morpheus.

The man rubbed his beard. "I'm playing chess on my chess set."

"Your chess set?" Andy had come over to join his friends; even an amoeba could have sensed Gary's annoyance through the Alliance bond.

"Of course—my chess set," the man said. "I bought it last year after winning the Bangkok Chess Open."

"Winning!" Gary said. "How can you say that? You were reading minds. That's cheating. And if you cheat, you're not technically a winner."

The man slapped Morpheus on the back, causing Morpheus to lurch forward a couple steps. "It was only on Morpheus here that I had to resort to telepathy. With humans, it's a matter of superiority."

"So you admit it. You cheated," Gary said.

The man tried to hold his smile, but it was fading—big time. "If you consider telepathy with another telegen cheating, then, yes, I suppose I cheated."

"Enough, enough," Morpheus interrupted. "Kids, I want you to meet Walker Pan, the buyer of the Ammolite chess set. Walker and I have been playing chess since last summer." He sighed. "It's part of the arrangement to keep the chess set here."

"So who wins?" Gary still eyed the man.

"We're pretty close to even," Walker said. "And, before you ask, I insist we use mind blocks."

"You should've insisted on that last year when you cheated your way to winning the Open," Gary said.

Walker's smile returned. "Gary Goodweather, if I had to guess I'd say you don't trust me."

Gary narrowed his already narrow eyes. "How do you know my name?"

Walker laughed. "Because Morpheus told me all about you and your friends. In fact, he mentioned you're a fairly decent chess player yourself." He raised an inviting eyebrow. "Perhaps we can play sometime?"

"I haven't mastered mind blocking like I'm sure you have." But even as he said it, Gary's scowl started to fade along with the annoyance in his mind.

"Perhaps one of your friends—say Benjamin Holt—could place a mind block for you." Walker looked to Benjamin. "He has one around his mind even now."

Benjamin wasn't sure how to respond. He was sure Walker had been following them around last year. Like turning up around every corner was all coincidence.

But the strange thing was that Benjamin hadn't placed the mind shield at all. Jack had put the shield up around Benjamin as soon as they walked into the store, but Walker didn't seem to know that. He'd assumed, for whatever reason, that Benjamin had placed the block. And now, once again, Benjamin saw just how important mind blocks could be. Benjamin sighed inwardly as he added it to the top of his list of things to improve at. Along with everything else.

But Benjamin never got a chance to respond. Walker turned to Morpheus. "Next week, same place?"

"Same time." Morpheus stepped out of the way before Walker could slap him on the back again.

Walker looked back at the students, smiled with about half his teeth, and then teleported away.

Gary threw up his arms. "What are you doing with him, Morpheus? Last year you admitted you didn't trust him. And now here you are, letting the enemy into your home!"

Morpheus patted his palms downward. "Calm down, Gary. I didn't trust Walker at first either. But my brother put in a good word for him; they've known each other for years."

It seemed not even sibling referrals were going to win Gary over. "But he read your mind—cheated—last year to win."

"All we do is play chess together." Obviously dropping the subject, Morpheus smiled at the students. "Now, what can I get for you today?"

Iva spoke up. "I'm looking for something made of Peridot. Maybe a ring or something."

"The stone of lost items," Morpheus said.

Iva nodded.

Morpheus put his finger to his mouth. "You know, I may have something in the basement. We can all go down and look."

They headed down the narrow steps in the back of the store. Shelves were filled with all sorts of...things, for lack of a better word. Iva picked up a jar, and whatever was in it moved. She jumped and dropped the jar, screaming as she did so. Just before smashing into the ground, it stopped. Andy levitated it back up and into his hands.

"Thanks," she managed to get out, still backing away from the jar.

"What is this anyway?" Andy brought it closer to inspect the slimy, purple creature.

Morpheus just about ran over and grabbed the jar from Andy's hands. "Someone gave it to me, I swear."

"You're smart not to admit to buying that on the black market." Jack teleported into the basement.

Morpheus nearly dropped the jar himself.

"Why?" Andy asked.

"Because it's a highly illegal genetically engineered species available only in Atlantis." Jack crossed his arms. "That's why."

"And rare," Morpheus said. "Extremely rare." He cradled the jar and placed it toward the back of the top-most shelf.

But Gary stared at the jar. "Wasn't that particular genus eliminated?"

"Why don't we look for our Peridot?" Morpheus suggested, clearing his throat. Apparently it was time

for another subject change.

"Hey, how about this?" Heidi said, walking over to a nearby shelf and picking up a green carved rose.

Morpheus squinted his eyes at it. "It is Peridot. But it's not a very strong telemagnifier."

Iva took the stone from Heidi and closed her fist around it. "You're right. This won't do at all. We need something way stronger."

"I keep the stronger telemagnifiers locked up over here." Morpheus walked over to a trunk draped in a thick black cloth. Lifting back the cloth, he unlocked the trunk with both a palm scan and an eye scan. "Some of these aren't really legal, so maybe we can just keep this between ourselves." He let out a nervous laugh.

Andy grinned like he'd just found a way to spy on Helios and Selene Deimos. "Oh, yeah, no problem. Your secret is our secret."

"The one I'm thinking of in particular is—" Morpheus began.

"—this one," Iva finished, reaching over to pick up the delicate golden ring with the small green stone. "It's perfect."

Morpheus smiled and nodded.

"So do you have anything in there that'll get us access to Geros?" Benjamin asked. He'd been thinking about the whole off-limits part of their problem, and given this box of contraband Morpheus had in his basement, he might have some way for them to get into the old capital city.

"Geros?" Morpheus said, and for a second, Benjamin thought it might pan out. But then Morpheus shook his head. "No way. Only the rulers give access to Geros. At

least these days. Back before they tore the ruins down, you might have been able to buy an access card, but now..." He shook his head. "No way."

"I told you that," Jack said.

"I know, I know," Benjamin said.

"Why?" Morpheus asked. "What's in Geros? From what I've heard, it's a whole lot of nothing."

Jack nodded. "Exactly. Nothing."

When they got back to the office after lunch, Nathan Nyx accosted them. "I need to talk to Benjamin alone if you don't mind," Nathan said to Andy.

"No problem." Andy pretty much ran out of the records room and vanished. Benjamin figured it would be time to go home before Andy turned up again.

"What's so important?" Benjamin said after the door had shut. Ryan hadn't turned up yet which left him alone in the awful room of records with Nathan.

"Your father had an important question for you," Nathan said.

"Couldn't he have just asked me on the way back from Mu?" Seriously. Benjamin had just seen his dad less than fifteen minutes ago.

"He's in a meeting," Nathan said. "So he sent me."

Benjamin crossed his arms. "Fine. What?"

"He was wondering if you took any records," Nathan said.

Benjamin's mind flew to the record. Sure, Nathan had gone over the secrecy thing every single morning. All information they looked at was classified. Nothing should leave the building. And technically, nothing had left the building. The record had been recycled. They'd only taken a copy.

"No," Benjamin said.

Nathan frowned. "You're sure?"

"Nothing. Why?"

Nathan twisted his mouth up. "There are some records which are unaccounted for."

Benjamin shrugged. "Maybe they got recycled?" Heck, he'd recycled hundreds of them just this morning.

But Nathan shook his head. "No. We checked the recycling reports."

"Maybe Ryan took them?" Benjamin said. If anyone needed to get blamed for anything, it was Ryan. He'd been the one who'd stolen the record from Benjamin in the first place.

Nathan paused and thought about that. "Very possible. It may have been him." And he turned to leave.

"Wait," Benjamin said. If this really was some super secret organization, maybe Nathan would be able to help out. "Can you get special access badges for anything?"

Nathan stood up a little straighter. "Probably. What?"

"Geros," Benjamin said.

Nathan laughed. "The old ruins? There's nothing there anymore."

Benjamin tried to laugh along with Nathan. "I know. But we still want to check it out."

Nathan Nyx put his finger to his mouth. "Let me see what I can do. I'll be in touch." And then he walked out the door to find Ryan.

Well that solved that. If Nathan could get them the access badge to Geros, Benjamin wouldn't have to bother

Helios Deimos with anything. Sometimes it was amazing how solutions presented themselves. And then he turned to the records, sank to the floor, and decided to take an after-lunch nap.

Benjamin had to give Nathan credit. The next morning as soon as they'd heaped sugar in their coffee, Nathan teleported into the records room. Ryan hadn't shown up yet which left Benjamin and Andy ready to start filing records for the day.

"What's up, Nathan?" Benjamin sat down.

Nathan smiled. "I got something for you."

Benjamin remembered the access badge. *"You got what I asked for?"* he asked telepathically.

Nathan winked and held up a card. *"Consider it an early birthday present."*

Benjamin smiled. Finally Nathan had done more than just order them around. *"Thanks."*

Nathan nodded. *"If you don't mind, I'd rather you didn't mention this to your dad."*

"So you didn't get it from him?" Benjamin asked.

Nathan shook his head. *"No way. But your father did enable a special credit line on the card."* He held it up. *"The access codes to Geros are masked inside it."*

"Oh, that's cool." At this rate, Benjamin thought he might get to a point where he could actually tolerate Nathan.

"How high is the limit?" Andy asked. Apparently, Benjamin's mind block had let Andy in. Not that Benjamin had tried hard to keep him out.

Nathan actually laughed. *"Let's just say it won't run out."*

With access to the off-limits capital city of Geros within his reach, Benjamin had a hard time thinking about anything else. And so, as soon as lunchtime hit, Benjamin and Andy took the elevator downstairs to meet Iva, Heidi, and Gary. They'd come to Wondersky City today, though strictly for fun, not to work.

"We're going on a little field trip." Benjamin held out the card.

Iva eyed it. "What's that?"

"What do you think?" Benjamin said. "Geros is waiting."

Heidi's eyes doubled in size. "You actually got access?"

Benjamin grinned. "Let's just say Nathan Nyx isn't totally worthless after all."

"We're going now?" Gary asked.

"Sure," Benjamin said.

So that was that. They all piled onto a public teleporter pad, Benjamin flashed the card in front of the scanner, and they vanished. And when the world rematerialized around them, it looked like the apocalypse had come.

CHAPTER 5

GEROS—TODAY

Benjamin looked out at the desolation. "So where's the Ruling Hall?"

Jack appeared and floated onto Benjamin's shoulder. "You mean where *was* the Ruling Hall."

"Right," Benjamin said. "Whatever."

"Beats me," Jack said. "I wasn't alive when it was destroyed."

Benjamin looked out over the city. Actually wasteland was more accurate; it was more like a desert made of dirt instead of sand. Piles of rubble lay around every so often, but they looked like scrap—everything nobody had figured out a use for yet.

"It was over that way." Gary pointed to the left.

Benjamin turned to him. "Please tell me you researched this, Gary."

Gary nodded, and a smile flew onto his face. "Of course. Last night I read everything I could on Geros." He pointed over to the right. "Did you know over there they used to have one of the biggest laboratories in the world?"

"No," Andy said. "And I didn't really want to."

They set out walking, Gary taking the lead. Except the problem with Gary leading was that every hundred steps or so he'd stop and point out some random pile of rocks and explain about some factory which used to be there. Really, with everything just looking like dirt anyway, did it really matter where the food generation plant or the toilet factory had been? Nothing mattered besides the Ruling Hall where some secret object had been hidden for Benjamin.

But when they got within range of the old Ruling Hall, Benjamin got a sick feeling in the pit of his stomach—identical to the pit he saw in front of him. And each step he took confirmed what he'd hoped he wasn't seeing. There was a hole in the ground. A hole at least sixteen stories deep and probably more.

"Someone dug it up." Heidi walked to the edge of the pit.

Benjamin swallowed, unsure what to say. So he just nodded.

"Look at how the soil looks different here," Gary pointed, "as compared to here." And he pointed again. "This was done recently."

"How recently?" Benjamin tried to figure out what Gary was pointing at but couldn't see any difference in the dirt spots.

Gary tilted his head. "I'm no expert, but I'd have to say probably yesterday."

"Yesterday!" Iva said.

Benjamin looked at her. "Can you sense anything? Can you tell who was here?"

She stood still and closed her eyes. But when she started biting her lip, Benjamin knew the answer even before she opened her eyes.

"You can't," he said.

Iva shook her head. "No. There's nothing here. It's like all imprints of the past have been removed."

"Fine," Heidi said. "So we just march up to Ryan and ask him who he told and what they found."

"Ryan might not have had anything to do with this," Gary said.

"Ryan found the record yesterday." Andy waved down at the pit. "Let's take a look and see what's left."

Benjamin read Andy's thoughts a millisecond before he fell over the side of the pit. And then he started falling.

"You pushed me!" Benjamin yelled after he managed to get the levitation under control a couple of stories down.

Andy grinned. "Can't you handle it?"

"Of course," Benjamin said. "But next time tell me."

"I did," Andy said.

Benjamin felt the ground under his feet, so he let up on the telekinesis. "Whatever."

"Aren't we down here to look around?" Jack teleported onto Benjamin's arm.

"Not like we're going to find anything," Benjamin said. "Look at this place. There's nothing here."

Jack floated over to the ground. "I don't know about that. Here are some footprints. Fresh ones."

Benjamin walked over. Jack was right. There didn't seem to be anything else down in this dirt pit, but there were footprints. But only one set by the look of things.

"Can you tell whose they are?" he asked Andy. After all, wanting to be a spy should be useful for something.

Andy knelt down and leaned in close. "No, but they don't move around a lot." He pointed off to the right. "They came from over there, walked right over here, and then disappeared."

"Like someone teleported away," Jack said.

"Ryan can't teleport," Benjamin said.

"You don't know that," Jack said.

"Can he?" Benjamin said.

Jack shrugged. "No. But he's pretty close. Like you."

"I already did," Benjamin said, "to Shambhala last year."

"That was a fluke," Andy said, but Benjamin felt the twinge of jealousy.

"Fluke or not," Benjamin said. "I did it."

"Whatever." Andy stood up. "All we know is someone who can teleport came down here, and then teleported away."

"Yesterday," Jack added.

Andy nodded. "Right. Yesterday."

They levitated back to the top of the pit, and Andy told Iva, Heidi, and Gary what they'd found.

"Why would Ryan want some secret object of Benjamin's?" Gary said.

"It doesn't matter," Andy said. "I'll take it as an excuse to pummel him."

Iva pursed her lips together. "It does matter. And no pummeling. The best thing to do is go back, act like nothing happened, and figure out what to do next."

Benjamin looked down the pit. "Which is what?"

Iva shook her head. "I don't know. But it better be something. I doubt your brothers will wait around forever."

Benjamin sighed. "Especially if someone else is looking for them, too."

CHAPTER 6

BENJAMIN GETS AN IMPLANT

But two more months passed back in Virginia filled with mundane, human stuff, and Benjamin didn't find a single clue. Finally it was time to head off to summer school. Benjamin walked into the family room to find his baby sister sitting over his backpack, furiously trying to unzip the front pocket.

"No, Becca. Don't do that." Though why he bothered saying anything he wasn't sure. It's not like she ever listened.

She ignored him the way only a two-year-old can and doubled her efforts to get the bag unzipped. The twins stood watching with their hands over their mouths.

Benjamin walked over to her and reached down. "Do you think she wants me to take her along?"

"Maybe," Douglas said, and then unable to control himself any longer, he burst out laughing. Derrick joined in, and the two of them fell to the ground.

"What's so funny? Did you shove a smelly diaper in my bag?"

Douglas perked up. "No, Benji, but that's a good idea. Stay here for a second."

"Nobody's getting any smelly diapers." Benjamin's mom walked in from the kitchen. "Benjamin needs to get going."

"What is Becca doing to your bag?" His dad came in just behind his mom.

Realization hit Benjamin, his mom, and his dad all at the same time. The twins' minds showed it clearly. There in the front pocket of Benjamin's bag was Becca's favorite red phone rattle, hidden beneath everything else.

It's not like this was the first time the rattle had gotten hidden. The twins hid it in the coffee maker, the oven, and even in the toilet, though no one mentioned that around company.

His mom whipped around and faced the twins. "Whose idea was this?"

Derrick and Douglas cowered under her gaze, even as they tried to stifle their laughs.

Benjamin unzipped the pocket and handed Becca her rattle. "Found it!" she said and grabbed it from his hand.

Benjamin knew summer school was only minutes away when his dad finally managed to corral Derrick, Douglas, and Becca and get them out of the house. "So what would have happened if I left with the rattle in my bag?" he asked.

His mom put her hand to her forehead and closed her eyes. "If Becca's skills are developing as quickly as the twins', there's no telling."

"Would she have found a way to Lemuria to get it?"

His mom nodded her head and reopened her eyes. "I'm willing to bet she would have at least found the teleporter."

The ugly velvet tiger picture that hid the teleporter transformed just like it had last summer. If it hadn't been such great camouflage, there wouldn't have been any other reason to keep something so random around the house.

Velvet pictures had gone out of style probably a century ago—if they ever really were in style to begin with. With a touch on the velvet, a holographic keypad appeared. Benjamin's mom entered a thirty-two number code—Benjamin noticed the code was different than last summer—and the teleporter came to life.

With a final kiss and hug, Benjamin put his hand on the picture and vanished into a pinprick of light.

"Welcome to Lemuria. Please step off your teleporter pad."

Benjamin turned and immediately recognized the same old man from last year supervising his arrival pad. It didn't seem possible, but the man's already oversized ears seemed to have doubled.

"You again," Benjamin said. "It's good to see you."

"What?" The man cupped a hand behind an ear.

Apparently just making someone's ears bigger didn't help their hearing.

"I said it's good to see you again," Benjamin said.

"No time for pleasantries," the old man said. "We don't want to spoil an on-time arrival with unnecessary conversation."

"Of course not." Benjamin walked off the pad and out of the arrival area.

"Benjamin Holt if I remember correctly," the man said.

Benjamin nodded his head.

"On time two years in a row. Very commendable. Pads four and five have been down for the last two hours. We've been hurrying students through so we can divert others to the working teleporters." He shook his head, and his ears flopped back and forth. "Still they haven't upgraded our numbers. Not in the budget this year they say. You'd think a 900,000 year-old civilization would be beyond budget constraints."

Benjamin didn't say anything; sometimes, it seemed, keeping quiet was the best choice.

"So, have a nice summer." And the old man moved back to the teleporter pad.

Benjamin sighed and walked to a kiosk to get his homeroom assignment. Homeroom 1110. Very binary.

Benjamin dumped his bag in the nearest luggage terminal and started down Primary Hallway Number One. Sitting on the first bench Benjamin passed was something familiar and green. And about six inches tall.

"Hey, Jack!"

Jack tapped his foot on the bench. "I've been waiting on this bench all day."

Benjamin raised an eyebrow.

"Fine. Not all day." Jack jumped and landed on his feet. "I met with Helios this morning, but then I came here."

"Why'd you meet with Helios?" Benjamin had thought about Helios Deimos, one of the rulers of Lemuria, a lot over the last year, but he certainly hadn't talked to him. Helios had been responsible for saving Benjamin's life not to mention keeping the shields intact around Lemuria and Atlantis last year.

Well, mostly responsible. Benjamin had played a small part in it too.

"Oh, you know," Jack said. "This and that."

Benjamin reached out to grab at the little man, but

Jack was too fast and teleported away, appearing a foot or so to the right. "This and that what?" Benjamin said.

Jack cleared his little throat. "I happen to have important matters to take care of with Helios. We Nogicals have to keep some of our secrets." And then he pointed. "Look who it is."

"Hi, guys!" Heidi hurried over. "You'll never believe it. I levitated my bags into the luggage terminal all by myself."

Benjamin laughed before he could stop himself. "You did not." Heidi could hardly lift a feather with telekinesis.

"Did, too." Heidi crossed her arms. "And I can lift more than a feather. Why do you always forget I can read your mind?"

"Because you're not supposed to?" Benjamin said.

"Well maybe you should practice a little harder on blocking your thoughts," Heidi said.

"She's right, you know," Jack chimed in. "Sometimes your mind is so wide open a human could read it. Have you thought about taking mind blocking as your elective?"

"Ha-ha. Very funny." Benjamin planned on taking something cool like Body Part Teleportation. Then he could make good on his vow to teleport Ryan's teeth from his mouth.

But Jack shook his little head. "Not kidding. You of all people should work on telejamming."

Heidi turned to Jack. "Telejamming?"

"Of course," Jack replied. "Telejamming—blocking telenergetic forces."

"Telenergetic forces?" Benjamin asked.

Jack smacked his forehead with his palm and shook his head in disbelief. "Didn't you learn anything last year?

 40

Telenergetic forces: all the extra cool stuff telegens can do with their minds."

And then Benjamin had a good idea. Jack wouldn't get off so easy. "Hey Heidi, what did Jack and Helios talk about this morning?"

Heidi blushed, looked to Benjamin, then back to Jack. And then she mumbled something.

"What?" Benjamin asked as Jack smiled.

"I can't read Jack's mind." Heidi managed to say it louder this time.

Benjamin's mouth opened but he could hardly form the right words. "You can read anyone's mind."

"Not mine," Jack said. And then he smiled.

"Is it because you're a Nogical?" Benjamin asked.

"It's because I'm so good at telejamming!"

Jack left before they got to Homeroom 1110. When Benjamin and Heidi turned down Tertiary Hallway Number One, a short line waited to enter a crypt-sized box in front of the classroom door. And so Benjamin and Heidi joined the line.

"What's going on?" Benjamin asked.

Heidi paused, obviously employing her telepathic genius. "No one seems to know."

The boy in front of them turned around. His dark brown hair matched his dark brown eyes which matched his dark brown shirt. It looked like someone had taken a giant brown crayon and colored him in. "It is 'edzup display," he said in a thick accent.

Benjamin narrowed his eyes. "What?"

"'Edzup display," the boy repeated.

Heidi smiled at the boy, and he smiled back. "What

exactly is edzup display?" she asked, but Benjamin could tell the kid had no idea. He'd bluffed enough times to know what it looked like.

"You 'ave not listened as you walked," the boy said.

Benjamin glanced at Heidi and then shook his head. "No, I guess not."

"'Edzup display is—" the boy began.

"Nicholas Konstantin," a voice called from the crypt.

"Ah, is my turn. I will see you in classroom." And the boy turned to enter the box.

"So you have no idea what we're in for?" Benjamin asked.

"None." Heidi let out a nervous chuckle. "Maybe they'll call you first."

Sure enough, Benjamin was next. He gave Heidi one last look before forcing himself to walk into the crypt thing.

"Identity confirmed—Benjamin Holt. Please step to the center of the cube and focus on the red dot of light. Do not blink your left eye."

"What?" Benjamin narrowed his eyelids to slits. "Why not?"

"Please do not move. Your new heads-up display will now be implanted in your left eyeball."

"Eyeball!" Benjamin squeezed his eyes closed. "I don't need something implanted in my eyeball." More like didn't want something implanted in his eyeball.

The voice spoke again. "Please open your eyes."

Benjamin thought of Heidi waiting behind him. He didn't want her thinking he was afraid of some eyeball implant. Not that afraid would have been the right word.

 42

Reluctant? He opened his eyes and looked at the red light. "Will it hurt?"

"It is done," the voice said. "Please exit straight ahead."

Benjamin blinked a bunch of times, and nothing felt different. But when he looked ahead and thought about the school, a map lit up in front of his face, showing his current location. He reached out, trying to touch it.

"Please exit straight ahead," the voice repeated in its dull monotone.

Benjamin stepped out of the cube, and decided to wait for Heidi.

She came out a minute later. "Pretty cool, huh?" Her hair which had been blond and straight just minutes before was now red and curly.

"Cool?" Benjamin snorted out a laugh. "What happened to your hair?"

Heidi pulled a piece of it around to see and sighed. Staring at the red curls, she changed them back into the straight blond strands she normally wore. "Guess I just got a little bit nervous."

Benjamin laughed. "Glad I'm not the only one. Let's go."

They walked into Homeroom 1110 and almost bumped into the boy who'd been ahead of them in line. "So that's a heads-up display," Heidi said.

"Yes." The boy brushed invisible dust off the front of his brown shirt. "'Edzup display. Will be very 'andy."

"What's Andy?"

Benjamin turned to see Andy, Gary, and Iva behind them.

"Hey!" Heidi gave them each a hug. She hadn't hugged

 43

Benjamin this time. Maybe he shouldn't have been so weird about it back over Spring Break.

Andy glanced at Heidi, but Benjamin noticed he had a hard time peeling his eyes off Iva. "We thought you'd never get here," Andy said.

Iva's smile turned bemused. "Yeah, I've been stuck listening to Andy brag about all his telekinetic displays of the last year."

"I was not bragging, Iva."

"Iva?" the boy with the accent said. "That sounds like language of Russia."

Iva turned to look at the boy, and even a blind man would have noticed their eyes lock. "Oh, yes, actually it is," she said. "My grandparents were agents in Russia when my dad was growing up. I'm Iva Marinina."

"And I am Nicholas Konstantin." The boy kissed her hand.

Andy's mouth dropped so far open, Benjamin thought a giant squid could fit in it.

"Do people call you Nick?" Iva asked. And then she giggled.

"It matters not what other people call me." Nicholas still held onto her hand. "Women as beautiful as you may call me whatever and whenever you like."

Benjamin looked again over at Andy. Andy looked like someone had punched him in the stomach. Not that Benjamin could blame him. Did anyone really act like this?

"What should I call you?" Andy ground his teeth together, hardly getting the words out.

The boy laughed. "Ah, my friends call me Nick."

"I'm not sure that clears it up," Benjamin heard Andy say telepathically. Heidi must have heard too as a huge smile broke out across her face.

Luckily a chime sounded, and the tall double doors to the classroom sealed shut. They walked to the desk area at the front of the classroom where Benjamin, Andy, and Gary chose seats behind Heidi and Iva. Nick didn't even hesitate. He walked over and sat down in the empty seat next to Iva. Andy opened his mouth, and for a split second, Benjamin actually thought Andy might say something. But he didn't. Thankfully.

"Guess you should have sat there," Benjamin said mentally to his friend.

"Whatever," Andy replied.

Proteus Ajax teleported into the classroom and smiled at the students. "Hello! For the lucky students who had me last year, guess what?" He didn't wait for an answer. "I've decided to move up a year."

This was met by some claps and hooting (from those who'd had Proteus last year) and some confusion (from those who'd never seen him before in their lives).

"If you didn't receive a heads-up display, now is the time to tell me." Proteus stopped talking and looked around. Nobody raised their hand. "Good. What do you think?"

Jonathan Sheehan raised his hand. He sat with Ryan just behind Julie Macfarlane and Suneeta Manvar, Julie's best friend.

"Yes, Jonathan Sheehan?" Proteus said.

"What exactly is the heads-up display?" Jonathan asked. "That machine said it implanted something in my eyeball."

Proteus nodded. "The heads-up display is equivalent to a computer stored in your eyeball. A projection system casts an image directly ahead of your retina. This image can be anything from the current weather to the results of your last science experiment."

"Fantastic!" Gary's eyes glazed over.

"Money on the fact that he was already checking the science lab," Andy said telepathically to Benjamin.

Heidi blinked a few times. "Does it ever come out?"

Proteus shook his head. "No, the heads-up display is there to stay. All Year Two Denarians and above are equipped with them."

Proteus looked around the classroom and answered a few more questions. Benjamin couldn't believe some of the questions people asked. Do Year Two Denarians have to do their own laundry? Are there special bathrooms for Year Two Denarians? Would Year Two Denarians really have to share the dining hall with Year Ones? By the end, every time a hand went up, Proteus answered through clenched teeth until finally, the questions stopped.

They picked electives next. Benjamin thought 'List of Electives,' and in front of his left eye scrolled his choices. There were lots of cool ones, like Telekinetic Muscle Building and Outer Space Telepathy; it was actually hard to decide. But like Jack had said, taking some sort of tele-jamming course made sense. He scrolled down the list and found what he was looking for. Telejamming—Blocking Telenergetic Forces. And he picked it.

Andy settled on Agent Training, Heidi on Empathy, and Iva on Dream Interpretation. And after ten minutes of debate with Proteus, Gary relented and picked only one elective—Genetic Engineering—instead of the three he'd originally intended.

Andy looked at Nick. "Let me guess, you're taking Dream Interpretation, too."

Nick shook his head. "Ah no, telegnosis is not my strong point."

Iva rested her chin on her hands and looked at Nick. "So what are you taking?"

"I know sounds silly, but I 'ave chosen Poetic Interpretation," Nick said. "I 'ave always 'ad fascination for poetry."

Benjamin wasn't sure what was funnier—the look on Andy's face, like he was going to throw up, or the ones on Iva's and Heidi's, like they both wanted to marry Nick and have his children on the spot.

Proteus looked around. "Well, I believe that's enough for one day. I'll see everyone bright and early tomorrow morning." And then he teleported out of the room.

 47

CHAPTER 7

A CHIP OFF THE OLD BLOCK

Level four telekinesis was no place for the weak, and when Benjamin walked out after the first day of class, his only consolation for feeling like he'd been beaten with a stick was that he'd won against Ryan in a Kinesis Combat. Sure, only once, and unfortunately Ryan had won once, also. Not to mention Andy had beaten Benjamin a couple times. Benjamin wasn't sure what was worse—losing to Ryan or losing to Andy.

Actually both were painful; he'd just have to practice more.

Just as they were about to walk into the dining hall for lunch, Benjamin glanced down a side hallway. Heidi was leaning against the wall talking to some guy. Alone. He had long dark hair that reached his shoulders, and he wore a black leather jacket over the standard t-shirt and jeans. Was that even allowed? And was that stubble on his face? How old was this guy? He had to be older than fourteen.

"Who's that guy talking to Heidi?" Benjamin asked Andy. As fixed as her eyes were on the guy, Benjamin doubted she'd be listening for other thoughts.

Andy shrugged. *"I've never seen him before."*

Just then Iva and Gary walked up.

"Where's Heidi?" Iva asked.

48

Benjamin nodded his head in the direction of the side hallway. "Down there."

"Whoa!" Iva said. "Who is that?"

"You think he's hot?" Andy said.

"Well, yeah. I mean just look at him." She glared at Andy. "And don't read my mind."

Andy scowled. "Don't broadcast your thoughts."

Just then, Heidi smiled to the boy, and they parted ways. She started walking but hurried up when she saw her four friends watching her. "Oh, sorry I'm late."

"Who was that?" Benjamin asked.

Heidi flushed red. Then she ran her hand through her hair, and it gave off small sparks.

That was new. Benjamin had seen it go from curly to straight and change colors but never give off sparks.

"Oh, some guy I met in Empathy this morning."

"Does he have a name?" Benjamin asked.

"Josh," Heidi said. "His name is Josh."

"It looks like you guys really hit it off." Benjamin prayed it came out less idiotic to Heidi than it sounded to him. "How old is he anyway?"

Heidi giggled. "Oh, he's actually fifteen. And we have Telepathy together tomorrow, also. Isn't that great?"

"Yeah, just great," Benjamin said.

"Wow, lucky you," Iva said. "As fate would have it, Jonathan Sheehan is in my elective this year."

Benjamin could hear his stomach carrying on a conversation in growls. "Can we get moving? I'm starving."

As they headed toward the dining hall, Benjamin relived fond memories of the food from last year. The automatic menus put out food better than any restaurant in the human world. But when they walked into the dining hall, a horrid scene descended upon Benjamin.

Long streams of kids queued up in food lines like the kind normal human cafeterias had. And the cleaning lady, Leena Teasag, was serving the food. He looked over and saw the same horrified expressions on Andy and Gary's faces.

"What's up with the lines?" Benjamin was almost afraid to ask but figured he had to know.

Gary's pupils dilated as he checked. "My heads-up display says the menus are out of order."

"So the cleaning lady is serving food?" Andy asked. "Doesn't she have toilets to scrub or something?"

"This means she'll have less time to talk to us," Heidi said. And then she sighed.

Benjamin looked at the lines. "Sounds like a blessing to me."

Heidi and Iva ignored Benjamin and got into line.

By the time he got through the food line, Benjamin wished he'd headed out to the city to eat instead. Or starved. Either would have been better. First, he couldn't decide what to get. There was the boiled mush that looked like it might have been meat in a previous life, the genetically engineered tuna noodle casserole complete with fish heads mixed in, or the strained spinach with extra iron. The boiled meat-wanna-be looked like swill, and the spinach smelled like metal, so Benjamin settled on the mutant tuna casserole. Maybe he could teleport the fish heads onto Andy's plate.

Leena Teasag slopped a tiny serving on his plate and helped the next person in line before he could ask for more—not that he really wanted any.

The line ran out of bread just before Benjamin, and the

milk machine only gave out soy milk. And the Jell-O dessert had bits of something in it that reminded Benjamin of science experiments gone wrong.

Mutant fish or not, Benjamin finished his casserole in two bites—except of course for the heads—and began to pick at the Jell-O.

"Can't you fix the menus, Gary?" Benjamin flicked something green onto the table from the Jell-O.

Gary smiled. "I appreciate your confidence. I already checked on my heads-up display, and it seems they're locked out with some security protocol."

"Does that mean no?" Benjamin asked.

Iva looked up from her spinach to take a sip of her soy milk. "Oh, are you done already, Benjamin?"

"Of course I'm done. I had like one bite of food." He looked at Heidi's plate and licked his lips. She still had three large pieces of the mush meat with an entire loaf of bread. Maybe he should've gotten the meat.

"You want to share any of that?" he asked her.

"I'm hungry," Heidi said and pulled her plate closer.

He looked around the dining hall and spotted Ryan sitting with Jonathan, Suneeta, and Julie. Julie stared at Ryan— her new apparent boyfriend, ignoring the untouched food on her plate. Without hesitation, the loaf of bread on Julie's plate began to levitate. Benjamin lifted it up high above everyone's head, and started moving it toward their table, hoping nobody would notice.

Just as it was halfway between the two tables, Suneeta looked up, spotting it. She looked at Julie's empty plate. "Julie, I believe your loaf of bread is levitating."

Benjamin held it in place, trying to decide if he should

continue moving it or return it back to the plate.

Julie looked up. "Oh, my bread! Ryan, do something!"

Benjamin felt Ryan began to exert his mind on the bread. Benjamin held on, not quite sure what to do. Ryan would know it was Benjamin. It tugged one way then back the other. Back and forth it went. Benjamin held on; at this point it was strictly as a matter of principle. He would not let Ryan beat him in another telekinetic duel, even if it was a piece of bread they were fighting over.

Benjamin had the bread almost directly above his own table. Ryan yanked it back. Benjamin again pulled on it, this time as far as he possibly could, and then he decided to let it go. With a final pull of energy, the bread snapped back, just like a slingshot, heading straight to the table from where it had come. With a solid thud, it hit Julie Macfarlane right in the eye. She fell off her chair, landing on the floor. Benjamin cringed.

Ryan's face turned white and his eyes grew wide. He glanced around the room before finally daring to look down at the moaning Julie. Both hands covered her left eye, and she cried like she'd just lost her puppy.

"Oh, my eye. Is it bruised? Is it horrible? Suneeta, can you see where it hit me?" And then she uncovered her face, bringing her hands down. Benjamin gasped and heard Ryan do the same. At least Ryan would be the one who had to look at her. Her left eye was black and blue, swollen and puffy, and was well on its way to swelling shut.

Suneeta looked at her friend. "Your eye looks like a rotten tomato that is about to burst," she said as if announcing the weather. "It is highly noticeable on your pasty complexion."

Julie's hand flew back to her face, and she broke into a

sobbing frenzy. When Benjamin turned back around, even Heidi and Iva were trying not to smile, and Heidi was cutting her loaf of bread in half for Benjamin.

"Hey. What ever happened with that DNA scanning stuff?" Benjamin asked, changing the subject. He'd almost forgotten about it. And after Iva's face fell, he'd almost wished he had.

Iva took the green Peridot ring off her hand and dropped it on the table. "Nothing. I found nothing."

"Maybe you were doing it wrong," Andy suggested.

She whipped her head around so fast Benjamin thought she might break her neck. "I was not doing it wrong, Andy. I know how to scan the earth for DNA."

Andy cowered. There was just no other word for it. He shrank so far back in his chair, Benjamin figured he'd slide under the table next.

"I didn't mean to suggest you didn't know how to do it," Andy said.

"How did you match the DNA?" Gary asked.

Iva paused before answering. "I used the part of Benjamin that got imprinted on my mind through the Alliance bond."

"Maybe you should try joining minds," Heidi said.

Gary nodded. "That's precisely what I was thinking."

"Joining minds?" Benjamin said.

Heidi nodded. "We were learning about it in Empathy. And it's nowhere near as hard as you might think. Josh and I practiced together."

"You joined minds with Josh?" Benjamin asked. "Isn't that kind of...oh, I don't know...personal?"

Heidi rolled her eyes. "Well of course it's personal.

 53

The very nature of Telepathy and Empathy is personal. Anytime your mind is connected that closely with someone it gets pretty intimate. Mentally of course."

"Wonderful." Benjamin looked back to Iva. "Let's get on with this DNA stuff. Iva, without being too intimate, what do you need me to do?"

Heidi shook her head and looked away.

The mind meld actually wasn't that bad.

Fine, it was awesome. Like he knew every thought in Iva's head. And not only thoughts. Their powers combined, too. Benjamin felt his telegnostic abilities reaching out across the entire school. Almost out across the whole continent of Lemuria. He could see Proteus Ajax. And his telekinesis teacher The Panther. And there was Morpheus Midas in the Silver Touch. It was like anything he thought about he could find. And this wasn't even the seeing-the-future part of telegnosis. Is this what it felt like in Iva's mind all the time?

Heidi had been right; combining minds was a personal thing. But Benjamin knew enough to keep his mouth shut and not mention it. Somehow, he didn't think Andy would be too happy he'd been that close mentally to Iva.

When they were done, Benjamin looked up and smiled. Iva smiled back. Andy did not smile. But he wasn't the only one. When Benjamin happened to glance to the next table, he noticed Ryan wasn't even looking at Julie and her grotesque black eye. Instead, his eyes were fixed on Benjamin. It didn't take a telegen as good at Empathy as Heidi to sense the hatred coming off him. And it was directed right at Benjamin.

 54

When Benjamin, Andy, and Gary walked into homeroom Friday morning, all the girls were clustered in the back of the classroom. Benjamin stood on his toes to get a better look. "What's going on back there?"

Andy looked hopeful. "Cat fight maybe?"

"Between who?" Benjamin said. "Julie and Iva?"

"Or maybe Suneeta and Heidi," Gary said.

Benjamin couldn't see over the gaggle of girls in the back of the room. They were all gathered around something. He, Andy, and Gary climbed up onto the table, and Benjamin quickly spotted Heidi and Iva in the front of the flock next to Julie Macfarlane. Their mouths hung open and their eyes were glazed over. Benjamin's gaze followed the direction of their eyes. There at the front of the group was Nick Konstantin.

> *"My 'eart is 'eld by the one*
> *Who, like a spider, a web has spun.*
> *It grows each day a little more.*
> *She is the one that I adore."*

"*Is he reciting love poems?*" Gary raised an eyebrow and looked sideways at Benjamin.

Benjamin nodded. "*He's doing something.*"

Andy hardly looked. "*What an idiot—up there in front of everyone.*"

Gary looked back at the gathering. "*The girls sure seem to like it.*"

> *"I think of 'er both day and night*
> *And then again at morning light.*

When I 'old 'er close, she will see
She 'as made a captive of me."

Nick finished the recitation, and the pack of girls erupted.

"Ah, thank you, thank you." Pompousness poured off Nick as he spoke.

"That was just so wonderful, Nick," Iva said.

Still not looking, Andy rolled his eyes so hard, Benjamin thought he might fall off the table.

"Ah, you liked it?" Nick asked Iva.

"Oh yes," she said. "Only a true poetic genius could make up poems with such feeling."

Every female eye in the class still focused on Nick. Some girls pushed forward, trying to interrupt Iva's conversation with him. Julie Macfarlane was standing right next to Iva, batting her mascara'ed eyelashes frantically.

"I would be more than 'appy to recite poetry each morning before class," Nick said.

This caused another loud uproar from the crowd of girls.

"You have got to be kidding me." Andy jumped down from the table and headed to the front of the room.

Benjamin hopped down and turned to see Ryan Jordan watching from a different table, his eyes locked on Iva. Seriously, could Ryan really still think he had a chance with Iva? Benjamin figured the moon was more likely to fall out of orbit if Andy or Julie had anything to do with it.

It took Proteus a good couple of minutes and some sharp telepathic thoughts to get the class under control. But finally the girls disbanded, and everyone sat down.

"Good morning, Year Two Denarians," Proteus said to the class. "We have a new student to the class—a young man by the name of Magic Pan."

"*Magic Pan,*" Benjamin said through the Alliance bond. "*Doesn't that sound familiar?*"

"Magic is the son of Lemuria's new government liaison, Walker Pan," Proteus went on.

"*Bingo,*" Heidi said.

"*Government liaison.*" Gary snorted. "*More like 'cheater' if you ask me. It's the guy from the chess tournament.*"

"*Seems kind of like a strange coincidence,*" Benjamin said.

"*Strange and weird,*" Iva said. "*And I don't believe in coincidence.*"

Proteus motioned, and someone who looked like a young version of Walker Pan without the full beard stood up.

"Welcome, fellow Year Two Denarians." Magic Pan waved across the classroom. "I wasn't going to even come to school this year until I heard about the problem."

"What problem?" Ryan called out.

Magic feigned shock. "Why the menus, of course. The rumors were confirmed to me this morning at breakfast. It will be my sole purpose this year to get the menus back online."

It only took a second and then the class applauded—except for Gary who gave Magic the evil eye. But if Magic could get the food menus working again, who cared if he was potentially the son of the enemy?

"How much longer must we walk through the food lines?" Magic said. "How much longer must we put up with sub-par service from unfriendly cleaning ladies? I tell

57

you, I've had enough. The menus must come back!"

This time the class erupted with cheering. And Magic became the most popular kid in homeroom.

CHAPTER 8

CHRONOLOGY IS CONFUSING

"Hey, watch where you're sitting." Jack spoke up just before Benjamin sat down on him in lecture. "Can't you see this seat's taken?"

Benjamin looked down at the small green Nogical. "You're too small. Get up."

"Are you saying just because I'm small I shouldn't have my own seat?"

Benjamin grabbed for the Nogical but missed. "No. I'm saying you shouldn't have your own seat because you're not a student. Anyway, all you ever do in lecture is fall asleep."

"That's not entirely true." But after evading Benjamin's reach, Jack levitated so Benjamin could sit.

"What part of it's not true?" Benjamin planted his bottom in the chair before Jack could change his mind.

Jack settled down on the arm rest. "I normally stay awake for at least the beginning. And I stayed awake the whole time last year when Mr. Hermes talked about genetic engineering."

Andy plunked down next to Benjamin. "That's because he kept using you as an example. If I remember right, you were standing on Benjamin's head so Mr. Hermes would notice you."

"I wasn't trying to get noticed," Jack said. "I'm just

very interested in genetic engineering, that's all. Anyway, tonight's lecture is going to be great."

"What's it on?" Andy asked.

Jack smiled. "I don't have the time to tell you."

A bell chimed, and Mr. Hermes called the lecture hall to order. "Quiet down. We have lots to cover."

Not that anyone really needed to be told. Lecture might be late at night, but it was always full of cool things they never learned about anywhere else.

"Who knows anything about chromosomes?" Mr. Hermes asked.

Gary's hand shot up like a rocket.

Andy whispered to Benjamin and Gary. "Don't boys have YY chromosomes and girls have XX?"

Gary shuddered, still waving his hand in the air. "It's XY that guys have and XX that girls have," he whispered back to Andy.

"Whatever," Andy said.

"You're on the right path, Andy." Mr. Hermes looked around, ignoring Gary. "Anyone else besides Gary Goodweather?"

Gary kind of lowered his hand, but threw it back in the air when Mr. Hermes sighed and looked at him.

"Yes, Gary?"

Gary smiled, and the words fell out of his mouth. "Everyone has twenty-three pairs of chromosomes. Twenty-two of these are matched and the final pair determines if someone is a boy or a girl."

Mr. Hermes crossed his arms. "Almost correct, Gary."

The smile evaporated from Gary's face. "What do you mean—almost correct?"

"Every human has twenty-three pairs. Every telegen has twenty-four," Mr. Hermes said.

"We have an extra chromosome pair?" Gary didn't even bother raising his hand.

Benjamin couldn't believe Gary didn't already know this. Gary knew everything.

Mr. Hermes pointed to a holographic display with little red and blue balls bouncing around on it. "The twenty-fourth chromosome pair is known as the temporal chromosome, and it determines if and how well a telegen can temporally phase."

Gary's chin fell so far it would have hit the ground if it hadn't been attached. "Temporal phasing! Are you kidding?"

"What's temporal phasing?" Andy asked.

A long line appeared on the holographic display. "Time travel," Mr. Hermes said. "The extra chromosome pair determines how well a telegen can time travel."

"See, I told you this would be interesting," Jack whispered in Benjamin's ear.

"Nobody thought temporal phasing was possible until the birth of a telegen named Kronos. Born in Atlantis, Kronos discovered early on the ability to displace himself in time." Mr. Hermes pointed to the display and a map of Atlantis appeared along with the image of a man in a white toga.

"Kronos the Greek god?" Iva asked.

Mr. Hermes nodded. "But not just Greek. He was known as Enki, Saturn, Shaneeswara, or even Nimrod. His control over time travel led him to be viewed as a deity—the god of time."

Heidi leaned forward in her seat. "So he made himself a false god just like the other Atlantian gods."

"Yes, and Kronos's mother was Gaea, the original false goddess," Mr. Hermes said. "In the midst of traveling every when in time, Kronos had six children, none of whom he could stand. I guess the feeling was reciprocated because one of the oracles of Delphi told Kronos his own child would kill him."

"So did they?" Andy asked.

Mr. Hermes shrugged. "Maybe. Maybe not. We enter the age old debate of whether time can be altered. Once a timeline presents itself, can any actions we do now or anything we think to do in the future change what the timeline will be? If we travel back in time, can we change the future as we know it now?"

Benjamin turned, half to Jack and half to Mr. Hermes. "So what's the answer?"

"The answer is that we just don't know," Mr. Hermes said. "It's impossible to tell if an action we make now would have the ability to change the past."

"Did Kronos try?" Heidi asked.

"Sure," Mr. Hermes said. "The story goes—and here I think we diverge somewhat into myth—that Kronos ate his six children, or at least the first five of them. When he ordered his wife to bring him the sixth and final child Zeus, she instead brought him a stone which he ate. Now I myself think I would know when I was eating a stone, but I also don't think I could eat another telegen whole. Or course, Kronos was fabled to be a Titan—a telegen who could make himself enormous. So I suppose Kronos could have enlarged himself, eaten his children, and then returned to normal size. But let's not get caught up with details. Zeus grew up and forced his father to throw up the stone and the other five children, all of whom were still alive inside Kronos' belly. The regurgitated stone supposedly was placed by Zeus at the center of the world and forms the cornerstone for one of the most powerful telegnostic cities of ancient times."

Iva's eyes bulged out. "You mean Delphi." It wasn't a question.

"Good, Iva," Mr. Hermes said. "Yes, Delphi was the city formed around this stone, known as the Navel of the World, and is probably best remembered for the oracles who lived there."

"So can anyone time travel?" Benjamin asked.

"It all depends on the flexibility of the temporal chromosomes." Mr. Hermes fiddled with the holographic control pad and the red and blue balls reappeared. "They need to bend every cell in the body out of phase during the process. Some telegens can time travel whenever and wherever and however often they want. Others are limited; their chromosomes need more time to bounce back. Most telegens can time travel only with the aid of telemagnifiers, and even then only on a limited basis." He stopped and thought. "Not that this is a bad thing. Time travel is kept under tight control by the government and all displacements need to be officially recorded in the ruling hall. Time travel telemagnifiers are not something you can buy; in fact, buying and selling them is illegal."

The image of Morpheus' basement popped into Benjamin's mind and apparently Andy's, also.

"I wonder if Morpheus has any in the trunk in his

basement," Andy asked.

"You know I can time travel as much as I want, and I don't need any telemagnifiers," Jack said.

"So do you ever do it?" Benjamin knew the answer. Really, nothing the Nogical did surprised him.

"Sometimes," Jack said.

"So what kinds of things is time travel allowed for?" Andy asked.

Images of dinosaurs and volcanoes and wars crossed over the screen. "Damage control," Mr. Hermes said. "The Department of the Preservation of Time is responsible for acting on tips received to track down rogue time travelers from both Lemuria and Atlantis."

"Do you think I'll be able to time travel?" Benjamin asked Jack.

Jack smiled. *"Definitely. And sometime you'll have to try it."*

"When?" Benjamin asked Jack.

Jack closed his eyes and sat back for the rest of lecture. *"Maybe sooner than you think. Or maybe later than you think. It's all just a matter of time."*

CHAPTER 9

BENJAMIN'S BROTHER MIGHT BE ON MARS

Magic Pan stood at the dining hall entrance Saturday morning greeting everyone who walked in. Aside from seeing him in homeroom, none of them had actually met Magic Pan. Sure, Benjamin was halfway convinced Magic's dad was a traitor to Lemuria but decided not to mention that small detail. Better to say too little than too much.

Gary extended his hand, and Magic Pan nearly pulled it off shaking it.

"Would you care to make a bet, Gary?" Magic asked while they shook.

Gary pulled back his hand. "What kind of bet?"

"On who can get the menus working sooner, of course," Magic said.

"The menus are locked out," Gary said. "They can't be fixed."

Magic put a finger to his chin. "So you're declaring me the winner already?"

Gary laughed a totally non-funny laugh. "I'd hardly call that winning."

"Ah, but that's where you're wrong," Magic said. "Even in school there are winners and losers. Much like chess." And then Magic winked at Gary.

Gary scowled. "If you cheat, it's not winning."

 65

Apparently Walker Pan had told his son about the chess game thing after all.

"I'm not saying I disagree," Magic said. "But, let's just say, sometimes cheating is necessary to assume the winning position."

Gary's scowl darkened a few shades. "What? Do you plan to cheat on fixing the menus?"

Magic shrugged. "Cheating or not, the food lines have come to an end."

Andy licked his lips. "No way! That's fantastic."

"Yeah, I've had about as much mush meat as I can stand," Benjamin said. "And I sure won't miss Leena." He gave an involuntary shudder at the thought of the lunch lady.

"Oh, she'll still be around," Heidi said. "Maybe not serving our food, but always around."

"So you're not kidding, are you?" Andy asked.

"Would I kid about a thing like this?" Magic said.

"So how'd you pull it off?" Benjamin asked. "How did you get the menus back online?"

Magic Pan smiled at them. "You may think of me as someone who can repair the impossible, obtain hard to find items, collect useful information. When you are in need, remember your Year Two Denarian friend—Magic Pan!"

Magic stepped aside so they could go on to the dining hall. Benjamin saw Leena Teasag across the room closing down the food lines. Looking over at Heidi, he saw her engaged in a blocked, telepathic conversation with Leena. If Heidi ruined the menu system somehow, he'd find some way to teleport her to Antarctica and leave her there.

 66

Once they sat down, Iva threw the Peridot ring onto the table. "This thing sucks."

"So I guess you didn't have any luck," Andy said.

Benjamin cringed, waiting for Iva to erupt like a volcano. But Andy was right; Benjamin kind of wanted to toss the ring across the room, also. How could she not have found anything?

"No, no luck," she said.

"Maybe Benjamin's brother is on Mars," Gary said.

Benjamin glared at him.

"Well, it is possible," Gary said. "Remember the base Lemuria has on Mars?"

"So why didn't this work?" Benjamin said. "Seriously, Iva, if you can't find something this way, I don't have any other ideas."

"You didn't come up with the idea in the first place," Iva said.

"Maybe you missed something," Andy said.

"No, I didn't miss anything," she said.

"You could've," Andy said.

"Look, I'm doing the best I can here. If I say I didn't miss anything, then I didn't miss anything," she said.

"Maybe their DNA is too different from mine to detect," Benjamin said. It was the only way he thought he could tactfully say she'd missed something.

"Maybe your brothers are dead, Benjamin." Heidi's voice was almost inaudible.

And there is was; Heidi had said it. The thing he'd been afraid of ever since Iva's lack of success. "I thought about that," he said.

"Me, too," Iva said. "But if they were dead, their DNA

signatures should still be strong enough, even after fourteen years; they would have shown up." She sighed. "Maybe I did do something wrong."

This was just heading down the wrong path, fast. Time for a subject change. "I've been doing some thinking," Benjamin said.

Heidi smiled. "Good idea."

Benjamin frowned.

"What?" Heidi said. "You're broadcasting it like a beacon."

Benjamin threw up a mind block. "*Fine. How's this?*"

"*Much better,*" Heidi said.

"*And...*" Andy said.

Benjamin looked at Heidi. "*Would you like to do the honors?*"

Heidi smirked but still sent out her thoughts. "*Benjamin thinks we should time travel back to Geros in the past to get whatever object someone stole.*"

Gary's eyes lit up. "*Time travel.*" And he looked like if he'd been able to go on the spot, he would have given up his left arm.

"*But how?*" Iva asked.

She was always so skeptical.

Benjamin sighed. "*I don't know that yet. I only just came up with the time travel thing after lecture the other night.*"

"*It'll work,*" Gary said.

"*How do you know?*" Iva said.

Benjamin leaned in. "*Simple. We find a way to get a time travel telemagnifier and travel back a thousand years ago to before the ruins were torn down.*"

 68

"So if we go back in time and get the object, does that mean whoever stole it recently won't ever get it?" Andy asked.

Benjamin looked at Andy and smiled. "*Maybe they never got it in the first place. Maybe we got it first.*"

But Gary shook his head. "*No, you guys heard Mr. Hermes the other night. It's no guarantee.*"

Iva stood up. "*It doesn't matter. It's the best idea we've had yet.*"

"*Hey,*" Benjamin said. "*I had the idea.*"

"*Sure,*" she said. "*But you haven't figured out how to do it.*"

"*And let me guess,*" Andy said. "*That's where the rest of us come in.*"

But after checking around, it seemed getting a time travel telemagnifier was actually harder than Mr. Hermes had suggested. Impossible would have been a better word; they were available nowhere. Benjamin stewed about it all night but still came up empty.

Along with an elective, all Year Two Denarians got assigned an enrichment activity, which for Benjamin and his friends turned out to be Archaeological Digs. On the morning of their first class, public teleporter access had been arranged, but Benjamin had a different idea. It was only after spending ten minutes convincing a skeptical Gary everything would be fine that Benjamin finally teleported them all naturally.

When they arrived on a sandy beach, relief poured into Gary's face. "That's it? That's all there is to it?"

"What did you think?" Benjamin asked. "You'd be able

to feel pink, squishy brain or something?"

Gary cleared his throat. "Fine. So it was no big deal. You've proven your point."

"And you've proven you can teleport us," Iva said. "That's terrific."

Heidi's hair had turned pitch black, which all things considered, looked pretty good on her. "And really cool too!" she said. "Now we can go wherever we want."

"It's the getting back through the dome part that'll probably be tricky," Benjamin said, remembering why Jack never teleported to see him during the past year.

Iva turned away. "We can worry about that when the time comes."

They gathered around with the rest of the class. Their Arch Digs teacher, Sci Omega, had already started talking.

"So you might notice we're still in boring old Lemuria today." His brilliant, blue eyes sparkled as he spoke. "But the history is rich here. Give it a few minutes, and you'll feel the vibes."

"What is this place?" Gary looked around.

They stood on a beach at the bottom of a bunch of cliffs. And really big cliffs, too—the sheer walls jutted into the sky. At the base of the cliffs stood large stone columns supporting elevated platforms, crumbling with age, and at the edge of the water sat enormous stone creatures with the heads of eagles and bodies of lizards. The creatures rested on their haunches, watching over the ocean, situated every so often, and went on, it looked like, forever.

"A portal for one of the previous capital cities," Sci Omega said. "Everyone who came to Lemuria had to pass through The Crags."

Iva cocked her head. "The Crags?"

Sci Omega waved with an arm at the giant statues. "The guardians you see before you. The Crags watched over the beach, protecting the tunnels inside the cliffs from invaders."

"How many capital cities were there in the past?" Benjamin asked. The Crags now made three including Mu and Geros.

Sci laughed. "A lot. But when it was here at The Crags, Lemuria was at war. Most people lived either in tunnels or underground."

"How many people lived in the tunnels?" Andy craned his head around to look at the platforms leading to openings in the cliff walls.

"Hundreds of thousands," Sci said. "They stretch underground for miles in all directions."

Gary shook his head. "That's a lot."

Sci inclined his head.

"So what are we supposed to do today?" Heidi asked.

Benjamin smiled. For some reason it made him happy knowing Heidi couldn't read everyone's mind.

"Explore," Sci said. "No digging; no excavation. It's prohibited in The Crags. Walk around. Listen to the stones. If you are quiet enough you can hear. The memories of hundreds of thousands of dead Lemurians are preserved here. But..." and here, his blue eyes pierced into each of them, "...don't venture into the tunnels." And the piercing look disappeared as quickly as it had appeared. "Meet back here at two o'clock. I'll be up there." He pointed to one of the elevated platforms at the top of a large column and teleported away.

They sat on top of a Crag's head to eat lunch. Benjamin noticed Andy position himself next to Iva—he always did, but either she didn't notice or didn't care.

"So I know where your brothers are," Iva said, catching Benjamin off guard.

"What?"

Iva looked down. "I figured it out last night."

And she'd waited until now to tell him? "Where?"

"Well I don't really know exactly where they are."

Andy stared at Iva. "What are you talking about?"

But Heidi smiled at Iva. "Maybe just try to explain it."

"Good idea," Benjamin said. "And then you can explain why we're here right now rather than going to get them."

Iva sighed. "We can't just go get them."

"Why?" Benjamin said. "Are they dead?"

But Iva shook her head. "Oh, no. I mean, not really." She paused. "Well, I guess kind of they are. At least I think so."

Benjamin stared at her.

"They're back in time," Heidi said, and Benjamin turned to look at her, then back at Iva.

Iva nodded. "Right. Based on all the scanning I've been doing for your DNA, it's the only answer. Someone hid them back in time. I figured it out when you mentioned traveling back in time to Geros."

"What about forward in time?" Gary said.

Iva shrugged. "Sure. Maybe they're forward in time."

"In which case they aren't dead," Gary said. "They just wouldn't exist."

"It doesn't matter," Benjamin said. "Wherever they are, we just time travel and go get them. Right?"

"Wrong," Iva said.

 72

"Why not?" Benjamin asked. Why was Iva always so pessimistic?

"Because if they did time travel, then we have no way of locating them," Iva said. "I can only trace their DNA with the Peridot in the present."

"Oh come on, Iva," Andy said. "There has to be some way."

"Even if we could locate them somehow, which we can't, how would we get them?" Iva asked. "Who knows if we can even time travel at all?"

"Jack thinks I'll be able to," Benjamin said. "And we can keep trying to find a temporal phasing telemagnifier. Maybe Nathan Nyx can get us one."

"You heard Mr. Hermes in lecture. You can't get TPTs," Iva said. "Let's just face it—it would've been better if I hadn't figured it out. We can't find them, and we can't retrieve them."

"I may be able to help you."

Five heads whipped around in the direction of the voice. There stood a girl just cresting the head of the large Crag. She had a white dress, olive skin, and long green hair braided into a million tiny braids. And though her eyes seemed to shift between colors, they looked green most of the time.

Benjamin stood up. "What did you say?"

"I said I may be able to help you." She grinned and took a few steps closer to them.

Iva glared at the girl. "How much of our conversation did you eavesdrop on?"

"Enough to know you need help." The girl flipped some of her green braids over her shoulder and smiled like she'd

 73

done nothing wrong.

"You know it's not polite to sneak up on people and listen in on conversations you have no right to listen in on," Gary said.

The girl scowled at them. "You guys are up on my Crag. And you didn't have any shields up. How was I supposed to know the conversation was private?"

Benjamin mentally smacked his head. Why hadn't he placed a shield around them? When was he going to learn?

"Your Crag?" Andy said. "What makes it your Crag?"

She pulled at a green braid and twisted it. "I come up here all the time. And nobody else ever comes up here." She laughed. "Nobody ever comes to this city. People are afraid of it—afraid of all the memories from the dead spirits. This place has lots of bad karma, what with the slaughter that happened."

Heidi's eyes grew wide. "Slaughter?"

"Look, we're not here for a history lesson," Gary said.

Benjamin almost laughed out loud. When was Gary not up for a history lesson? When was Gary not up for any kind of lesson?

"Who are you anyway?" Heidi said. Her hair was still black but ringlets were forming on the sides.

"Yeah, and what makes you think you can help us?" Benjamin said.

"I'm Aurora." The girl's green eyes flashed violet, then settled back on green. "You know—like Aurora Borealis. And I can help you because you have trouble with time."

Andy narrowed his eyes. "So what can you do about it?"

Aurora walked closer and sat down. So Benjamin sat

back down, also. He sensed a super-strong mind block being placed around all six of them.

"I'm not a student like you guys," Aurora said telepathically. *"I live here in Lemuria."*

"And...?" Andy said.

"And my Dad is a special agent."

Andy's face perked up. *"A special agent doing what?"*

"He works on special assignments for the Department of the Preservation of Time."

"He time travels?" Benjamin said. His heart had started pounding as soon as she said time.

"He's a temporal phasing agent," Aurora said. *"He time travels all the time."*

"Does he know how to locate telegens in the past or future?" Iva asked.

"Of course," Aurora said. *"That's what his job is all about. He goes mostly back in time to catch rogue time-traveling telegens. He's supposed to do what he can to keep time from being changed."*

"So how do they do it?" Iva asked. *"How do they find people elsewhere in time?"*

"They use special devices," Aurora said. *"Devices that can track DNA and locate it anywhere in time."*

Iva fiddled with her ring. *"Like the Peridot can track anywhere on the Earth?"*

"Exactly," Aurora said. *"Except way more powerful. These aren't the kind of telemagnifiers you can buy at any old store."*

"Do you have one?" Iva asked.

Aurora laughed. *"No, I've never even seen one. But my dad has, and he's told me all about them."*

"*So where do we get one?*" Benjamin hoped his thoughts didn't sound too eager.

"*You don't get one,*" Aurora said. "*They're huge. And there aren't that many. No—chronolocational telemagnifiers don't move from where they are.*"

"*So where are they?*" Iva asked.

"*There are only three I know of,*" Aurora said. "*Two are under heavy protection at DOPOT, so you wouldn't be able to get to those.*"

"*And the third?*" Iva asked.

"*The third is kept in the Ruling Hall; it's your best bet,*" Aurora said. "*It's kept near the ruling chamber.*"

"*So even if we could somehow get into the Ruling Hall and use this telemagnifier, once we locate my brothers, how do we time travel?*" Benjamin asked remembering they had no telemagnifier to help them.

"*That's the easy part,*" Aurora said. "*All you need for that is a TPT.*"

"*And we can buy that at the store?*" Andy asked.

"*No, of course not,*" Aurora said. "*But if you know where to look, and teleportation isn't a problem, they're easy to come by.*"

"*How?*" A flicker of hope flashed into Benjamin's mind.

"*According to my dad, Kronos keeps these things hidden all over the Earth, all the time, no pun intended,*" Aurora said. "*So you just find a place where Kronos hid one, and voilà, you can time travel.*"

"*The Earth's a pretty big place,*" Gary said.

"*Not for Kronos,*" Aurora said. "*He keeps mostly to his places of worship. Any temple or sculpture of Kronos is sure to turn up a telemagnifier, especially if you're looking.*"

 76

"*Why?*" Heidi asked.

"*Because all Kronos wants to do is cause trouble in time,*" Aurora said. "*He is the ancient god of time after all. The more issues with time, the more he's needed. He loves when people travel back in time and screw things up. It's the kind of thing that keeps my dad up late at night.*"

"*So you're saying we just teleport to any old Temple of Kronos, and we'll find a TPT?*" Benjamin asked.

"*Exactly,*" she said. "*If you know what to look for, you can't miss them.*"

CHAPTER 10

Benjamin Gets Contraband

Andy took charge of the Ruling Hall heist. Okay, so it wasn't really a heist. They weren't stealing anything. All they needed to do was get in, use the telemagnifier, and leave. Simple and almost not against the rules at all. Almost.

Friday, they sat in homeroom going over some last minute details. At least the guys did. Heidi and Iva had run off to the back of the classroom to listen to Nick Konstantin recite his cheesy poem of the day.

"Do you think he ever gets sick of that?" Andy teleported a marble back and forth across the desk. Not like Andy was better at teleportation than Benjamin. It was the single last thing Benjamin was better at. He could feel the annoyance needling at Andy every time he teleported and Andy didn't.

"Gets sick of what?" Gary's eyes glazed over as he stared at his heads-up implant.

"Gets sick of standing up in front of all those people spouting ridiculous love poems," Andy said.

Gary blinked away from his display and looked to the back of the room. "Are you kidding? The guy is up in front of twenty hypnotized girls. All he has to do is make up some corny poem and recite it."

Gary had a good point. Every single glassy female eye was locked on Nick. And he'd just started another recitation.

"My love drew me close, and I knew the time was
near.
As I felt 'er breath, I saw she was sincere.
With 'er arm around me, the truth was oh so
clear.
'Er eyes spoke of love as I whispered in 'er ear."

Nick motioned for Iva to come up to the front. She giggled and got up, sitting on the chair Nick held out for her.

"What is he doing now?" Benjamin turned his neck to see better.

Andy didn't even acknowledge the question. "If for some reason, someone finds out we've broken in to use the chronolocational telemagnifier...good God, can we call it something else? I can't even say that without taking a breath. Anyway, if someone finds out that it has been used, I don't want anyone to be able to trace it back to us."

"How about CT?" Gary's eyes glazed back over. "We could call it the CT."

"Fine. Anything but chronolocational telemagnifier," Andy said.

Benjamin could hear Nick continue the recitation in the background, though he tried to filter it out of his mind. But it persisted.

"And then 'er eyes closed as she drew in for the
kiss.
My life I 'ad lived for the culmination of this.
This love of mine I knew I would never dismiss.
And then our lips met, and I knew that this was
bliss."

79

"My lovely ladies," Nick began.

Man, was this guy a cornball or what?

"This is poem of love's first kiss." He walked behind Iva, placing his hands on her shoulders. He pulled back her hair and leaned his head down close to her.

"Are you guys watching this?" Gary blinked away from his heads-up display again.

But Andy was already on his feet, making his way back to the swarm of girls.

Nick leaned over and began to whisper in Iva's ear. She giggled again.

Benjamin and Gary jumped up to follow Andy, but Andy had already pushed his way through the first layer of girls. With the erratic thoughts pumping through Andy's mind, Benjamin had no idea what Andy was going to do. All he knew was it was going to be something totally stupid.

"*We need help now!*" Benjamin's telepathic voice boomed in Iva's and Heidi's minds.

Iva turned, startled out of her daze. She looked to see Andy, Benjamin, and Gary staring at her, and her face flushed bright red.

"*And what exactly do you need help with?*" Her question sizzled through the telepathic link.

"*If you guys would get over here, we could explain,*" Andy said before Benjamin even had time to think about a response.

Iva ignored Andy and stood up. "I fear I must go now, Nick."

"Alas, as I was afraid," Nick replied. "Until next time." He lifted her right hand to his mouth and kissed it.

Iva giggled, as did the twenty other girls. Except,

Benjamin noticed, Julie Macfarlane. She didn't giggle at all.

Iva and Heidi left the back of the room and joined the guys at a round table. "What is so important?" The sizzling stayed in Iva's voice.

"What's so important is our plans for tonight," Andy said. "Or have you forgotten? I know you have your mind on other things." He nodded his head toward Nick.

"Oh, cut it out." Iva sat down. "You guys are so pathetic. Can't we have a little time to listen to some poetry?"

"Oh, sure," Andy said. "You know come to think of it, maybe we guys can handle it ourselves. We don't need your help anyway."

"Can we please get down to business?" Benjamin said.

Iva crossed her arms. "Anyway, you need my help to use the Chronolocational Telemagnifier."

Andy gritted his teeth but didn't deny it. "We're calling it the CT now."

"Whatever," Iva said.

"I have our plans all mapped out except for one small detail," Andy began. "At midnight we're going to teleport to the outer entrance of the Ruling Hall."

"And by 'we' you mean...?" Benjamin asked.

Andy blew out a breath of annoyance. "I mean you can teleport us all there."

"Why don't we teleport inside the Ruling Hall?" Iva asked.

"They have sensors in place," Andy said. "Once we teleport there, Gary opens the infrared entrance using the keypad he found the other day, and we make our way to the throne room."

"Why the throne room?" Gary asked.

"Secrets of the trade." Andy smiled. "We enter the room. Now comes the tricky part—the part I haven't quite figured out yet. There's a bunch of infrared light beams all over the room. If we get in the way of their path, the alarm sounds, and the chamber seals. So what we need is an infrared deflector to block the beams from being disrupted."

"Where do we get the infrared deflector?" Gary asked.

"This is our problem." Andy tapped his fingers on the table. "I've checked with Morpheus Midas, but he can't get us one. I asked Proteus if he knew anything about them, but he didn't."

"Can we make one?" Gary asked.

"Not in the next sixteen hours." Andy blew out his breath. "So unless we can find one, I'm not sure what to do."

The chime sounded. Homeroom was over.

"All right. Let's all think about it and talk again at lunch," Benjamin said.

Benjamin stewed through telekinesis; Ryan Jordan beat him in every single Kinesis Combat. It would have been humiliating if Benjamin hadn't been so preoccupied. Actually, it was still humiliating. After class, Benjamin and Andy parted ways. Andy was off to look for an infrared detector from a possible source he wouldn't divulge, so Benjamin headed to the dining hall.

Rounding the corner, he saw Heidi and Josh in their normal spot, talking in the hallway. Josh had his usual black leather jacket and unshaven face. Heidi leaned against the

wall, smiling at him.

Benjamin did his best to ignore them, walking straight into the dining hall. He reached up and felt his chin. There wasn't a hair in sight. Could he somehow use his mind to start growing facial hair? Maybe that's how Josh already had enough hair to look eighteen. Getting a black leather jacket might be easier. He did have the extra credit line Nathan had given him, but it was so hot outside. Who in their right mind wore a black leather jacket in the summer anyway?

Since everyone had pretty much ditched him for lunch, he found an empty table and sat down. But then a shadow moved across his plate, and he looked up to see Magic Pan.

"Are you enjoying the menu system being back online?" Magic asked.

"More than you could ever believe," Benjamin said with a full mouth. "And I have to say I'm impressed. You promised you'd get the menus back online, and you did."

"I'm happy you're happy," Magic said. "As I said before, you may think of me as someone who can repair the impossible, obtain hard to find items, collect useful information. When you are in need, remember your Year Two Denarian friend—Magic Pan!"

Benjamin's mind started turning. "So what kind of hard to find items can you obtain, Magic?"

"There is nothing I haven't been able to find when asked," Magic Pan replied.

Benjamin leaned forward. "There's this thing I need. And I need it by tonight."

Benjamin told Magic Pan about the infrared deflector.

Not what they were planning on using it for, of course; just that they needed it and needed it soon.

"But you can't tell anyone," Benjamin said.

Magic shook his head. "Of course not."

"Not even your dad," Benjamin said. The last thing they needed was Walker Pan figuring out they planned on breaking into the Ruling Hall.

Magic pulled an invisible zipper across his lips. "No one. Do you need it before dinner?"

"No. Why? Can you get one?" Benjamin said.

"It is never a question of whether I can obtain the item," Magic said. "Meet me outside the back entrance to the dormitories after dinner. Don't be late, and come alone."

Without another word, Magic Pan stood up and left the dining hall.

Benjamin smiled and finished his lunch.

Later that night, Benjamin returned from meeting Magic Pan and held out his hand so they could all see the small square tile.

"That's all there is to it?" Iva asked.

"Well, what'd you expect?" Gary said. "All it has to do is deflect a tiny beam of light."

"So what did Magic want in return?" Andy asked.

"Nothing," Benjamin said. "He just said to remember this gift as a token of his appreciation, and return it to him when he asks for it."

"Magic Pan is a little strange." Heidi motioned to the infrared deflector. "He acts all innocent, but come on. How did he get this thing?"

Andy took the deflector and pocketed it. "It doesn't matter how he got it, just that he got it. Wear black and meet back here at midnight."

CHAPTER 11

WAKING UP THE RULING HALL

They met at the school exit and teleported in two groups. Benjamin couldn't even see the secret infrared door, but by the time Benjamin got there with the second group, Gary already had it open.

The Ruling Hall was empty as a tomb, so when they got to the throne room, they went on in. Talk about dark. Benjamin adjusted his eyes and saw the two thrones up on the platform. And before Benjamin could stop him, Andy walked over and sat down on a throne, putting his arms on the rests beside him.

"What are you doing?" Benjamin said under his breath.

"I'm working," Andy said.

"No you're not," Benjamin said. "You're sitting down."

"Watch and learn." Andy placed his feet flat on the ground, and with his back straight against the chair, he flipped open a panel under his right arm. A holographic display materialized, and Andy entered a sequence of numbers. The throne slid back, revealing a staircase underneath.

"Whoa," Gary said.

"Where'd you get the code?" Iva asked. Benjamin could tell she was impressed. He was even impressed, though it pained him to admit it.

Andy grinned. "While you were busy flirting with Nick, I was gathering information."

"I do not flirt with Nick," Iva said. "I like to hear his poems. That's all."

"Whatever you say," Andy said. "Okay, one at a time, walk down the staircase."

Benjamin went first, followed by Iva, then Heidi, then Gary. Andy jumped into the opening below, and the throne slid back into place. It was just as dark down here as it had been above. Actually, Benjamin thought it was even darker. But apparently, Gary disagreed.

"Look at that grid," Gary said.

Andy threw his arm across the opening to a room. "Nobody move."

"What grid?" Heidi said.

"The grid of light beams." Gary pointed. "You see?"

They all shook their heads.

"Doesn't anyone see them?" Gary said.

"I see nothing," Benjamin said, glad he wasn't the only one.

"They've used the Leokadia Theorem for light refraction," Gary said. "By tracing the theorem backwards, the starting point becomes obvious."

"I don't care about some theorem," Andy said. "Just tell me where they originate."

Gary followed whatever invisible light beams only he saw with his head, bobbing it up and down, back and forth. He then looked down at the threshold. "Sure. Right here." He pointed just inside the doorway.

Andy handed over the infrared deflector. "Good. Stick this on the wall where the lights start. But don't

touch anything else."

Gary nodded. "The deflector should mimic the play of lights around the room and provide a continuous circuit."

"That's what I heard," Andy said.

Gary took the infrared deflector and squatted down. Without hesitating, he stuck it to the wall and stepped away. And then the chamber lit up like a sun, and Benjamin heard Iva suck in her breath.

There in the center of the room was an enormous, glowing, green sphere. Easily three yards in diameter, it sat on a bronze pedestal with eight legs spread below it on the ground like a giant octopus.

"Look at that," Gary said.

Iva's mouth opened and closed, trying to formulate words. Finally she said, "Can we go in?" But she didn't wait for an answer and didn't even see Gary nodding his head. Stepping into the room, she crossed the distance over to the sphere.

"The Chronolocational Telemagnifier," she said.

"CT," Andy said.

Benjamin walked in also. "Now I see what Aurora meant when she said nobody moves these things. It's huge."

Iva reached out with a delicate hand and touched the orb in front of her. It flickered and thrummed with her touch. Encouraged, she placed both palms on the sphere and ran her hands over its smooth surface. "It's the most beautiful thing I've ever seen."

"Do you think you'll be able to use it?" Heidi asked.

Iva nodded and kept her hands on the sphere. "Definitely."

Andy stepped in beside her. "Let's not waste time then."

It was at this point that Iva took over. She directed them to sit on the ground around the sphere. Even though the tentacle legs stretched nearly to the walls, they found spots to sit between them. Iva herself walked around the sphere, as if trying to find the perfect spot. She ran her hand along the circumference and finally stopped between Benjamin and Heidi. Without a word, they moved farther apart, making more room for her.

Iva turned and looked at them. "You guys need to be totally quiet. It might take a while."

"What's a while?" Andy asked.

"As long as it takes." Iva closed her eyes and placed both hands on the CT. It continued to flicker and thrum as she did so, and she remained still for nearly five minutes. But then, she gave a disgusted sigh and opened her eyes.

"It's not working. I can't find anything." Iva took her hands off the CT, and it stopped thrumming.

"Do you think it would help if Benjamin touched it also?" Heidi said.

If anyone else had made the same suggestion, Iva would have probably blown up; but it was Heidi.

Iva thought about it and then nodded. "I guess it can't hurt."

Benjamin stood up and walked to the opposite side of the sphere from Iva. He placed his hands on it, and Iva replaced hers. She closed her eyes, and the sphere again began to flash and pulsate. It started slow, but gradually increased, until pretty soon, Benjamin felt like he was at some kind of heavy metal rock concert stuck next to an

amplifier. Andy jumped to his feet, but to his credit, remained silent—not that anyone would have heard him over the noise. Heidi and Gary also stood, and the three of them backed away from the telemagnifier.

Just when it sounded like it was going to explode, the light vanished and the sound silenced. Benjamin and Iva flew backward and landed across the room. Heidi rushed over to Iva, followed by Andy and Gary.

"Are you okay?" Heidi asked, squatting down to her level.

Iva remained on the ground, but Benjamin stood up and brushed himself off. He walked over to join his friends.

"Yeah, I'm fine. I think." Iva tried to stand up, but quickly sat back down. "My legs are still a little wobbly."

Benjamin brushed off his pant legs. "I'm okay, too, in case anyone was worried."

Heidi rolled her eyes.

"It felt like getting an electrical shock," he added.

"A pretty high powered electrical shock I'm willing to bet," Gary said. "Did you see that thing? It looked like it was about to explode."

Andy squatted down next to Iva. His voice was gentle— actually gentle—when he spoke. "I know you're shook you up, but we need to get going." He put out his hand for her to grab and helped her to her feet.

"Did you get the information you needed?" a voice from near the doorway asked.

All five heads turned to face the intruder. A tall figure stood shadowed in the dark doorway.

"Oh, crap!" Andy said.

But when the shape stepped closer, Benjamin immediately recognized it, and a weird mixture of relief and nausea washed through him. They'd been caught red-handed by one of the rulers of Lemuria, but at least it wasn't somebody else.

"Don't worry, Andy," Helios Deimos said. "Let's just be thankful this chamber is soundproof. As you know, the chronolocational telemagnifier can make a lot of noise."

"CT," Andy managed to say.

Helios nodded. "Yes, it is a mouthful."

"How long have you been here?" Benjamin asked. "I didn't hear you come in."

"You looked occupied," Helios said. "I'm happy to see you aren't idling away your time practicing for school. So let me ask again. Did you get the information you needed?"

Benjamin looked over at Iva, and she looked back. They both smiled. "Yeah, we got it," he said.

"Then let's be going," Helios said.

When they filed out of the room, Helios reached down and unattached the infrared deflector. He held it up and looked at it. "Where did you manage to get one of these?" He handed it over to Benjamin. "No, don't answer that; I probably don't want to know. Andy, you researched this place pretty well. You got most of the critical information for a successful break in."

"Most of it?" Andy asked.

"What's not so easily accessible is the fact that any time the 'CT' comes to life for even the smallest amount of time, Selene and I are immediately notified," Helios said.

Andy groaned. "Figures."

Helios led them through a hallway at the back of

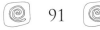

the throne room until they came to a private teleporter. "Benjamin, I need you to stay back for a few minutes."

Benjamin looked at his friends. "I'll meet up with you guys back at school." And so, one at a time, Gary, Iva, Heidi, and Andy teleported away.

"How have you been?" Helios asked Benjamin once everyone had gone.

"Oh, pretty good I guess, considering everything that happened last summer," Benjamin said. "Where is Selene, by the way?"

Helios pursed his lips together. "Away on important business."

"Alone?" Benjamin asked.

Helios nodded. "It's why there are two rulers of Lemuria, instead of just one."

"Makes sense, I guess," Benjamin said.

"So do you need help with anything?" Helios said. "Keeping in mind the block placed on me though. I still can't tell you any more about your siblings, though it looks like you are on the right track."

"Finally." Benjamin shook his head. "You know, I was in Wondersky City over spring break doing this really horrible filing work. Why are so many things kept and filed anyway?"

"Bureaucracy." Helios sighed. "You were saying..."

"Right," Benjamin said. "We happened to stumble across a record with my name on it."

Helios raised an eyebrow. "What did it say?"

So Benjamin explained the whole Ancient Lemurian thing and the old capital city of Geros. "But when we got there, it was gone."

 92

Helios shook his head. "You should have come to me for access badges."

Benjamin laughed. "The thought crossed my mind—for a second."

"And?" Helios said.

"And you're just way too busy," Benjamin said. "Not to mention how would I ever get in to talk to you? Walk in while you're holding court and cut to the front of the line? Or call you on the telecom?"

Helios actually laughed. "No, nothing like that. But we should do a couple telepathy exercises before you leave, so your mind can easily identify and single out mine." And then Helios looked Benjamin right in the eye. "So what are you going to do now?"

Benjamin smiled. "I'm going to travel back in time to Geros to get whatever the secret object is."

"And then?" Helios asked. "What did the chronolocational telemagnifier tell you?"

Benjamin sighed. "Not everything."

Helios raised an eyebrow. "Enough?"

"Enough to find one of my brothers," Benjamin said. "So I'll travel back in time and find him."

"And the other one?" Helios said.

"I don't know," Benjamin said. The CT had only shown him where one of his brothers was in time. There had only been one DNA signature matching his own. Which meant when it came to finding his other brother, he still had no clue. "I guess I'll cross that bridge after I cross this one first."

CHAPTER 12

SUNSPOTS CONTROL LIGHT ON EARTH

Benjamin teleported straight back to the dorms, hoping his head wouldn't spin off with all that had happened. As if breaking into the Ruling Hall hadn't been enough, Helios had caught them doing it. But apparently the night wasn't over yet. Benjamin rounded the corner to his dorm room and found the hallway already occupied.

Benjamin froze in place. "Magic?"

"Hello, Benjamin." Magic Pan smiled and walked toward him, and Benjamin had a weird urge to teleport away. Not like Magic couldn't find him.

"What are you doing here?" Benjamin said.

Magic shrugged. "I came for the infrared deflector. What else?"

Without thinking, Benjamin reached down into his pocket and found the small square. "I thought you gave it to me."

"I did," Magic said. "But unless you give it back to me now, I'll never be able to give it to you in the first place."

That seemed odd. Why would Magic need it now to give to Benjamin in the first place? And then it hit him—hit him like a giant chronolocational telemagnifier. And he knew he had to hand it over to Magic.

"You time traveled to get it?" Benjamin said—not like

 94

it was really a question. There was no other explanation.

Magic took the square from Benjamin's hand. "I can't reveal secrets of the trade. But just remember—you may think of me as someone who can repair the impossible, obtain hard to find items, collect useful information. When you are in need, remember your Year Two Denarian friend—Magic Pan!"

And then Benjamin found out he was not the only Year Two Denarian who could teleport, because, before Benjamin could say another word, Magic Pan teleported away.

Heidi and Iva weren't alone when the boys arrived at the Deimos Diner the next morning. In the booth sat Aurora, the girl they'd met at the Crags a week earlier. Except instead of green hair, today it was orange and her eyes matched yet again.

"What in the world are you drinking?" Andy asked as he slid into the booth and positioned himself next to Iva. Iva's drink was dark and thick and green and looked like something ogres might drink.

"It's Amoeba Juice." Jack teleported onto the table and stood next to the drink. "Packed with kumquats." He licked his lips. "You don't mind do you?" he asked Iva, though he didn't wait for a reply. Putting his tiny lips to the straw, he started drinking and didn't stop. The glass was as tall as he was and twice as wide, but before Benjamin knew it, the Amoeba-Kumquat Juice was gone.

"How can you drink so much?" Benjamin asked.

"Yeah, where do you put it?" Heidi said.

"Hey, that was my drink," Iva said and then shuddered. "But I was done with it anyway."

"I love Amoeba Juice," Jack said. "But it's getting harder and harder to find."

"We have barrels of it in the lava tube," Aurora said.

"The lava tube?" Gary asked.

"Yeah," Aurora said. "Lava tube. My dad and I live in one."

"How can you live in a lava tube?" Heidi said.

"It's big," Aurora said. "Way more space than the two of us need."

"Where's your mom?" Gary asked.

"Gone," Aurora said. "My dad says she ran off just after I was born."

"Wow, I'm sorry to hear that," Iva said. "That must have been hard."

Aurora smiled. "I'm sure she had her reasons. I don't let it drag me down."

Benjamin immediately thought of his birth mother, dying after giving birth to triplets. She'd been so heartbroken at having her three babies taken away that she'd given up living. And Aurora's mother had run off? What would make someone do that?

"Which volcano?" Heidi changed the subject. "Don't you worry that it might erupt?"

Aurora ordered another Amoeba Juice, this time with chipotle peppers. It appeared on the table red as blood and thick as sludge. Jack teleported in front of it and immediately started drinking it until Aurora yanked the straw away. "It's up north in the Ring of Fire, and it's not going to erupt for another three thousand years."

"How do you know?" Gary asked.

Aurora took a giant sip of the drink. "You know. The

time travel thing and all. We've actually gone forward and watched it erupt. Erupting volcanoes are my favorite thing to watch." She paused. "Well, maybe my second favorite."

"What's your favorite?" Andy asked.

"Yeah, what could be cooler than watching a volcano erupt?" Gary asked.

"Watching the Aurora Borealis from just outside our lava tube."

"The Northern Lights?" Benjamin said. "That's right. If you live that far north, you can probably see them every night."

"Not every night," Aurora replied. "It depends on sunspots and all."

"Sunspots?" Benjamin said.

"Of course," Gary said. "The more sunspots there are, the stronger the Aurora Borealis. They tend to follow an eleven year cycle."

Aurora crossed her arms. "So anyway, what's up? I'm sure you guys had a reason for asking me to meet you."

Benjamin remembered to put up a mind block this time. Talking about sunspots was one thing. Talking about unauthorized time-traveling trips was another.

"*We plan to time travel,*" Benjamin said in his mind.

"*Cool,*" Aurora said. "*Did you figure out when to?*"

Benjamin nodded his head. "*We actually need to make a couple of trips.*"

"*We need to go back about three thousand years,*" Iva said.

"*That's the second trip,*" Benjamin said. "*First we need to go back a thousand years.*"

Aurora didn't even blink—or flinch when she took

another sip of her drink. *"Good. And just to clarify—none of you guys has ever time traveled, right?"*

They all shook their heads.

"So you'll want to do the thousand years back trip first—kind of as a test run," Aurora said.

"I thought telegens could only temporally phase once a year," Gary said. *"The chromosomes need time to realign, right? I read that in the DOPOT warnings."*

Aurora laughed. *"Not that long. They just say that to scare people."*

"So how do TPTs work?" Gary asked. *"It's impossible to find information about them in the library."*

"Then you're going to the wrong libraries," Aurora said. *"Each TPT can transport a handful of telegens backward or forward in time. It's a two-way trip. You keep it with you when you jump back, and then use it to move forward again whenever you're ready. You know, time and all isn't really an issue."* Aurora laughed at this.

"Sounds perfect," Benjamin said. *"How do we get one?"*

"Oh yeah. It's not that hard, but it can get complicated. Kronos is always trying to screw things up. He thinks it makes him and his job more valuable." She consulted her heads-up display. *"It's probably too late to get one now. You'll have to wait until next Saturday. Even though telegens aren't supposed to time travel, and no one's supposed to know about the TPTs, people do, and they get snatched up pretty fast."*

"From where?" Andy asked.

"Well it kind of works like this—in general," Aurora said. *"Each Saturday morning, Kronos goes around leaving TPTs at his places of worship around the Earth. Then, tele-*

 98

gens come and collect them, time travel, create havoc on the timeline, and voilà, once again, Kronos is in business."

"So you're saying that what we need to do is wake up early next Saturday, teleport to some temple of Kronos, and look for a TPT?" Gary said.

"Exactly!" Aurora replied. "But you have to use it that day."

"Why Saturday?" Andy asked.

"Because Saturn is another name for Kronos, and it's Saturn's Day—get it—Saturday—Saturn's Day." Aurora said.

"Oh, yeah, get it," Andy said.

Which made about one thing Benjamin understood. At least he had a week to figure out what to do next.

Using a ridiculously long game of Rock, Scissors, Paper, they decided Heidi and Gary would get to time travel with Benjamin for the first time. Sure, the game was unfair, but finding a random method among a bunch of mind readers all connected through the Alliance bond was pretty much impossible. So now all there was to do was wait.

When Friday finally rolled around, Andy and Gary went to bed early. Benjamin plugged his ears to tune out their snoring, but he still couldn't sleep. So he stepped out of the dorm room to practice telepathy.

He could hear tons of people still up around the school, and pretty soon, he tried to zero in on some of them. First he decided on Ryan Jordan. Ryan was probably practicing telekinesis in private somewhere.

Benjamin opened his mind to all the thoughts he could

around the school and tried to single out Ryan. He found Jonathan Sheehan in their dorm room, but Ryan wasn't there. He continued looking, but Ryan wasn't in the school. Extending his mind a little more, he searched nearby.

It wasn't long before he found Ryan, perched on a roof of a nearby building. Though Ryan was pretending to be looking up at the night sky, there was only one thing on his mind—and surprisingly, it wasn't Julie Macfarlane who sat next to him. It was Benjamin.

Why was Ryan thinking about Benjamin? Did it have something to do with the record? But then Benjamin felt the mind block go up. Ryan had detected him which was so not good. Benjamin still had a long way to go. But how had Ryan detected the snooping so soon, unless he'd been working on telejamming also?

Benjamin decided to check on someone else to see if the Alliance bond made eavesdropping easier. He scanned the school. Heidi was just getting back to her dorm. Where had she been all this time? Benjamin felt around in Heidi's mind, making sure not to trigger any of her usual alarms. The regular blocks she always had in place were up, but there was something new. She was bubbling over. And she was thinking about that guy from her Empathy class, Josh. No way! Had Heidi been with Josh?

Benjamin felt his heart speed up. He didn't like the thought of Heidi on some sort of date, but why should he care? Heidi was just one of his friends. But still—what was she doing wasting her time hanging out with Josh? She had way more important things to be doing. Things like trying to help Benjamin figure out where his brothers were.

He'd definitely mention it tomorrow. See what she had

to say about it.

Heidi opened the door to her dorm room and stopped. She took in the situation for a moment then ran over to Iva's bed where Iva was lying face down on her bed crying. Okay, this was getting way too personal, but Benjamin couldn't drag himself away.

"Iva! What's wrong?" Heidi said.

Iva only cried louder. She hid her face in her pillow, trying to muffle her sobs.

"It's okay," Heidi said.

"It's not okay," Iva managed to get out between sobs. "I had another dream."

Iva was having dreams? Why hadn't she mentioned anything about them?

"I can't stand to even go to sleep anymore," Iva cried. "And Jonathan's there trying to eavesdrop on every dream I have."

Jonathan Sheehan was eavesdropping on Iva's dreams?

"You have to ignore him, Iva," Heidi said. "He has nothing to do with any of this. He's just trying to show off. And you have to ignore the dreams. They're only dreams. Not real."

"But they are real," Iva said. "I see it in the future."

"That's only one possible future," Heidi said.

"But you die in every single dream. Every single dream! And Andy. And Benjamin. Horrible deaths." Iva was now sobbing.

"Iva," Heidi said. "We're not going to die. They're only dreams. Nothing more."

Benjamin froze in place. Iva was having dreams about him dying? And dying a horrible death? Why hadn't she

said anything? And what about Gary? She hadn't mentioned Gary dying a horrible death.

"I'm so scared, Heidi," Iva cried. "I don't want to go through life without you guys."

"You'll never be alone, Iva. And just because you see something in a dream doesn't mean it's going to happen. Your mind is just focusing on the worst. Your dreams are not the future."

Iva tried to wipe her eyes. "But what if they are? What if my dreams do come true?"

"Your dreams will only come true if you let them," Heidi said. "Just because you're really good at telegnosis doesn't mean every dream you have is real. I have no intention of dying anytime soon, and I'm sure Andy and Benjamin don't either."

She could say that again. Benjamin almost telepathically agreed but managed to stop himself in time.

"You have to get past this, Iva," Heidi said. "You're destined to be the high oracle; I know you are. You can't let these dreams get in your way."

Iva leaned over and hugged her friend hard. And then Benjamin felt Heidi think about what Iva had said. About the horrible death thing.

Benjamin jumped back, and left her mind, severing all telepathic links. He felt dirty all over—like he shouldn't have been listening to the conversation at all. If Iva hadn't told him about the dreams, there was probably a good reason. Truthfully, now that he knew what she was dreaming about, he almost wished he didn't. What kinds of horrible deaths had she dreamed for him? And who was killing him?

But still, even with his curiosity, he shouldn't have

been listening. Talk about just plain wrong. Iva always had a reason for everything she did. At that moment, Benjamin decided, unless it was absolutely necessary, he would never intrude on his friends' privacy again. Ever. Turning out the light, he headed back to the bedroom to get some sleep.

CHAPTER 13

THE TOURIST ALMOST STEALS THE TPT

"Couldn't you guys try to be on time just once?" Iva glared at them when they walked in for breakfast five minutes late. Seriously, with the way she tapped her foot, you'd have thought the world would come to an end.

"Couldn't you cut us some slack just once?" Andy said. He'd hit snooze like five times, but seeing as how he wasn't the one time traveling, Benjamin kind of understood.

Benjamin opened his mouth to agree with Andy when he remembered the conversation from the night before—the one he'd eavesdropped on. It was hard to forget how upset Iva had been. It was also hard to forget she thought he was destined to die in some torturous way.

So instead Benjamin laughed. "You know, maybe we could try to be on time, just once. It probably does get annoying having to wait around all the time."

Heidi and Iva said nothing—just looked at him like he'd told them the dome was imploding.

"Who's ready for a little temporal phasing?" Gary looked like he might start dancing at any moment.

"Shhhh!" Iva said. "Do you want the whole school to know?"

"Iva, the whole school is asleep," Andy said. And then he yawned just for effect.

Gary angled his ear upward. "That's not quite true. I can hear at least twenty Year Two Denarians up already."

"Yeah, well I'm pretty sure they aren't spying on us," Andy said.

"If everything goes well, it won't seem like we're gone long at all," Benjamin said.

"And if everything doesn't go well?" Iva asked.

Benjamin shrugged. "Everything will be fine. We're only going back a thousand years."

"Just be careful," Iva said.

"Yeah, and bring us a souvenir," Andy added.

"Seriously, Andy, it's not like we're going back in time to shop," Heidi said.

Andy laughed. "I thought girls always wanted to shop."

Heidi smartly refrained from answering, and Andy smartly refrained from saying anything else.

"So you're sure these are the right kind of clothes?" Benjamin motioned down at the baggy pants Gary had insisted he put on.

Gary nodded. "Everyone wore baggy pants back then. Trust me."

Which Benjamin was prepared to do. If Gary had taken the time to research fashion trends from one thousand years ago, who was Benjamin to argue?

"Ready?" Benjamin reached out and grabbed Heidi's hand. He placed his other hand on Gary's shoulder. And before anyone could change their mind, he teleported them away from the school.

A pile of rocks crumbled under Benjamin's feet when they arrived. He fell and only managed to keep himself

from hitting head first by grabbing hold of a round piece of column. But his weight threw it off, and it started rolling down the hill.

"Wow!" Heidi said.

Benjamin thought she must've been talking about the giant column rolling away, but she wasn't even looking at it. And once he looked up, he saw why. Green grass grew up around the ruins of the giant temple, and a statue as big as a Titan stood over them.

"So this is Tunisia," he said.

"It's not as popular as some of the temples in Rome," Gary said, "but this was one of the most important temples in ancient Tunisia. It's rumored to be built on the ruins of an even older temple to the god Baal-Hammon."

"Right, Gary," Benjamin said. "Good information." No matter the situation, Gary always had useless trivia to supply.

The ruins were big, but totally in shambles. There probably used to be tons of columns, but now there were six; only the outline of the temple was still intact.

"Iva was right about there not being too many visitors here," Gary said.

"We have to watch out for other tourists." Heidi motioned with her head to the columns on the other side of the ruins.

"Hey, where'd he come from?" Gary asked.

"He walked up from over the hill," Heidi said. "I saw him just when we reached the perimeter."

"Well one tourist shouldn't be too hard to avoid," Benjamin said.

The tourist, a young guy with dark, curly hair, looked

up across the ruins, smiled, and waved. They waved back, and he turned away.

Benjamin pointed at a bunch of rocks that looked like at one point they might have been a wall. "Let's say the TPT is inside the temple boundaries. Assuming that, let's walk the perimeter and see what we come up with."

But after a half hour, they'd found nothing. Benjamin sat on a broken off column and wiped his dripping sweat with the "Nogicals Rule" t-shirt Jack had given him for his birthday.

Gary sat beside him on a low wall. "Does it ever fascinate you guys to think this used to be a state-of-the-art place of sacrifice and worship built two thousand years ago?"

Benjamin thought for a moment before answering. He used to think recorded history was only eight thousand years old. But Lemuria went back 900,000 years, which really changed his views on everything.

"You know even though Lemuria is older than dirt, it's still cool to be somewhere like this." Benjamin nodded at the ruins. "This used to be a really important place, and now it's just a crumbling ruin. Two thousand years is nothing compared to Lemuria. But here we are walking where others before us dreamed their dreams and worshipped their gods. Someone took the time to build this temple which was a big thing; I mean—look at this place. The temple was probably perfect when it was built. And now it's in ruins. And we come along and wonder about the people. What would they say now if they saw their temple destroyed?"

Benjamin stopped talking and realized both Heidi and

Gary were staring at him.

"Whoa," Gary said. "That was really deep."

"Yeah. Really intense," Heidi said. "I didn't know you had it in you."

Benjamin felt his face heat up. Great. With the emotions he'd been putting off through the Alliance bond, Heidi probably thought he was some kind of softie.

"I've always thought history and archaeology and stuff were pretty cool." Benjamin hoped it didn't sound as dopey as he knew it did. "We'd never really visited anywhere like this before. And now we go to a different archaeological dig each week. But this seems so real, so perfect. Like a moment of time that's been captured and preserved." He cleared his throat. "Anyway, let's keep looking. Where's our tourist?"

They looked up. The tourist was ten feet away from them holding a shiny brass plate. Benjamin felt the telenergetic power sparking off it.

"*That's it!*" he thought to them. "*He's got the TPT.*"

It took a moment for realization to dawn on Heidi and Gary.

"*What do we do now?*" Gary asked.

The tourist looked up at them, still holding the plate. "Are you kids here all alone?"

Benjamin hesitated. What kind of creepy question was that? Was this guy some rogue time-traveling telegen also looking for TPTs?

"Uh, no," Benjamin said. "We're actually part of a field trip."

The tourist passed the plate back and forth between his hands. "Funny. I haven't seen anyone else."

"They're down the hill," Heidi said. Guess she felt the creep-factor, also.

Benjamin pressed on the man's mind. Nothing. It felt like a blank slate. Okay, so this guy wasn't a telegen. But he still had the telemagnifier. And who wouldn't walk away with an ancient Tunisian brass plate given the chance?

The man looked down at the plate again. "Did you kids see this rock?"

"What rock?" Benjamin asked.

The man held up the plate. "This one. It looks like it should be heavier than it really is."

"He must see the plate as a rock," Gary said silently. *"He doesn't know it's a telemagnifier."*

"Oh, that boring old rock," Heidi said. "Yeah, we saw it. Talk about ugly."

"I was thinking it may be petrified feces," Gary said. "Which would explain why it's so light."

The man smiled. "Well in that case..." and he tossed it Frisbee-like clear across the ruins.

Benjamin watched as it sailed away, hit the ground, and started rolling down the hill. The tourist looked at them and winked. "I hope you enjoy the rest of your field trip." And then he walked away.

Once he was out of earshot, Benjamin jumped up and started running toward the plate. "Maybe only telegens can see it's a telemagnifier." Either that or the man was blind. Not that it mattered. They needed to get to the plate before it vanished. Benjamin didn't bother to look behind him; he knew Gary and Heidi would be following. And when he ran down the hill and saw the sun reflect off the bronze, he smiled, reached down, and picked it up.

 109

"Got it," he said.

"Good." Gary walked up. "Kronos put this thing here for us to use."

"So let's not disappoint him," Benjamin said.

"Aurora told us to think of the time and place we want to go, and then just hold on to the telemagnifier," Heidi said.

"So just to be sure, we're all thinking about Mu, capital city of Lemuria, one thousand years ago. Right?" Gary asked.

"Right," Benjamin said.

They grabbed onto the brass plate. Looking around, Benjamin made sure the dark-haired tourist was gone. Which he was. After all, who would want petrified feces?

"Okay, ready, set, go." Benjamin began to concentrate on the location and time they were seeking. In his mind, through the Alliance bond, he felt Heidi and Gary doing the same. He felt some of his energy transferring to the TPT, and then the world changed.

CHAPTER 14

THE CHESS SET GETS TRADED

The first thing Benjamin noticed was his shadow get smaller. And then he felt his body start to bend—almost like it was collapsing in on itself. But before Benjamin could think too long on it, he felt a giant crunch and heard a snap, and then everything disappeared.

The world only vanished for a second, but when it re-formed, everything had changed. Benjamin felt the crunching again—actually kind of decompressing this time—and then it was over. He looked down at himself. Everything seemed to be in place, and nothing hurt. He'd wound up in a park surrounded by a bunch of trees, and Gary, Heidi, and he still had the plate. So far so good.

"Are we really in the past?" Heidi asked.

Benjamin didn't answer for a second but then replied, "Check your heads-up display. Looks like it gets updated with the local time."

"No way!" Gary's eyes glazed over. "You're right. It must synchronize itself to a global satellite."

"You're telling me it's backwards compatible to one thousand years ago?" Heidi said.

"Or that it's forwards compatible to one thousand years in the future," Gary said. "I guess it's just how you decide to look at it."

"Do you think the Deimos Diner was in business now?" Heidi said.

"I doubt it since it's named after the current—I mean the future—rulers of Lemuria," Benjamin replied. "Any ideas who the rulers are now?"

"Of course," Gary answered. "If we really are exactly one thousand years back in time, then the rulers aren't twins but actually a married couple—something pretty much unheard of."

"Why?" Heidi asked.

"Well, history shows us that when the rulers are married to each other, it ruins the objectivity each of them would otherwise provide," Gary said. "The current rulers only stayed in office for a few years, at which point they were forcibly overthrown."

"You're kidding, right?" Heidi asked.

Gary shook his head.

"So you're telling me that here, in Lemuria, the rulers were overthrown?" Heidi said.

When Gary confirmed her statement, Heidi continued. "Lemuria is just so advanced. I just can't imagine rulers getting deposed."

"Look at history everywhere," Benjamin said. "It happens all the time. People won't stand for bad government."

"How do you know all this, Gary?" Heidi asked. "How do you know that the current rulers are going to be overthrown?"

"I read a book on the governmental history of Lemuria," Gary said.

Just then, Benjamin noticed someone watching them. The man must've overheard. Why hadn't Benjamin put up

a mind shield? Seriously, when would he learn?

"*Look, let's stop talking about it,*" Benjamin said. "*I don't want to cause the next revolution.*"

The eavesdropper hurried off.

"*It may be too late for that,*" Gary said. "*I'm pretty certain that telegen was Ichabod Icter—the man history credits with starting the revolution.*"

"Well, if they deserve to be overthrown, who am I to stop it?" Benjamin said.

"So now what?" Heidi asked.

Benjamin smiled. "The Silver Touch. We need access badges to Geros."

The surprising thing about the past was how few things had changed; it made one thousand years seem like no time at all. They walked down Mu Way until, just like in their own time, they found the three dimensional floating cube hanging in the air.

Heidi headed to the front door and it automatically opened, and Benjamin and Gary followed her in.

"Amazing," Benjamin said. "The world outside is in the middle of the crusades, and the doors here in Lemuria open on their own."

"Remember, Benjamin, one thousand years is only point one one percent of the timeline of Lemuria," Gary said.

Benjamin nodded but didn't say anything. He left most wise-cracking comebacks to Gary's vast fountain of knowledge up to Andy.

Once they got inside The Silver Touch, they found it empty. But at this Silver Touch, not even the shopkeeper was around. Heidi made a beeline for a display case full of

jewelry. Benjamin shrugged, and he and Gary followed her.

"Doesn't anyone work here? Because I totally need to look at that." Heidi pointed to a hideous, green star bigger than Benjamin's palm hanging on a rope.

"You're kidding, right?" Gary asked. "Because that thing is uggg-lyy."

"Ugly! I've been looking for one of these forever," Heidi said. "They're so rare and so hard to come by. If I don't get this one now, I may never find another one."

Benjamin kept to himself the fact that it might be a blessing. "I thought we weren't here to shop," Benjamin said, but only got a smirk for a reply.

"What's it for?" Gary asked.

"I don't know," Heidi said. "But I saw a picture of it in our Empathy study guide."

And then the chime sounded. Someone had come into the store. Benjamin turned to look, expecting to see a shopkeeper, and froze. He knew the man who'd just walked into the store. Walker Pan—Magic Pan's dad, and the owner of the Ammolite chess set.

Benjamin's reflexes took over. He wasn't sure how it happened, but without giving it more than a microsecond of thought, he teleported himself, Gary, and Heidi to the opposite side of the store behind two bookshelves.

If Walker Pan hadn't just walked into The Silver Touch, the looks on Gary and Heidi's faces would have been priceless. Heidi was still staring down at the ugly green star which was no longer there. And Gary was grimacing. But then they looked up.

"Don't say a word." Benjamin threw up the strongest mind block he could—which was pretty strong, if he did

say so himself. Telejamming had paid off after all.

Thank God his friends were smart and caught on to things quickly. There was no "What are you talking about, Benjamin?" or "How did we get way over here, Benjamin?"

"*Who just came in?*" Heidi asked.

"*Take a look,*" Benjamin said.

They peeked their heads out from between some books. And then Benjamin actually heard Gary's heartbeat speed up.

"*What is he doing here?*" Gary asked.

"Ah, my friend," a voice said, coming from the far back of the store. "You'll have to excuse me. I was down in the basement and didn't hear you come in. My door chime has been acting up. I hope you weren't waiting long."

The man looked like Morpheus—kind of. More like Morpheus on steroids. With long hair.

"I actually just arrived." Walker looked around, and Benjamin could have sworn his eyes rested on the bookcases for just a second longer than necessary. But then they moved on. "I have a business transaction I would like to make. Is the store empty?"

The shopkeeper smiled and nodded. "If it is privacy you would like, then it is privacy you shall get."

Benjamin watched as the door locked and the windows blacked over.

"Minnolo Midas at your service," the bulky Morpheus-look-alike said.

Walker strode to the counter and then teleported an object from somewhere else to directly in front of him.

Benjamin kicked Gary when Gary sucked in his breath.

 115

"It's the chess set," Gary said.

"I can see that," Benjamin said.

"Just be quiet you guys," Heidi said.

But Gary couldn't have been heard anyway over the gasping of Minnolo Midas. "There's no way I will ever be able to afford this."

Walker smiled and tented his fingers. "Perhaps we could make a deal then?"

But Minnolo didn't reply. He was too busy running his hands over each of the pieces and rubbing the board.

Walker cleared his throat.

Minnolo took a moment to recover. "Oh, yes, a deal. What kind of deal did you have in mind?" He looked around his store and scratched his head. "Though I'm not sure everything in here put together could pay for this exquisite piece of art."

If Minnolo was trying to bargain, he wasn't doing a very good job.

"Perhaps you have some more unique items elsewhere," Walker said.

Minnolo glanced to the back of the store, to the steps Benjamin knew led down to the basement. And then he looked back at the chess set. If Benjamin had to guess, he would have said at that moment in time, Minnolo would have traded his soul for the chess set.

Minnolo licked his lips. "What kind of unique items are you interested in?"

"I'm in the market for telemagnifiers." Walker tapped his fingers together. "TPTs in particular."

"It's illegal to have temporal phasing telemagnifiers," Minnolo said, looking back to the basement steps.

"And perhaps some telejammers and an infrared deflector," Walker continued as if Minnolo hadn't said a word.

"*An infrared deflector!*" Gary thought.

"*That's what we got from Magic Pan,*" Benjamin thought back.

"Infrared deflector," Minnolo mused and picked up another chess piece.

"Ah, yes," Walker said. "And possibly a teleportation booster and a teleportation scrambler—but a large one."

"*What's a teleportation scrambler?*" Heidi asked.

"*Sounds like something to block teleportation signals,*" Benjamin said.

Minnolo didn't reply. Walker again looked around the store and at the front door. Did he know they were in the store? He couldn't possibly; they'd arrived before him.

"So, do we have a deal?" Walker Pan asked.

Minnolo placed the two chess pieces he was studying—the rook and the bishop—back on the board. "Let me just go check in my basement. It may be the case that someone has snuck the items you're interested in into my store."

It seemed like an eternity but was probably only about ten minutes before Walker finally left. But then it got even worse. Minnolo took painstaking care setting up the chess board on a display table near the front of the shop. After the first eight pieces, Benjamin couldn't take it anymore. He teleported them out of the shop onto a bench.

"That was close," Heidi said.

"Way too close," Gary agreed. "What was he doing back

here one thousand years in the past?"

"Selling the chess set it looks like," Benjamin said.

"But why?" Gary asked. "Why time travel all the way back here to sell the chess set only to buy it back one thousand years in the future?"

"Good question," Benjamin said.

"Maybe to get those telemagnifiers and the infrared deflector." Heidi started walking across the street, back to The Silver Touch.

"Where are you going?" Benjamin asked.

She stopped and grabbed his arm, dragging him with her. "I'm not leaving without that star telemagnifier. Not to mention we still need our access badges to Geros."

They didn't mention the chess set when they walked back in, and Minnolo didn't bring it up either. Benjamin wasn't sure what he could say without giving away the fact that they'd eavesdropped on the entire transaction.

"What may I help you with?" Minnolo Midas asked, but Heidi was already pointing out the telemagnifier.

"This," she said, and grabbed for it when he took it out of the display case.

But he pulled it back. "How would you like to pay?"

"Pay?" Heidi said.

A wave of panic swept into Benjamin's mind. They were back in time, but had no way to buy the access badges they needed. And it's not like they had a priceless chess set to trade.

"Yes, pay," Minnolo said. "That is the general idea of shopping."

Benjamin was about to open his mouth when Heidi beat him to it. "Do you take credit?" she asked.

Minnolo laughed. "Of course. Credit. Denari. We take anything."

Heidi looked over at Benjamin. "Benjamin, use your credit account your dad gave you to pay, will you? You did transfer it to your heads-up display, right?"

He looked back at her. Was she nuts? They were one thousand years in the past. There was no record of his credit back then. But the heads-up displays seemed to work, so maybe the credit would, too.

Minnolo swiped the bill in front of Benjamin's left eyeball, and it clicked green instantly; the transaction had gone through just fine. Heidi was now the proud new owner of the ugly, green star. Which solved their first problem in ancient Lemuria.

"Hey, Benjamin," Heidi said. "Did you ever get a birthday present?"

Benjamin looked down at his t-shirt. "Only from Jack."

"*Nogicals Rule*," Minnolo read. "Interesting. Anything else you think you might like?"

"Last year I got a Geodine." Benjamin pulled the small globe out of the pocket of his baggy pants. "I take it with me everywhere."

Minnolo's eyes almost popped out of this head. "May I please see that?"

"Sure." Benjamin handed it over.

Minnolo studied the small globe. "Amazing. The idea of putting a Geodine inside a tiny globe. If only I'd thought of it myself. May I ask where you purchased this particular item?"

"Here of course," Benjamin said just before Heidi

kicked him sharply in the shin. "Ow!" he said. "*What'd you do that for?*"

"*Idiot!*" she thought to him. "*We aren't supposed to tell anyone we're time travelers.*"

"Here?" Minnolo asked. "I can guarantee we've never sold anything like this in the Silver Touch. I've never seen anything like it before."

Benjamin grabbed the small globe back from Minnolo. "Oh, I mean, I think I was wrong. I found it somewhere."

"Isn't that the Geodine we made together in science class, Benjamin?" Gary asked.

"Oh, yeah, of course," Benjamin replied. "We made it. That's right."

"Would you mind if I used its design to make some more?" Minnolo asked.

"Sure." Benjamin stuffed it back in his pocket. "I mean there's nothing special about it."

"Of course there's not," Minnolo said.

"*And so the globe Geodine is invented,*" Heidi thought. "*At this rate, the whole timeline is going to change. We'll be lucky if the school still exists when we get back.*"

"*Not if it was destiny for Minnolo Midas to invent it,*" Gary said. "*Maybe that's how it always was.*"

"Back to your birthday present," Minnolo Midas said. "I have a wonderful item for you." He led them over to a display cabinet packed full of random objects. Benjamin had no clue what any of them were. Minnolo reached in and pulled out a small, glass rod. At least it kind of looked like it was made of glass.

"The ultimate spying device," Minnolo said. "A lumitube."

Benjamin reached out and took the glass rod from

Minnolo. "A lumitube? What does it do?" As he turned the rod over in his hand it started glowing yellow from inside. He rolled it over again, and it changed to blue.

Minnolo smiled. "It's a universal eavesdropping device. It can tap into some of the most advanced systems in Lemuria." He looked around. "I don't really have anything around here to show you how it works, but it's pretty simple. You just plug it into a lumitube socket when you want to tap information."

Benjamin looked again at the rod which was now green. "Why does it change color?"

"It's looking for a socket," Minnolo said. "When it's red that means there's a socket close by."

"It's great. How much do I owe you for it?" Would his credit line ever run out? Nathan Nyx hadn't told him how much was in it. But maybe with the time travel thing and all, there was actually more money on it—like none of it had been spent so far.

"Consider it my gift to you for the design of the globe Geodine." Minnolo turned to Gary. "And is there anything I can help you with?"

Gary shook his head, but Benjamin took a deep breath. Here went nothing. "There is one more thing."

Minnolo was not idiot. With a flick of his hand he blacked the windows over—again—and leaned close. "Yes?"

"We need access to Geros," Heidi said.

Minnolo laughed. "You're kidding, right?"

"Uh, no," Benjamin said. "Why would we be kidding?"

"Because you're the second person in here today looking for access cards," Minnolo said.

 121

"We are?" Benjamin said.

"Who was the first?" Gary asked. "That guy who just came in?"

Minnolo's eyes flew to the chess set. "What guy?"

But apparently Gary wasn't up for playing games. "Don't act like you don't know. The one you just traded a bunch of illegal stuff for this chess set with. Walker Pan."

Minnolo's eyes grew wide. "How could you know—?"

But Heidi was on top of things. "It doesn't matter, Gary." She smiled at Minnolo, and Benjamin could just about feel the positive emotions shooting from her. Maybe she was using some of her advanced Empathy techniques to make Minnolo happy again.

Whatever she was doing, it worked. Minnolo smiled. "That's true. It doesn't matter. Business is business, and it just so happens I do have another access badge to Geros somewhere around here." He reached under the counter and when his hand came back up, he had a circular plastic disk in it.

Benjamin smiled. "Perfect." He reached out to take it, but Minnolo pulled his hand back.

"Not so fast," Minnolo said. "There's still the matter of payment."

Benjamin sighed. "How much?"

But Minnolo shook his head. "Not money. No, this time I want something besides money."

"You already got the design for the Geodine," Gary said.

Minnolo put his finger to his mouth. "True."

"What then?" Gary said.

"How about I go easy on you," Minnolo said. "How

about we just settle on a little telepathic energy."

"Telepathic energy!" Heidi's hair flashed and turned bright red.

But apparently this didn't faze Minnolo. He smiled at her. "I need someone to open an eavesdropping portal to Atlantis for me." And then he stared right at Heidi. "Someone who is good at telepathy."

"No," Heidi said.

"Just a small amount of energy would do," Minnolo said.

Heidi met his gaze, and their eyes locked. "I'm not giving you any of my energy."

"What's the big deal?" Benjamin said.

But immediately he was sorry he asked. Heidi whipped around to look at him. "It's mine, Benjamin. And it's not for sale."

Minnolo crossed his arms, and held the access badge in clear sight in his fingers.

Benjamin turned back to Heidi. "Heidi, we need the Geros access badge. Can't you just expend a little?"

Heidi stood there for a minute, and Benjamin could sense her internal battle through the Alliance bond. But he didn't say anything else. She needed to decide on her own.

"Fine," she said to Minnolo.

"Fine, what?" he said.

She glared at him. "Fine. A tiny amount." She started walking to the back of the store. "Show me where the spying portal is."

Waiting for Heidi felt like eternity, though it was probably closer to ten minutes. Sure, Gary kept himself occupied staring at the chess set, which left Benjamin wandering

around the shop trying to guess what different things were. And wondering who else had gotten a Geros access badge. Walker Pan was the obvious answer, but he hadn't mentioned it, and they'd watched the whole transaction. But who else could it have been? The odds that some random stranger had decided to visit Geros today of all days were pretty close to zero.

When Heidi walked out of the back room, Benjamin hurried over. "What took you so long?"

"We can talk about it later," Heidi said.

Minnolo walked to the door. "If there is nothing else…" And he pulled the door open.

Benjamin held out his hand. "Aren't you forgetting something?"

Minnolo smiled. "Of course." He reached into his pocket and handed Benjamin the Geros access badge. "Might I say it's been a pleasure doing business with you."

But before Benjamin, Heidi, and Gary had hardly taken a step out the door, it had closed and locked behind them.

"Guess he's excited to go spy on Atlantis," Gary said.

"Good for him," Heidi said. "Let's go."

Benjamin nodded. "Right. Let's get to Geros. Good God, Heidi. You took forever. Whoever went to Geros before us could've died of old age by now."

CHAPTER 15

Geros—Then

Compared to Geros of their own time, Geros in the past looked like a metropolis. Sure, a crumbling metropolis, but at least instead of holes in the ground there were buildings standing everywhere in various states of disrepair. And speaking of the big hole in the ground, Benjamin looked over to where the ancient city's Ruling Hall had been.

"It's still here." Benjamin let out the breath he'd been holding.

Heidi nodded. "Now just to find whatever it is we're looking for."

Gary squinted. "Who's that?"

"Who?" Benjamin looked toward the building.

"The heat signature from inside," Gary said. "Can you see it through the wall?"

"You see a heat signature?" Heidi said.

Gary nodded. "Sure. I mean look at this place. There's nothing else generating heat around here to get in the way."

"So you're saying someone is inside the Ruling Hall?" Benjamin said.

"Yep," Gary said. "But they're just standing there."

Benjamin sighed. "You know, can't anything be easy? Just once? We try to get the object in our time, but someone beats us to it. So we travel back a thousand years, and we

have the same problem." He started walking toward the old building. "Might as well get this over with."

But Heidi smiled. "I don't think they're trying to beat us to getting the object."

"They?" Gary said. "I only see one heat signature."

"You can read their minds?" Benjamin said.

But Heidi shook her head. "No, not really. I mean kind of." She blinked a couple times. "Oh, let's just go see who it is." And she set out ahead of Benjamin.

He shrugged and followed her. Maybe this wouldn't be so hard after all.

When Benjamin walked through the crumbling door of the old Ruling Hall, he realized why Gary hadn't seen a second heat signature; it was too small.

"Helios? Jack?" Benjamin said.

Jack smiled and winked. "See, I told you you'd be able to time travel," the Nogical said from Helios' shoulder. "And nice t-shirt."

Helios looked over at Benjamin's t-shirt. "*Nogicals Rule?*"

Jack beamed. "Why thank you, Helios. I couldn't agree with you more."

"So you're the ones who got the access badge," Gary said.

Helios nodded. "Let's just say there are extenuating circumstances."

"With what?" Benjamin said.

Helios motioned to the ruins around him. "With the object you came to get."

Benjamin felt relief pour through him. "So it's still here?"

"Let's hope so," Jack said. "Otherwise things will really

be messed up."

"What kind of extenuating circumstances?" Heidi said.

Benjamin raised an eyebrow in question.

"What?" she said. "They're blocking their minds."

Helios smiled. "The object needs special care."

"What?" Benjamin said. "Do I need to feed it or something?"

"No, nothing like that," Helios said. "Once you've retrieved it, we can talk about it."

"So where to?" Jack levitated in the air.

"The record said sixteen floors down and in a hidden chamber." Benjamin looked around. "Any idea where the stairs are?"

"Or where they used to be?" Heidi said.

Helios walked toward the center of the room. "They used some special sort of lifting machine back when Geros was capital."

"Like an elevator?" Heidi asked.

Helios nodded. "Right. But it was powered from a nearby volcano." He stopped walking at a circular hole in the ground. "But, unfortunately, that volcano hasn't erupted for thousands of years. It's one of the reasons Geros was abandoned as the capital city."

Benjamin looked down the hole. It was a straight shot, pitch black, and somewhere partway down, something massive blocked the path. "So what now? Do we levitate down?"

Heidi shook her head. "No way. You can teleport us."

"Into a mass of unknown rubble?" Benjamin said. "I don't think so."

"Benjamin's right," Helios said. "The only safe way to

go from here is levitation."

"I guess that means me and Heidi stay up here and keep watch," Gary said. Even since the start of school, Heidi's and Gary's telekinesis abilities had improved about as much as the California coastline shifts each year.

"Maybe there's another way down," Benjamin said, but looking at the sides of the shaft, he wouldn't have wanted to scale down. "Maybe I can levitate you. Or Jack can."

But Heidi shook her head. "No. Just go ahead and go without us."

And so Benjamin, Helios, and Jack levitated down the lifting shaft. Really all was fine except that every so often Benjamin got the image of the volcano coming to life and exploding them back up the chute. But what were the odds? An extinct volcano generally stayed that way—at least for a while. And aside from being flattened intentionally, Benjamin couldn't remember any stories of the ancient capital city exploding.

When they got to the thing in the middle of the path, they stopped; Benjamin and Helios settled down on it, and Jack rested on Benjamin's shoulder.

"What now?" Benjamin asked.

Helios smiled. "Now we teleport around it."

Jack went first. Given he was the littlest, the odds of him teleporting into a rock were the smallest. When he teleported back with a smile on his face, Benjamin decided he'd go next. But once he got to the other side, every bit of light vanished.

"How do we see where we're going?" Benjamin asked once Helios had joined them, but then he remembered his birthday present. He pulled the glass tube from his pocket

 128

and it started glowing bright yellow.

"Where'd you get a lumitube?" Jack held his hand out.

Benjamin handed it over to the Nogical. "Back in Mu. It's a birthday present." He looked at Helios. "Did you know credit works back in time?" he asked as they started levitating downward.

Helios smiled. "Of course. I tried to use it to buy the access badge, but the owner of the shop insisted on a trade."

"So what'd you trade?" Benjamin asked.

Jack laughed. "He tried to trade me, but I can be pretty rotten when I want to. So, instead the owner settled on some random telemagnifiers."

"I traded way more that the access badge was worth," Helios said. "But wasting time squabbling with a shop owner isn't how I normally spend my time-traveling days."

"You time travel a lot?" Benjamin could see ground coming up fast now, so he slowed his levitation.

"Only when I need to." Helios settled on the ground. "And now..."

"And now we need to find a hidden chamber," Benjamin said.

What Benjamin really needed was Iva. With her telegnostic skills, he should have insisted she come along for the trip. But then again, Heidi's telepathic skills had come in pretty handy with Minnolo back at The Silver Touch. Without her, they might not have gotten the access badge.

"Any idea where we're going?" Jack asked.

"No," Helios said. "But I'm willing to bet whoever hid the object wants you to find it. Let's just keep our eyes open and look around."

But it turned out it wasn't as straightforward as all

that. When Benjamin looked around, all he saw were walls. Walls covered with picture after picture after picture.

He looked over to Helios and Jack. "It was an art gallery?"

"*Did you find anything yet?*" Benjamin heard Heidi's voice in his head.

"*Lots of art.*" Benjamin walked over to the closest picture. It looked like a bunch of feathers twisted into some sort of contraption which covered the sun. "*At least I think its art.*"

"*Just don't forget about us up here,*" Heidi said.

Jack levitated over to another picture. "Hey look. A tribe of Baingels."

"Baingels?" Benjamin looked at the picture. Baingel seemed like as good a name as any; they each had twenty arms and apparently no head. "What's a Baingel?"

"A genetic engineering experiment." Helios looked at Jack and narrowed his eyes. "One that never should have been performed."

Jack threw up his hands. "What can I say? Nogicals got lonely. It's not easy being the perfect species, you know."

"So you made yourself some pets?" Helios said.

But Jack shook his head. "Not me. I wasn't alive back then. And they weren't really supposed to be pets."

"They look more like roaches to me." Benjamin looked around. "Do we split up? This place is huge."

Jack nodded. "Sure. I'll take everything way up high."

"And I'll start over here." Helios motioned to the left.

Which left Benjamin with everything on eye level on the right. Probably only about a thousand pictures or so. He walked to the first one and looked at it. Really, it looked like nothing. Sure, it was fine art and all, but how it was supposed to help Benjamin find a hidden chamber with a secret object in it, he had no idea.

"*This may take a while,*" Benjamin told Heidi and Gary, trying to pull the picture away from the wall. Maybe someone had hidden something behind it. But the picture was glued to the wall. So he moved on to the next one.

"*Why?*" Heidi asked.

Benjamin laughed. "*Because I have no idea what I'm doing.*"

"*I can tell,*" Heidi said.

"*Why don't you go about it methodically?*" Gary said.

"*Okay,*" Benjamin said, not that it helped. The most methodical way he could think was to move from one picture to the next and look at each one. "*But I don't even know what I'm looking for.*"

"*Look for something written in Ancient Lemurian,*" Gary said. "*Someone may have left you a message.*"

So Benjamin decided to do a quick pass first—checking each picture for writing. Not that he'd be able to read it. He'd been putting off learning Ancient Lemurian strictly on principle. But the first pass turned up nothing. And so he went back and started over. He must've missed something.

The first ten pictures turned up nothing. So did the next ten. And the next ten. It was only around about the ninetieth picture that something finally caught Benjamin's eye. Not Ancient Lemurian symbols like he'd been looking for, but a different symbol—one that he recognized as soon as he saw it. How had he missed it the first time?

The painting was of a giant head—like the ones Benjamin had seen pictures of on Easter Island. And on

the forehead of the giant stone figure was a symbol of three hearts intertwined. It was kind of messy and scratchy, but it looked just like the symbol which had been on the record they'd found back over Spring Break. Benjamin reached out and touched it with him thumb, and when he did, the painting shifted until the background had vanished and only the head remained. And then it spoke to him.

"What do you want, Benjamin Holt?"

Okay, so talking pictures shouldn't be a surprise to Benjamin. But the fact that this talking stone head in this painting in a long dead capital city knew Benjamin's name caught him off guard.

"I asked what you wanted," the statue said again.

"Maybe you should tell him," Helios said.

Benjamin turned. He hadn't even heard Helios walk over, but there he was with Jack floating in the air beside him.

"I came to get something," Benjamin said.

"What?" the talking head said.

"I don't know," Benjamin said.

The talking head frowned. "You don't even know what you want."

"It was hidden for me," Benjamin said.

The talking head closed its eyes. "I can't give it to you then."

"What?" Was it kidding? Benjamin hadn't traveled back in time to have some stupid painting refuse to give him what was rightfully his. "Why not?"

"Because if you don't know what it is, then you won't know how to handle it," the head said. "It's dangerous."

Helios stepped forward. "That's why I'm here. I'll tell Benjamin how to take care of it."

"And not to use it?" the talking head prompted.

Helios nodded.

"And what about proper storage?" the head said. "He should not touch it."

Helios pulled out a small metal box. "I came prepared." He handed the box to Benjamin who took it.

"Does anyone want to tell me what's going on?" Benjamin said.

"Not yet," Jack said. "Helios has it all worked out. Actually the two of you worked this out together."

Benjamin's mouth fell open. "You guys are from the future?"

"Duh," Jack said.

"No, I mean even more in the future than I am," Benjamin said.

"Like I said. Duh."

"So do we have a deal?" Helios asked the picture.

The talking head looked at Benjamin, then at the box in his hand. "You take full responsibility?" it finally said to Helios.

Helios nodded. "Yes."

And then the talking head vanished, and in its place a gold coin appeared, no bigger than a quarter. Benjamin reached out to take it, but Jack was on his hand faster than lightning. "Did you hear anything the talking head just said? Don't touch it."

Benjamin turned to Jack. "So how am I supposed to get it out then?"

Jack smiled. "That's where I come in."

Benjamin stared at him.

"Yep, I can touch it, but you can't. It doesn't have any

power over Nogicals." Jack reached out and pried the golden coin from the painting. He held it up and looked at it, and then dropped it into the box in Benjamin's hand. Benjamin snapped the box shut.

"Well that wasn't too bad," Benjamin said. They started back to the shaft. "What is it?"

But Helios shook his head. "It's called a life force disk. And that's all you need to know."

"But you told the painting—" Benjamin said.

"I told the painting I would tell you how to take care of it," Helios said. "Which is simple. Don't touch it. Don't talk about it. Don't take it out."

Benjamin stared at the box holding the coin. "So what do I do with it then?"

"Put it in your pocket," Helios said. "Forget you have it. You'll know when you need it. But until then, just leave it alone."

When they got to the top of the lifting shaft, Heidi and Gary stood at the edge waiting.

"You guys took forever." Heidi looked over at Gary. "Gary's been nice enough to tell me about every old library that used to exist in Geros."

Gary puffed his chest out. "Only the ones in the Ruling Hall."

Heidi gritted her teeth. "It felt like a million." She looked back to Benjamin. "So I guess you found it?"

He nodded then looked at Helios and Jack. "Yep, but before you ask, I don't know what it is, don't know how to use it, and can't touch it. So, no, I can't show it to you."

Heidi's face fell. "You're kidding, right?"

But Benjamin shook his head. "Look at Helios. Does he look like he's kidding?"

Helios smiled and put up his hands. "I do what I can."

Heidi looked at Helios and then shrugged. "Well, at least you got it. And you know, we've been gone forever."

Gary glanced down at himself. "Yep. Maybe it's time to go back."

Benjamin looked at Gary. "I'm sure your temporal chromosomes are fine," he said after reading Gary's thoughts.

"I hope so," Gary said. "All I know is it's been a long day."

"For us, too," Jack said. "We're going now." And before Benjamin could ask him or Helios another question, the two of them teleported away. Which left Benjamin, Heidi, and Gary in the ruins of Geros alone.

"You know, like I said, it's way past time for us to go." Gary pulled out the TPT, and they all reached out and touched it. Benjamin thought of present day, and of the ruins in Tunisia where they'd started, and in an instant, the crunching and bending began, and Benjamin felt his body compress.

When it stopped, the telemagnifier was gone. Benjamin shook his head and took a moment to reorient himself. He looked over just in time to see the tourist crest the hill and head toward them.

"You know, come to think of it, I am going to take that rock with me," the man said.

"It's gone," Benjamin said.

The man pursed his lips together. "I threw it over here just a minute ago."

"That was a minute ago," Benjamin said. "A lot can change in a minute."

135

CHAPTER 16

TIME TRAVELING IS DANGEROUS—FOR GIRLS

You'd have thought they'd been gone for days. Andy sat in the dining hall drumming his fingers on the table.

"It's lunch time," he said. "What took you guys so long?"

"Lunch?" Benjamin said. "Feels like dinner to me."

Heidi yawned. "Or bedtime."

"With time travel, you should've been back hours ago," Iva said.

"Well, we had to find the TPT in Tunisia, and that took a while," Benjamin said. "And then there was this tourist who almost took it."

"The actual traveling to the past didn't take any time at all," Gary said. "When we got back to Tunisia, the sun had hardly moved in the sky."

"So what was it like?" Iva asked. "I want to hear everything."

They relayed the story as best they could, constantly interrupting each other to add forgotten details.

"So you're telling me that Walker Pan traveled back in time, sold Minnolo Midas the Ammolite chess set, then traveled back to our time, cheated to win the Bangkok Chess Open last year, followed us around all summer, and then bought the chess set from Morpheus Midas," Iva said.

Gary nodded. "That sums it up."

"Or maybe he sold Minnolo Midas the chess set then traveled forward in time," Andy said. "Maybe he's really from the past to begin with."

"Could be," Benjamin said. "All I know is Walker is not what he seems."

"I disagree," Gary said. "He seems like a snake; he is a snake."

Benjamin wasn't going to bother disagreeing. And Magic wasn't anywhere to hear. "So we had to negotiate for the access badge," he said.

"Minnolo needed me to open some Atlantis spying portal for him," Heidi added.

"And?" At the word spy, Andy's eyes had stopped blinking, and if Benjamin hadn't known better, he'd have sworn Andy stopped breathing.

"I got a telepathic peak into Atlantis. It was depressing." And then Heidi's mind froze, and Benjamin felt it too.

He held his breath. "You recognized something."

Heidi nodded. "A feeling. I didn't realize it until right now."

"What?" Iva said.

Benjamin looked at Heidi, and their eyes locked. He knew exactly what she'd recognized. "Reva." He could sense the evil through the Alliance bond.

Heidi nodded. "Right. Reva—the woman who used to rule Xanadu until she was thrown out. But nobody thought of her as Reva."

And then Iva sucked in her breath. She must've felt it too. "They thought of her as Gaea."

"The first of the false gods?" Gary said. "She should've

been dead millennia ago."

But Heidi shook her head. "The presence I sensed in Atlantis is the exact same one from Xanadu. Reva is Gaea, and a thousand years ago, she was back in Atlantis."

Benjamin's mind flew to his experience in Xanadu. He'd found the second key of Shambhala there—after a horrible test that involved his mom and his twin brothers almost dying. Ananya—the current ruler of Xanadu—had told him it was just a test. That Reva was imprisoned and most likely dead. But Heidi and Benjamin had sensed her presence when they were leaving. And whatever presence Heidi had sensed in Atlantis had been the same.

Harsh reality hit Benjamin. "Reva is Gaea, and if she's really out, then I know she's responsible for that awful test from the caverns."

Heidi reached out and put her hand on his arm. And the weird thing was it didn't feel awkward at all. If anyone understood what he'd been through, she did.

"She wasn't alone," Heidi said. "There was another strong presence nearby." And her eyes narrowed and focused on Benjamin. "And you know, come to think of it, there was something about it that reminded me a lot of you."

Benjamin held his breath. What was she getting at? "You think it was one of my brothers?"

But Heidi shook her head. "No. I don't."

"My ancestors?"

Heidi shook her head again.

"You think it was his father," Iva said.

Heidi nodded. "Exactly. At least that's what every part of my mind is telling me now." She looked right at Benjamin. "Your father was in Atlantis a thousand years ago."

 138

Really, Benjamin wasn't as surprised as he could have been. He'd known his biological father was probably from Atlantis. So apparently, he'd just traveled back in time the same way Benjamin had. No big deal. Back in time was better than here in the present day hunting Benjamin down.

They finished eating and got up to leave the dining hall, when Benjamin spotted someone walking toward them. His skin started to crawl at the sight of Nathan Nyx.

"What is he doing here?" Andy asked.

"I have no idea," Benjamin said.

"Benjamin." Nathan waved as he called out.

Benjamin reached out and waved back. "Hi, Nathan." Why was Nathan bothering him? "Thanks for the credit account by the way. I got a pretty cool birthday present."

"What'd you get?" Andy asked.

"Oh, I forgot to tell you guys." He reached into his pocket and pulled out the small, glass rod. "It's called a lumitube. It's supposed to be some sort of eavesdropping device."

"A lumitube," Nathan said. "Those are impossible to come by. Impossible because they're illegal."

"Illegal!" Iva said.

Nathan nodded. "They have been for about the last seven hundred years." He licked his lips. "Do you mind if I look at it?"

Illegal. Great. Now Benjamin had contraband on him. He looked down at the lumitube in his palm. "Sure, I guess." He handed the rod over to Nathan.

Nathan took the lumitube and studied it. "Wonderful. Just wonderful. This is in excellent condition. Where in the world did you get it?"

 139

None of your business, Benjamin thought as he stuffed the lumitube back into his pocket. He felt the small metal box with the thing they'd gotten back in Geros in there, too, so he switched the lumitube to the other pocket. If he wasn't supposed to touch the thing, he didn't want to take any chances. "Just at some shop downtown."

"I hope whoever sold it doesn't get caught," Nathan said. "Anyway, Benjamin, I was hoping to be able to speak to you." He looked at everyone else. "Privately."

Benjamin shrugged. "Sure, I guess so. I'll catch up with you guys in a minute."

After Andy, Gary, Heidi, and Iva walked away, Benjamin turned to Nathan. What did he want this time? Had he figured out they'd gotten a copy of the record? Had he realized they'd recycled more records than they'd filed? "What's up?"

Nathan leaned close. "Your father is worried about you."

"Worried about what?" Benjamin asked. "I'm fine."

"He's worried there may be people exerting a negative influence on you."

Instantly defenses went up around Benjamin's mind. Whatever he and the members of the Alliance may think—whoever they thought was evil—was none of Nathan Nyx's business. Why did his dad trust this guy so much? Was there something his dad knew that he didn't?

"Who would be exerting a negative influence on me?" Benjamin asked, hoping his voice sounded calmer than he felt.

"He's not sure," Nathan said. "Have you met anyone new this year? Anyone who's trying to get close to you?"

 140

"Of course I've met new people," Benjamin said. "I have new kids in my classes, new teachers."

"Benjamin, the enemy could be anywhere," Nathan said.

Had his dad told Nathan that Benjamin was adopted? Or that he didn't know who his birth parents were?

"What enemy, Nathan?" Benjamin asked. "Why would I have any enemies?"

"Benjamin, your father asked me to keep an eye out for you," Nathan said. "I'm smart enough to realize you're important, and others will be smart enough, too. Your father sent me to warn you to be careful who you trust. Nothing happens by coincidence, Benjamin. There are no chance encounters."

Benjamin's mind flew to Morpheus Midas and Walker Pan. Then to Leena Teasag. Joey Duncan even crept into his mind. He shook his head. "What am I supposed to do? Stop going to classes and barricade myself in my dorm room?"

"No, of course not," Nathan said. "Just heed the warning. Friends may not really be friends after all."

"Thanks for the positive words, Nathan." What an idiotic thing for Nathan to say. "I think it's time I go catch up with my friends. Unless of course they're spying on us right now and planning their next chance encounter." Benjamin started walking away, leaving Nathan in the corridor.

As Benjamin walked, he tried to put Nathan Nyx out of his mind. Unsuccessfully. The last thing Benjamin needed right now were doubts about his friends.

Why did his dad keep sending Nathan on these little errands anyway? And his dad had asked Nathan to keep an eye out for him. Nathan had been fine when he gave

Benjamin the credit account and the access codes to Geros, but now he was just annoying. Benjamin kept forgetting to mention it to his dad when he talked to him on the telecom; things just always were so rushed. Next time he would remember to say something for sure.

When Benjamin caught up to his friends, they'd decided to split for the day. Gary insisted on going to one of the libraries attached to the Ruling Hall to research Greek history. Iva headed down to the telegnostic levels to practice. Heidi decided to head off to the Crags by herself. And Benjamin didn't feel like doing any of those. Okay, maybe he wouldn't have minded hanging out with Heidi, but she had said alone. So he and Andy decided to wander around the city for the rest of the day.

"So really, Benjamin, who gets to time travel next weekend?" Andy asked.

Benjamin didn't say anything at first. Sure, he'd been thinking about it, but he'd been trying to keep his thoughts quiet. They walked down Mu Way, heading nowhere in general. It was only after Andy stopped and stared at him that he finally replied. "We're talking about three thousand years ago," Benjamin said. "Don't you dare tell Heidi or Iva I said this, but I'm scared for either of them to travel that far back in time when we have no idea what to expect."

Andy made a victory sign with his arm. "Yes!"

"I know, I know. Convenient for you," Benjamin said. "But I'm serious. Do you know what was happening back in ancient Greece three thousand years ago?"

"Gary's the right person to answer that," Andy said. "That's why he's at the library."

"Well it's a good thing Gary will be going, too," Benjamin said. "What I'm talking about is the Trojan War. That's what was happening three thousand years ago."

"You're telling me we're going to time travel back to the Trojan War?" Andy said.

Benjamin nodded.

"Like with Homer and Odysseus and Achilles?" Andy asked.

Benjamin nodded again.

"And with the Trojan Horse and everything?"

Benjamin continued nodding.

"Awesome!" Andy said. "We get to go back in time and witness one of the most famous wars ever."

"And one of the most ruthless and bloody wars ever," Benjamin said.

"Oh."

"So now you can see why there's really no choice but for it to just be you and me and Gary," Benjamin said.

"Iva and Heidi are gonna be furious," Andy said. "Especially if they find out your reasoning."

"I'm just not going to tell them," Benjamin said.

"How in the world are you going to keep Heidi from reading your mind?"

"I haven't figured that out yet," Benjamin said. "I don't think I can hold a mind block from now until next Saturday straight."

Andy laughed. "Then you better prepare yourself for their wrath."

Benjamin sighed. "Yeah, I know. Just something else to look forward to."

CHAPTER 17

BENJAMIN SEES A FAMILIAR FACE IN DELPHI

Sunday relaxation was not on the menu. Just after breakfast, the location for the day's archaeological dig was transmitted to their heads-up displays.

Iva shot up from her chair. "Awesome! We're going to Delphi!"

"In Greece?" Benjamin asked.

Iva gave him the you-are-an-idiot look. "Of course in Greece."

"Hey isn't Delphi the place where Kronos puked that stone up?" Heidi said.

"What?" Andy said.

Gary nodded before Heidi had a chance to respond. "You know—what we learned about in lecture. Kronos thought it was one of his kids. Mr. Hermes called it the Navel of the World."

Andy yawned. "I don't remember that."

"That's because you were sleeping," Iva said.

"I remember," Benjamin said. "I wasn't sleeping."

"You know Delphi was the most telegnostic place ever," Iva said. "The most famous oracles in ancient times—well normal earth ancient times—used to live at Delphi and work for the god Apollo. People came from everywhere to see what the oracles would say."

 144

"Yeah, in ancient times on Earth oracles were super respected," Heidi added.

"But didn't oracles used to look for the future in pig intestines?" Gary asked.

"Maybe the ones who weren't telegens. No true telegnostic would need to sacrifice an animal to see a possible future." Iva danced back and forth in place. "Let's go already."

From the minute they arrived at Delphi, Iva's eyes grew as big as saucers. She could hardly stand still.

Their teacher Sci Omega stood by a temple when they arrived. Ryan Jordan and Julie Macfarlane teleported there holding hands. Following closely were Jonathan Sheehan and Suneeta Manvar, definitely not holding hands. Julie glared at Iva as she walked by, but Iva didn't notice. Her eyes had narrowed, and Benjamin saw that Jonathan caught her eye and smirked as he walked by. Iva shook her head and looked away. Was he still spying on her dreams? Benjamin felt his blood heat up as he thought about it, but what could he do? He wasn't supposed to know.

"You all need to stay within the boundaries of Delphi." Sci's blue eyes bore into them as he spoke. "Also, we went over this in class, but I need to say it again. The forbidden doorway is off limits. It's secured shut, so please don't try to pry it open; you'll only trigger an alarm." He looked right at Andy. "If you need anything, I'll be in the arena." He teleported away without another word.

Iva sighed. "I think I'll just wander around on my own for a little bit." She barely got it out before walking away. But Benjamin did notice she walked the opposite direction from Jonathan.

"I guess she wants to feel the experience." Heidi turned to the guys. "So where to?"

Benjamin looked at Andy, and they both smiled.

"Where else?" Andy said. "Let's go check out the forbidden doorway."

Benjamin didn't look at Gary; he didn't want to listen to the argument, but it came anyway.

Gary put his hands on his hips. "You heard what Sci Omega just said. The forbidden doorway is off limits."

But Andy had already started walking, and Heidi and Benjamin quickly followed. Benjamin turned to look just in time to see Gary shake his head, sigh, and then run to catch up.

The forbidden doorway was hidden in an underground temple near the top of a hill, and it was in near perfect shape.

"So this is how Atlantians really used to sneak out of the barrier shield around Atlantis?" Heidi asked.

Gary looked over his shoulder to make sure no one was watching. "This is just one of many doors. The leaders of Lemuria sometimes find these doorways scattered around Earth even now."

"It's no wonder agents from Atlantis can still get free of the dome," Andy said. "These doors are virtually undetectable."

Benjamin looked at Andy. How in the world did Andy know something like that?

Andy shrugged. "We learned all about these doors in agent training. Sometimes Lemurian agents need to use them." He gave the door a final look. "Let's go check out the stone Kronos puked up. That sounds pretty cool."

 146

"And pretty fitting," Benjamin said.

"It's actually in the museum now." Heidi started walking back down the hill. "But according to the map, it used to be down there in the center of the temple."

"You know Kronos didn't actually puke the stone up here," Gary said. "It's told that once he did throw it up, Zeus saved it and then used it to mark the center of the world."

"How would he know this was the center of the world?" Andy asked as they started after Heidi.

"He released two eagles from Mount Olympus which flew in opposite directions and met here at Delphi," Gary said. "He placed the stone here as the mark for the center of the world."

"Hence the name 'The Navel of the World', right?" Benjamin asked.

"Exactly," Heidi said, overhearing the conversation.

"The stone is also called the Omphalos, which actually means navel," Gary added.

"Really, Gary, where do you get all this information?" Andy asked.

"I read about it," Gary said. "It's also interesting to know that before Apollo set up his oracle here, it was occupied by a goddess named Ge. Apollo had to kill her son, a giant snake god named Pytho to claim Delphi."

"Anything else interesting?" Andy asked. Benjamin could tell Andy couldn't have cared less. Since leaving the forbidden doorway, all Andy seemed to be doing was craning his neck around looking for Iva.

"I think it's interesting, Gary," Heidi said. "When did Apollo set up his oracle here?"

"Earth history only records Apollo's site here from the

eight century BC, but Lemurian history puts it here much earlier than that, probably around the twentieth century BC," Gary said. "I'd be willing to trust the Lemurian records."

"So where in Ancient Greece will we be traveling back to?" Heidi asked.

Benjamin tightened his mind shield—keeping Heidi out. "Troy. And we haven't decided who's going yet."

"I know," Heidi said. "But I guess it would probably only be fair if Andy and Iva went along with you this time."

Benjamin nodded. "Good point." He kept the mind block solid which was becoming a permanent fixture around his thoughts.

"Speaking of which, let's find Iva," Andy said. "Maybe she can make some divine predictions on the future for us."

Benjamin walked a little farther when he looked down and saw Heidi's ugly, green star on the ground—the one she'd gotten from the past. He bent down to pick it up. Man, it was ugly. Why had she bought this thing?

"Hey, Heidi," he called ahead to her.

She turned to look.

"You dropped this." He held it out. The black rope it hung on had broken.

"Oh! My pendant." She reached to her neck. "It must've fallen off."

"You almost lost it," Benjamin said.

"And that would have been a real pity," Andy added.

Heidi glared at Andy. "Can you hold it for me? These pants don't have any pockets."

"Sure," Benjamin said, cramming it into his front pocket.

They kept walking, looking around. It was in the back of a temple that they finally found Iva—cross-legged with

her eyes closed.

Andy sat down next to her. "What are you doing?"

Her eyes snapped open, and she shot him a dirty look. "Well, what I was doing before I was interrupted was communing with the stones around me."

They all just stared at her. Then Benjamin, Andy, and Gary busted out laughing.

"And how exactly were you doing that?" Gary asked.

Iva rolled her eyes. "Don't you guys ever listen? Sci Omega spent like an hour last week explaining how the earth stores memories of everything that goes on around it. I was listening to the stones."

"Oh yeah," Gary said. "Now I remember. I figured he was making up the whole thing."

"I can tell you with certainty that he was not making it up," Iva said. "Probably only those gifted in telepathy or telegnosis would understand."

"Maybe I should try." Heidi sat down across from Iva. "Actually Josh and I were talking just the other day about nonvolatile memories in inanimate objects. He's very talented at retrieving not only actual memories but the feelings associated with them. He's a very empathic person you know."

"No, I didn't know," Benjamin said. "Do you and Josh actually listen in class or do you just talk?"

"Of course we listen," Heidi said. "Why would you ask that?"

"Oh, well it's just that you're always talking about all these things you and Josh talk about," Benjamin replied.

"We do talk every day after class you know," Heidi said.

"Yes, I know," Benjamin said.

 149

"Hey, why don't you all give it a try," Iva said. "Maybe someone will be able to sense something."

"Maybe." Gary sat down.

Benjamin sat, and immediately felt the big, ugly star pendant in his pocket, cutting into his leg. He stood up and took it out of his pocket and sat back down.

Andy turned to Iva. "So what am I supposed to do?"

Iva closed her eyes and placed her hand on Andy's; his eyes shot open.

"Close your eyes, and open your mind," she said. "Listen for anything—thoughts, emotions, voices. But whatever you do, try not to say anything for at least five minutes."

Benjamin did what she said and closed his eyes. In order to really open his mind, he needed to lower some of the shielding around it. He didn't want to be so vulnerable but really didn't have much choice. He relaxed his mind and thought about his surroundings. Images began to fill his thoughts. He could see multitudes of people from all walks of life. Some dressed and manicured perfectly; others with clothes hanging by threads. And all of them were coming to Delphi.

In his mind what had before been ruined remains was now a thriving though secluded city. The temples were perfect, gilded in brilliant colors—gold, red, blue. He saw the temple they sat in now, but instead of a crumbling floor, it was covered in a complicated mosaic of a sun, polished to a shine. A solitary female in a white dress walked alone. She had her eyes closed and her long, dark hair hung down straight around her head. A jeweled necklace was woven into her hair, and bracelets adorned her arms.

 150

There was something familiar about her, but Benjamin couldn't quite put his finger on it. She walked with purpose heading out of the temple. He could read her thoughts and knew this girl was heading to the oracle's seat to prophesize for the throng of people gathering outside.

But just before exiting the temple, she stopped. Her eyes snapped open, and she turned and looked Benjamin directly in the face.

Iva!

With a small, forced smile, she closed her eyes again and left the temple. Benjamin couldn't take his eyes off her. His hands felt hot and sweaty. He watched as she walked down the slope to the dais where the oracle sat. The large Omphalos—the Navel of the World—sat on the grass in front of her. What in the world was she doing here, back in ancient Greece at Delphi? He kept watching, but she didn't turn back.

And then Benjamin realized his hands weren't just hot. They were burning. He could smell his skin starting to singe. He snapped his eyes open, breaking from the trance. The ugly green pendant was red hot in his hands. He threw it across the room where it hit against the wall and started smoking.

"Benjamin!" Heidi moved over to him. "Are you okay?"

"I'm fine," he lied. His hands hurt like he'd juggled hot coals, and his head pounded from the rush of blood. What had just happened?

"You're not fine," Heidi said. "Look at your hands."

He looked down. The skin of his palms was red and blistered and hurt. He immediately started the healing exercises they'd gone over in science class and the blisters

 151

began to fade. But his head still ached.

"Sorry about your pendant." He motioned with his throbbing head over to the far wall.

Heidi turned to look and gasped. The pendant which had been glowing red just a minute before had burned away to nothing but ash.

"What just happened?" Andy asked.

"I saw you here, Iva," Benjamin said. The pounding blood in his head started to subside. "I saw you here in Delphi a long, long time ago."

Iva's mouth fell open. "What?"

"You were an oracle."

Iva shook her head. "I didn't pick up on anything like that. You must be wrong."

"I'm not wrong," Benjamin said. "I watched you walk out of this temple and head down below to the oracle spot. You sat in the chair down there and started telling people their futures."

"Maybe it wasn't Iva," Heidi said. "Maybe it just looked like Iva."

Benjamin shook his head. "No, it was Iva. She opened her eyes and looked at me. There's no doubt it was Iva." He thought about the forced smile she'd given, but decided not to mention it. He looked back at the wall. "I think it was that pendant. It just kept getting warmer and warmer."

"What kind of telemagnifier is that—I mean was that—anyway?" Gary asked.

"I've been trying to figure that out," Heidi said. "It was some sort of empathic telemagnifier, but I hadn't gotten it to work."

"Guess you won't be able to now," Andy said.

 152

Iva creased her brow. "I don't have any plans of being an oracle in ancient Delphi. And we won't even be traveling back here next week. We're going to Troy, right?"

"I know," Benjamin said. "It doesn't make any sense. All I know is that I saw you here in ancient Delphi, and you were an oracle."

"Did you see anyone else?" Iva asked. "Was there anyone else you recognized around?"

"No," Benjamin replied. "Did anyone else see anything?"

They all shook their heads.

"So does what you say about telegnosis hold true for the past too?" Benjamin asked.

"What's that?" Iva said.

"You said that in telegnosis what you're able to see is only one possible future of many. Is what I just saw only one possible past?" he asked.

Iva pursed her lips. "I don't think any of us can answer that question."

"Yeah, that gets way into the whole temporal phasing debate," Gary said. "Can we change time by going back, or do the things that occur happen the way they do whether we interfere or not?"

"Like were we destined to change time and so we do?" Andy said.

"Exactly," Gary said.

"I have to be honest," Iva said. "Having Benjamin see me in the past here at Delphi kind of freaks me out."

"You'd be crazy if it didn't," Andy said. He turned to Benjamin. "Was she a lot older or anything?"

Benjamin shook his head. "No. She looked exactly like she looks right now."

CHAPTER 18

COINCIDENTAL EAVESDROPPING

The week ahead dragged, so to pass it faster, Andy started tutoring Heidi and Gary in telekinesis. He and Iva had pretty much told Benjamin not to help. Not so directly, but that was definitely the message.

Benjamin sat with Iva at a back table studying. Okay, actually, he was watching. It still irked him that Andy was tutoring Gary and Heidi. It still bothered him that Andy was better than him at telekinesis and that everyone thought so. Especially Andy.

Andy stood up in front of Heidi and Gary. "Maybe think of it like this." A chair began to levitate beside him. "If I couldn't levitate objects, how would I be lifting this chair?"

"You'd walk over and pick it up," Heidi said.

"Exactly. I would make contact with it using my hands and pick it up. Let's compare this to our Internet connections at home. Most of us have wireless connections, but you know when you go to the libraries and the computers are all plugged into a wall jack?"

"Yeah, but that's really old technology," Gary replied.

"And so is me walking over to pick up the chair. It's old technology. If a computer is hooked to a wire into the wall to get the Internet, the signals flow down the wire. If a computer is wireless, the signals flow through the air. It's

the same with telekinesis. A telegen sends electrical signals over to the chair without using a wire. Get it?"

"Yes, I get it," Heidi said. "But that doesn't make it any easier to do."

What in the world was Andy talking about? Wireless technology? Was he trying to help Heidi and Gary or just confuse them even more? Benjamin tried to force himself to look back down and study, but couldn't.

"*I'm sure you could be as good as Andy if you practiced more,*" Iva said silently to Benjamin.

"*Whatever.*" Benjamin didn't even bother looking over at her.

"*And you have more important things to do than to teach telekinesis,*" she continued. "*You have to save the world.*"

"*No, we have to save the world, Iva. Not me. And wouldn't me helping my friends improve at something be good for the Alliance? It's ridiculous that I have to sit here and watch Andy. I'm totally better than he is,*" he lied.

"*It's not about who's better,*" Iva said.

"*Yes. It is. If you hadn't thought he was better, you would have let me teach them.*"

"*Andy doesn't have two brothers he needs to find.*"

"*Yes he does. My brothers. He has as much to do with it as I do,*" Benjamin said.

"*Benjamin, this is ridiculous,*" Iva said. "*Heidi and Gary don't need that much help. It's really not that big of a deal. You're making so much of it. If you want, we can talk about Saturday's plans.*"

"*There's nothing to talk about. I'm traveling with Gary and Andy, and that's all there is to it.*" Standing up, he tele-

kinetically shoved his chair aside and walked away.

Benjamin left the practice room. Turning the corridor, he ran into Jack.

"Telekinesis got you down?" Jack said.

"How did you know?"

Jack smiled. "I can read your mind. Remember?"

"Do you think Andy's better than I am?"

"Yep," Jack said.

Benjamin sighed. "That's not supposed to be your answer."

"I can sense your ability levels though," Jack said. "You could be better if you tried. But you never try at anything. That's your problem."

"That's not true," Benjamin said.

"It is true, and you know it," Jack said. "You've coasted through life at everything so far, and if you don't change your habits, you'll coast through life in the future."

"So what?" Benjamin said.

Jack threw up his hands. "So telegens who coast through life never amount to much."

"But I'm destined to save the world," Benjamin said.

"You're not going to save anything if you don't start applying yourself," Jack said.

They walked in silence for a while. Actually, Jack levitated. Was Jack right? Was Benjamin really a coaster? Life had been pretty easy so far, and aside from being annoyed that Andy was better and Ryan Jordan was nearly as good, Benjamin hadn't worked any harder trying to improve.

Continuing to walk, they finally sat on a bench. "Can I learn to sense other telegen's ability levels?" Benjamin asked. "That seems pretty cool."

"Of course," Jack said. "I can teach you if you want. I could teach you lots of things if you're interested."

Benjamin nodded his head.

"How do your evenings look?" Jack asked with a smile.

Benjamin grinned back as thoughts of Andy and telekinesis moved to the back of his mind. "Let's just go ahead and start now."

Funny enough, when Saturday morning rolled around, Iva didn't complain about not time traveling.

"That's okay," she said. "We have plans with Aurora today, anyway."

"So take your time." Aurora walked over to join them at the Deimos Diner.

Andy raised an eyebrow. "You're not mad?"

Iva shook her head. "So where are you guys getting the TPT this time?"

"The Temple of Saturn in Rome," Andy replied. "It's probably the most popular place for Kronos worship around."

"Won't that make it hard to find the telemagnifier?" Heidi asked.

"Maybe," Gary replied. "But maybe it's popular enough that Kronos leaves more than one TPT lying around."

"What are you going to wear?" Aurora asked.

Benjamin looked down at his ripped jeans and t-shirt, then looked back up. "This?"

"Three thousand years ago!" Aurora laughed. "I don't think so."

Gary's face fell. "That's a good point. We can't travel back to ancient Greece wearing jeans and gym shoes."

"So what are we supposed to do?" Andy asked. "It's time to go."

"We could stop by the lava tube," Aurora said. "My dad has so many costumes from different times we trip over them. I think my entire closet is jammed with ancient Greek stuff." She stopped and thought. "Isn't that about the time of the Trojan War?"

"Exactly," Benjamin said.

"Then we'll have to dress you like fierce warriors."

Once they'd teleported to the volcano, Benjamin wasn't sure what he thought. Even with the lava flow going through the middle of her living room, Aurora swore to them the volcano was safe. And since her dad happened to be time-traveling back to the hippie era for work, they had the place to themselves.

Aurora stood up and stepped into the outer tunnels. "Make sure you guys duck. My dad gets bummed out when any of the stalactites or stalagmites break off. They have thoughts and stuff stored in them."

Iva glanced around at the emptiness. "What kind of thoughts would there be in a lava tube? Does anyone else live around here?"

Aurora laughed. "Not hardly. But this volcano is part of the advance warning system around Lemuria. You know—the Ring of Fire."

"Really?" Heidi asked.

Aurora nodded. "Yeah. So all the thoughts the volcano receives are transferred to Wondersky City for analysis."

"Aren't your thoughts transmitted, also?" Andy said.

"If we're here in the outer tube they are," Aurora said. "But we spend almost all our time in the inner chambers.

There's a special barrier around our place."

Aurora put her finger to her lips as she led them through the network of tubes. She smiled and motioned at the stalactites and stalagmites again. And that's when Benjamin's felt his pocket start vibrating.

"Hey, why'd you stop?" Andy ran into the back of Benjamin.

Benjamin didn't reply. He wasn't sure why he'd stopped. He reached into his pocket, trying to figure out where the buzzing had come from, and pulled out the lumitube.

Not only was the small, glass rod vibrating, it threw off such a beacon of red light, Benjamin actually had to squint his eyes.

"Where'd you get that?" Aurora grabbed the lumitube out of his hands.

Benjamin had the strong urge to grab it back but didn't. "I got it as a birthday present."

"No way!" Aurora ran over to the wall and slammed it into a hole Benjamin felt pretty sure was a lumitube socket like Minnolo Midas had mentioned. "My dad would kill me if he knew what we were doing."

Benjamin walked over to join her. "What are we doing?"

"Spying!" Aurora said. "What else?"

"But how'd you know what it was?" Heidi asked.

"I used to have one," Aurora said. "Then my dad lost it on one of his trips back in time. In most of Lemuria, that wouldn't matter, but here in the Ring, it was a bummer to see it go."

"What's the difference?" Gary asked.

"It's the technology," Aurora said. "Most of Lemuria is built with new technology—so new the lumitube won't

work." She looked at the lumitube socket and smiled. "But in The Ring, things are different. Here, we still have the old technology and lumitubes work great." She motioned to a holographic screen materializing on the wall. "See what I mean?"

Benjamin glanced over and saw the images.

Andy's eyes were glued to the holograms. "How do you control it?" He reached up to touch the screen.

"Simple," Aurora said. "You just think about who you want to spy on, and then you touch the screen."

Gary—of all people—walked over and slammed his palm on the screen. "Show me that snake Walker Pan," he commanded the lumitube screen.

And true to Aurora's word, Walker Pan appeared on the screen.

Heidi sucked in her breath. "What's he doing there?"

The screen showed Walker Pan sitting in the Ruling Hall—with Helios and Selene Deimos, Joey Duncan, and Magic Pan.

"What's Joey doing there?" Benjamin said. "And Selene isn't even around these days."

"And what's Walker doing in the Ruling Hall?" Gary said. "Doesn't Helios realize he's sitting with the enemy?"

"Just watch," Iva said.

But it seemed that whatever meeting had been going on had come to an end. Walker stood up and stared at Joey. "Just make sure you don't screw up your part of the plan."

"What plan?" Andy said.

"Shhhh," Aurora said.

Joey stood and got right up into Walker's face. "Don't imply that I'm not capable of the job." Joey looked over to Helios, then back at Walker. "If anyone screws anything

up, it won't be me."

"Boys," Selene said, "must we argue over every little detail? As long as everyone knows what part they play, there won't be any problems."

Walker glared at Joey. "There better not be." And without another word, Walker Pan left the Ruling Hall with Magic in tow, and the holographic lumitube screen went blank.

"What happened?" Gary asked.

Aurora hit the socket, but it didn't come back to life. "It must've run out of power. That's the problem with these old lumitubes. They only have a certain amount of power and it takes them a while to recharge."

"Wonderful. So it told us nothing." Benjamin pulled the lumitube out of the socket and stuffed it back into his pocket. "Anyway, where's your closet?"

By the time they changed, Benjamin was more than ready to teleport away. "I feel ridiculous." And really, with the short tunic and leather belt, the only consolation was that neither Ryan nor Jonathan was around to see him. But at least he had a sword. And a shield.

Heidi smiled. "I think you guys look brave and handsome."

"You do?" Well that changed everything. Brave and handsome. That didn't sound too bad.

Andy said nothing. He'd set his shield down and flexed his muscles at it to see his reflection.

Iva nodded. "Definitely. In a very fierce kind of way."

"So when we're done, should we come back here?" Benjamin asked. "Please?"

"We won't be here," Aurora said. "Meet us back at the Deimos Diner. We'll bring your clothes."

CHAPTER 19

X Always Marks the Spot

They arrived at the Roman Forum around noon.

"What makes this temple so special?" Benjamin asked as they walked toward the columns in the distance. He tried to ignore the stares their costumes drew—from everyone.

"Well, it's really old and really big," Gary said. "It was built around 500 BC, but actually, it got destroyed a couple times after that. The Romans just kept rebuilding it. They kept all their money here under a podium."

"But there are rumors the podium actually leads to the ruins of the previous temples underneath," Andy said.

Gary inclined his head. "Where do you hear your rumors, Andy?"

Andy put on a sly smile. "I have to keep my sources secret. Otherwise, they wouldn't be good sources anymore."

They walked right past the surrounding temples. Sure, Mercury and Jupiter were famous, but they weren't the reason they'd teleported to Rome. It was for Kronos and his temple alone.

Andy looked around. "You said the last telemagnifier you found was a plate?"

Benjamin and Gary both nodded.

"So where do we look?"

"Just anywhere," Benjamin said. "But maybe away from tourists."

"That's gonna be kind of hard," Gary said. "Don't you see how they're all looking at us?"

Sure enough, they'd drawn a crowd. Whether it was the shields, the swords, or the entire ensemble, people gawked.

"I feel like we should take out our swords and start fighting." Benjamin's hand moved to his sword though he kept it sheathed.

"That's not a bad idea," Gary said. "I always wanted to join the Society for Creative Anachronisms."

"We should keep moving," Andy said. "And I want to check out the podium first."

"It's closed to the public." Benjamin nodded his head toward a sign.

"Exactly." Andy moved toward it, stepped over the chain barrier, and they were in.

At the bottom of the ten steps, the tunnel curved to the left.

"How far in are we going?" Gary asked.

"As far as we can or until we find the TPT." Andy led them through the series of tunnel, down more steps, around more corners until they came to a dead end. In front of them was a wall inscribed with a giant X.

"Is this like X marks the spot?" Benjamin asked. "Because there's nowhere else to go."

"Yeah, maybe we should head back and look around outside," Gary said. "Last time the telemagnifier was sitting out in plain view."

"But you even said there was no one around last time," Andy said. "There are probably two hundred people walking around out there. It's gotta be down here."

Gary's eyes glazed over as he consulted his heads-up display. "You know the X is a symbol for Kronos. It's the Roman numeral for ten and the symbol for time."

"Useful information," Andy said, and for once, he wasn't being sarcastic.

"So we're on the right track," Benjamin said. "But there's no way our swords will cut through this wall."

Andy walked up and felt along the sides. "I think it's a door." He put his shoulder against it and tried to push it, but even when Benjamin and Gary joined him, it didn't budge.

Gary backed away and looked up. "I don't think it pushes in. I think it slides up." He pointed above the door.

"I can teleport us to the other side," Benjamin said. So they stepped together and he tried. But after disappearing, they reappeared in the exact same spot.

"It didn't work," Gary said.

Benjamin scowled. "Very observant, Gary." And then he tried again.

"Maybe you did it wrong," Andy said when it didn't work for a second time.

Benjamin looked back at the door. "I didn't do it wrong. There's something not letting me teleport, but I can use telekinesis to lift it."

"This wall must weigh three tons," Gary said. "You can't lift it."

"Yes I can," Benjamin said.

"And so can I," Andy said. "And I'm going to be the one to do it. Not you."

"You've got to be—" Benjamin began, but Andy put up his hand to stop him.

"It has nothing to do with who's better at telekinesis,"

Andy said. "I'm just thinking you need to save as much strength as you can. We have a war ahead of us, a brother to find, and then you need to teleport us all back. You need to conserve as much energy as you can."

Benjamin opened his mouth to argue, but closed it again. Andy was right; he knew it, but it still made him furious.

"Fine," he said. "Just lift it, and let's get on with it."

Andy didn't say anything; he just turned to the large X. Benjamin felt telenergy flowing toward the wall, but it didn't so much as vibrate. Andy closed his eyes and took another deep breath. The wall gave, just a little, unsettling the sand beneath it as it shuddered under the telekinetic forces. But it still didn't lift.

"Maybe we both need to do it together," Benjamin said.

"And I could help too," Gary added.

But Andy said nothing. He didn't even acknowledge the suggestions. Instead he walked closer to the wall, until he was only a couple of feet away from the center of the large X. Closing his eyes, he shook from the force he exerted. The wall grudgingly gave way, lifting off the ground a few inches. A trickle of blood began to flow from one side of Andy's nose, trailing down his chin and landing on his tunic. But he didn't even notice. The wall lifted more. It was at about this point that Benjamin gave up any thoughts of competition with Andy. He cheered Andy on, joined by Gary. Benjamin wanted Andy to succeed. He knew Andy could do it.

Blood began to flow out of Andy's other nostril as he gave one last final telekinetic effort toward the wall. It glided up, flush with the ceiling, and locked into place. And then Andy collapsed to the ground.

 165

CHAPTER 20

THE TIME TRAVELER'S VISIONS

Benjamin ran over to Andy and rolled him onto his back. Had lifting the door killed Andy? Benjamin remembered the very first science lecture they'd ever had in Lemuria. Mr. Hermes talked about the importance of understanding limits, and now it looked like Andy had gone way beyond his.

But then Andy started breathing again, and so did Benjamin. At least Andy wasn't dead—yet. But with all the blood pouring out of his nose, it might only be a matter of time.

"Do you think he's okay?" Benjamin asked Gary.

"I don't know." Gary leaned close. "He looks pretty pale."

"*I'm fine.*" Andy's voice in his head shocked Benjamin. "*Just give me a few minutes.*"

"After lifting five tons, even I would need a break."

Benjamin's head turned around in the direction of the voice. In the center of a large room was an old man; his curly grey hair reminded Benjamin of someone, but he couldn't quite put his finger on it.

Andy sat upright. "Five tons." He pinched his nose, trying to stop the flow of blood. "No wonder I feel so bad."

Benjamin felt five tons lift off his shoulders. He turned

back to Andy. "Dude, I thought you were dead."

"Not this time," the old man said. "Come sit with me over here in my nice warm resting place."

"*Said the spider to the fly*," Gary quoted.

The old man laughed. "Ah, but I will not dine upon you for lunch. You're always the cautious one, Gary Goodweather."

Gary narrowed his eyes. "How do you know my name?"

The old man gestured with his hands. "Maybe I just picked it from your mind."

"Or maybe you know who we are, and you led us down here," Gary said.

"Yes, that's right," the man said. "I made you dress up in your little costumes and teleport all the way from Lemuria just so you could open my door."

"I knew it!" Gary said.

The old man laughed. "I'm kidding. But since you're already here and your friend Andy obviously needs to rest before you travel back to the Trojan war, you may as well come join me."

"How do you know where we're going?" Against all common sense, Benjamin walked over. The whole purpose of the excursion was to find the TPT, and Benjamin would have bet his shield this old man knew where it was.

"I saw you back then," the man replied. "Of course, I was younger. But not as young as when I saw you in Tunisia."

"You're Kronos!" Gary said.

"Or Saturn," Kronos said. "I don't really care."

"The god of time," Gary said. "No way."

Benjamin's heart sped up. "You were the tourist at the temple last Saturday."

Kronos nodded. "I thought I'd have to hit you in the head with that plate for you to find it."

Benjamin sat down. "So can you tell us what happens when we travel back now?"

Kronos put his finger to his chin. "Oh, I guess I could. But it might change what you do. Or it might not." He laughed. "I love making decisions based on the flow of time. It's so much fun to play around with the fate of the world."

"So are you going to tell us?" Andy walked over and joined his friends.

"Doing better, Andy Grow?" Kronos asked.

"My head still hurts," Andy said. "But you didn't answer my question. Are you going to tell us what happens?"

Kronos laughed then regained his composure. "Why don't I show you something first? A vision of time. Then I'll let Benjamin Holt decide if he wants to know what happens in the past. In Troy."

"Of course I want to," Benjamin said. "Knowing ahead of time will help us."

"Watch first. Then decide."

There was no point in arguing. Andy needed to rest, and Kronos hadn't given them a telemagnifier. "Fine." Benjamin sank to the ground. "Let's just hurry."

"Afraid you'll run out of time, Benjamin Holt? That should be the least of your concerns." Kronos waved his arms, and a green, crystal ball appeared in the center of their circle. The lights in the room went out, and the ball began to glow.

Benjamin looked at the crystal ball—not so much because he thought it would do anything, but more because, with the lights out, there was nothing else to see. And then the images started.

Benjamin saw himself at his house back in Virginia. He immediately recognized his twin brothers and the telekinetic car chase they were having. He remembered this day; it was the day he'd teleported away to summer school for the first time. And then the image flickered and changed.

Benjamin saw himself walking inside a long, dark tunnel. From the stone walls around, Benjamin knew it was underground, but he didn't remember ever being there. He walked alone with Heidi, and they held hands. That was a little bit strange. Benjamin felt his face heat up when he realized Gary and Andy were seeing the exact same thing as he was. He looked up, caught Andy's eye, and quickly glanced back down. But it had been enough to see the smirk on Andy's face. And then the image flickered again.

This time Benjamin remembered the vision perfectly. He and Andy sat at elementary school graduation, playing pranks on the principal and other kids. That was back when telekinesis had been just for fun. When they were the only ones around who could do it. Those were the days. And the best thing was that no one—at least no one besides their parents—knew who was causing the cell phones to ring in the audience. The image flickered.

Benjamin found himself back in Xanadu. Back inside the cavern where he'd had the test for the second key of Shambhala. He shuddered as soon as he saw the place. It was just as he'd remembered it—even though it had only

been a test. The ledges on the wall, the cell with bars. But thankfully, this time the place was empty. His mom and his twin brothers were nowhere to be found. And the water hadn't run up above its banks. Flicker.

Benjamin stood on a platform next to Andy and Heidi. But they all had their hands held behind their back. It only took a second for Benjamin to realize they had some kind of invisible restraints holding their hands together. A huge crowd was gathered, and every eye was on the three of them. Benjamin looked at Heidi and saw tears streaming down her face. And then he looked out in the crowd and saw Iva and Gary. What in the world was going on? "Let the executions begin!" a voice boomed over the crowd. And the image flickered.

Benjamin found himself at a party of some kind. He'd never been to this place before, but someone had obviously spared no expense, and Benjamin himself was dressed like he was going to the prom. He sat alone at a bar and turned to see a beautiful girl walking up to him in a gorgeous red dress. He couldn't help but smile. Flicker.

Benjamin looked around and knew he was in Delphi. It was just as he had remembered it, except it was nighttime. And strangely enough, he was with Heidi again. Only Heidi. This was the second time he'd been alone in a vision with Heidi. But this time they weren't holding hands at least. She looked at him and smiled. And the image flickered.

Benjamin found himself being held in a prison of some kind. A cell with no windows and no door. And he was alone. And hungry. His clothes were torn, and he felt like he hadn't showered in weeks. How long had he been in here anyway? His stomach growled just as he looked to

the floor at an empty plate. He walked over and kicked it, though where he got the energy to do so, he wasn't sure. And the image flickered.

And the green, crystal ball turned off.

By the time the lights came back up in the room, Benjamin felt like his head was being used as a roulette ball. He almost felt like leaning over and throwing up but managed to hold his focus by staring at Kronos.

"Well?" Kronos asked.

"Well, what?" Benjamin said.

"Well, what is your decision?" Kronos asked.

"My decision?" Benjamin's head kept spinning. "I have no idea what you just showed me."

Kronos shook his head. "You misunderstand, Benjamin. I've showed you nothing. Everything you saw came from your own mind. From time. I have no control over what the Temporal Orb shows." And on cue, the green, crystal ball—the Temporal Orb—vanished.

"So how did Benjamin dream all those images up?" Andy's nose wasn't bleeding anymore, and the color had returned to his face.

"I didn't," Benjamin said. Holding hands with Heidi? Dressed up and at a party? Executions?

"They are not dreams," Kronos said. "They just are. They may be. They may not be. Time doesn't tell. It only shows...possibilities."

Andy blew out a breath in disgust. "So the images tell us nothing."

Kronos cocked his head. "One could interpret it that way."

"So anything you tell us about the past might not

 171

even be what ends up happening?" Benjamin said.

Kronos smiled. "You catch on quick. So what is your decision? Do you want to know about the past? Or do you choose to head into it with an open mind?"

"Is there really any choice?" Benjamin asked.

"Of course," Kronos said. "You always have a choice. That's one of the things that makes time so wonderful. Any choice we make, even the smallest one, could potentially change everything."

"My choice is no," Benjamin said. "We'll let the past determine itself." Really, he trusted Kronos as much as he trusted Leena Teasag. Even if Kronos told them about the past, there'd be no way Benjamin would believe him.

"You're sure?" Kronos said. "You don't want to gamble with Fate? I know her pretty well."

Benjamin nodded. "Yeah, I'm sure. Now where do we get the TPT?"

"Up there." Kronos pointed his finger to way up high on the wall. "In the loculi."

Benjamin turned his face upward and looked. He'd been so focused on Kronos and the Temporal Orb that he'd forgotten to even look around. Maybe he should've signed up for Agent Training after all.

"I've been wondering what those are." Andy still held his head in his hands. "But that doesn't really clear it up for me."

Like a beehive, the walls were honeycombed with individual alcoves. Bricks and tiles covered some of them, but most had fallen apart.

"What are loculi?" Benjamin asked.

"They're catacombs," Gary said. "They put dead people there."

"You mean we're surrounding by hundreds of dead people?" Andy whistled out a low breath.

"Four thousand and ninety six to be exact." Kronos put on a smug smile.

"Who's buried in them?" Gary stood and walked over to a wall and began peering inside one of the openings.

"My priests and priestesses," Kronos said. "Just because they work for me doesn't mean they can escape the grips of time. Time stops for no one. Except me."

"This is fascinating." Gary's head was halfway inside one opening. "Look at the state of the bones in here. It's remarkable."

Benjamin shook his head. "No thanks. Just tell us which one it's in, and we'll be going."

"Actually I have a previous engagement." Kronos stood up. "So I'm afraid I really must be going. Have a nice time." He looked at the large stone door Andy had lifted.

Benjamin felt the telenergetic forces before he could do anything—not that he probably could have done anything, and the next thing he knew, the door was back down. And then Kronos teleported away.

CHAPTER 21

Surprises in the Loculi

The first thing Benjamin did was try to teleport—which worked out as well as it had before. They ended up exactly where they started.

"Great." Andy sat down. "Now what? I'm not lifting that door again. And we have no idea which loculi to look in."

"Loculus," Gary said.

"What?" Andy asked.

"It's loculus. That's the singular for loculi," Gary said.

"Whatever."

"So do we just each pick a wall and start looking?" Benjamin's eyes scanned the graveyard room.

"I guess so." Andy shook his head. "But this is gonna take the rest of the day."

"Why don't you just do what Iva would do?" Gary said.

"Listen to poetry?" Andy asked.

"I'm not sure that would help," Gary said. "No, what I mean is use telegnosis to find out exactly which loculus the TPT is in."

Benjamin brightened. "Great thinking, Gary. I don't think I'm as good as Iva at telegnosis—no scratch that. No one is as good at telegnosis as Iva, but it's worth trying. Let's all give it a shot."

Andy shook his head. "Not me. I'm still beat from lifting the door."

"Yeah, you try alone first," Gary said. "I don't want my thoughts interfering."

Not that he thought he had a chance, but Benjamin went ahead and sat and stretched out his mind, reaching it high into the alcoves above. He had no clue what he was looking for, but he knew it had to have telenergetic forces. Closing his mind, he felt something. It came from his left. He angled his body in the direction and reached out again.

There it was again. Like a pulsing of energy. He could see it in his mind. It was high—on the top row he thought. He isolated his thoughts once more, and within a few moments, his mind settled on a single loculi or loculus or whatever it was.

"Up there." He pointed to the alcove. "There's something in that one."

Gary tilted his head way upward. "Figures. Guess I won't be going to get it."

"I'll go." Benjamin didn't give Andy a chance to offer. Without another word, he levitated to the top—to the loculus he'd isolated. When he got there, he looked down. Andy and Gary were far below, looking up at him. And then, because it felt like the thing to do, he waved.

The tiles were almost completely intact—all except for one—luckily. Benjamin shined his lumitube inside to look. Even if the power was too low to eavesdrop, it still put off a pretty strong light.

"*I can't see anything,*" he told Andy and Gary. "*Not like I know what to look for.*"

"*Just reach in and feel around,*" Gary said. "*It's got to be in there.*"

 175

Benjamin reached his hand inside the dark loculus hoping his telegen DNA had a built in cure for spider and snake bites. He moved his hand around until he felt something hard. It had to be the telemagnifier.

"I got it." Benjamin tightened his grasp around the object and pulled it out of the small opening. "Ahhh!" Benjamin dropped the object and heard it clatter far below.

"Did you just drop a leg bone on Andy's toe?" Gary asked.

Benjamin shuddered. *"I don't know what part of the body it came from. I thought it was the TPT."*

"It was a femur." Gary obviously thought Benjamin must care which bone he'd dropped. Sometimes Gary just didn't get it. Actually most of the time Gary just didn't get it.

Benjamin reached his hand back in through the missing tile, trying to ignore the bones. He visualized what he felt, and found it was a human or telegen skeleton laid to rest, now missing a leg bone of course. It lay on its back with its hands folded across its chest. Benjamin felt up the arm bone to the hand and realized the hands gripped an object which had been laid on the chest.

Benjamin touched the object and smiled when he felt the energy pouring off it. This was his telemagnifier.

When he pulled it out, he didn't drop it like he had the leg bone. Instead he studied the short, golden dagger with a hilt almost totally covered in sapphires. By the way it gleamed, there was no way it had been in the catacombs for thousands of years. This had just been placed here.

"I found it for real this time," he said.

"Great. Get down here, and we can get going," Andy said.

When Benjamin settled back on the ground, he handed the dagger over to Gary.

Gary whistled. "It looks like it should be in a museum."

Andy took it from Gary. "It's a good thing you didn't drop that on us. I'd have probably lost my toe."

Benjamin laughed. "How do you feel? Are we ready to go?"

Andy nodded. "As ready as I'll ever be."

"Yeah. Trojan War, here we come," Gary said.

They gathered close and each placed a hand on the gleaming dagger.

"This one feels different than last time," Gary said. "More powerful."

"Maybe Kronos is trying to help us," Benjamin said.

Gary laughed. "You really think so?"

"No. Probably not," Benjamin said. "Okay, focus your thoughts. Three thousand one hundred ninety years ago. Troy—on the west coast of Turkey."

The telemagnifier glowed; Benjamin felt the crunching and heard the snap. And then everything shifted.

"Arghhhh!"

Benjamin just had time to look up as the warrior came charging straight for them. Without thinking, he teleported the three of them away—somewhere else. Anywhere else.

They ended up about fifty feet away.

"So much for not teleporting in front of humans," Gary said.

"Given the choice, Benjamin did the right thing," Andy said.

"Are we dressed like the enemy or something?" Benjamin looked down at his ridiculous costume.

Gary adjusted his shield so it rested over his chest. "I don't think so. Maybe we just startled him."

Benjamin raised an eyebrow. "So he tried to kill us?"

"It is a war," Andy said.

"Then how do we look around without fighting?" Benjamin said.

Andy shrugged. "We walk around and look busy. As long as we look like we know what we're doing, no one will stop us."

Thankfully, the silly costumes Aurora had picked out were appropriate, and after Benjamin grew his hair a couple inches, he fit right in.

"Let's head to the camp." Andy motioned about a half mile away. "We can look around and ask questions."

They didn't run but walked fast and only slowed down when they reached the camp. After the warrior had nearly killed then, an onslaught with someone seemed almost unavoidable.

"We're in the Greek camp, right?" Benjamin asked.

"Spartan," Gary said. "The war was Sparta against Troy."

Benjamin watched a troop of soldiers drilling. "Some of these warriors look younger than us."

"That's because they are," Gary said. "In ancient Sparta, males were sent off to military school when they were seven. They trained their entire lives until sixty when they could finally retire from the warrior life."

"Seven!" Benjamin said. "What if they were too little?"

Gary pursed his lips. "Sick and weak babies were left

on a hillside to die."

"You're kidding, right?" Andy asked.

Gary shook his head. "The government enforced it."

"Glad I wasn't born in Sparta," Benjamin said.

"Maybe you were," Andy said. "Maybe it's really you who time traveled to the future. Maybe someone left you on a hill because you were too weak, and a telegen came along and teleported you away."

Benjamin smirked. "Maybe you were born in Sparta, and they had to dress you up like a baby girl and sneak you out of the city."

Gary rolled his eyes. "Knock it off. We have work to do, don't we?"

"Yes, yes, Gary," Andy said. "*Hey, didn't all the Spartans die in the end?*"

Gary nodded. "*The war wiped out lots of them. Even though they won, the story is that the Greek gods and goddesses took revenge on them and caused them to die. Hundreds of thousands were dead at the end of it all.*"

Benjamin looked around. "*There's like a million people here. Do we just ask if anyone has seen a kid—I mean a fierce warrior—who looks a lot like me?*"

"*Let's just keep looking first,*" Andy said. "*We still have time before we need to travel back to the present.*"

"*As long as no warriors try to kill us.*" Benjamin shook his head. "*That guy looked ferocious.*"

"He should. He's Achilles," a voice replied in their heads.

The boys stopped dead in their tracks. Benjamin wasn't sure it he should put up a solid mind block or leave his pathways open. He tightened his current block a little but didn't cut out all communication.

"*Who said that?*" he asked.

"*Meet me in the green tent on the edge of the camp.*"

Benjamin looked at Andy who looked at Gary.

Gary shrugged. "*Sounds like a good start.*"

Benjamin increased his mind block. "*Let's just be cautious. Whoever said that isn't necessarily from Lemuria.*"

While they walked across the camp, Benjamin checked over his shoulder every time they passed a tent. Aside from trash and camp fires, he didn't see much of anything. But then finally, at the edge of camp, sat a small, green tent. The entry flaps were closed, but they opened as soon as the boys approached.

The man who walked out looked familiar, but Benjamin couldn't place his unshaven face, long brown hair, or annoyed look.

"You're too late," the man said. "Cory's gone."

"Who's Cory?" Benjamin asked.

"You're brother. He's gone."

"Gone like dead?" Benjamin dropped his mind block. This man knew why they were here.

"Did he get killed in the war?" Andy asked.

The man shook his head. "No, of course not. Not Cory. He was the best. He rivaled Achilles for bravery and skill."

"So where is he?" Benjamin asked.

"You missed him by a few weeks," the man said.

"How do we find him?" Gary asked.

"You travel back three weeks ago and get him."

"Really?" Benjamin asked. Had they really mistimed the arrival time by three weeks?

The man sighed. "Kronos probably tricked you."

"So you know my brother...Cory?" Benjamin liked the

name. It had a strong feel to it. He felt so close to actually meeting him.

"Of course I know your brother. I raised him after all." The man seemed to remember himself. "I'm Hexer by the way."

"Hexer!" the three boys said in unison.

"You've heard my name before?"

"Yeah. We've met you before," Andy said. "Except there were two of you."

Hexer frowned. "Two of me? Like twins?"

But Benjamin now recognized him. There couldn't be a mistake. The face was the same, but when they'd met Hexer a year before, he was older. And there had been two of him. They—the Hexers—were the guardians of the Emerald Tablet.

"I'm not really sure," Benjamin said. "But they were you."

"No mistake about it," Andy agreed.

Hexer shook his head. "That ought to be interesting."

"You raised my brother?" Benjamin asked. "Did his guardian give him to you?"

"I am his guardian," Hexer said. "When I took Cory as an infant, I traveled back in time and placed him in Sparta with a couple who took care of him for about a year. Raiders from Athens attacked the city one day, and they raided the farmhouse. I saved Cory, but not his parents. I'm pretty sure it was the Atlantians who did it, but I never had proof. Not that it mattered. From that day forward I vowed to never let Cory out of my protection. I almost lost him that day. If I hadn't made it to the farmhouse in time, he would have died along with them. He

 181

was my responsibility. My duty. And I will never fail him again."

"Why the past?" Benjamin asked.

"Because no one would think to look here, in the past," Hexer said. "Unless temporal phasing became much more prevalent, Cory would be somewhat safe." Hexer sighed. "At least those were my thoughts."

"But what about this war?" Andy asked. "You guys were actually fighting in it?"

"Stupid war. All these people dead over some prince kidnapping a woman. And she isn't even that pretty—that's the funniest thing about it. At least not pretty like your friends Heidi and Iva."

"You know about Heidi and Iva?" Benjamin felt his heart speed up at the mention of their names. Why would Hexer—at least this younger Hexer—know about Heidi and Iva?

"Because they were here with you a few weeks ago," Hexer said. "It was the two of them, Andy, and you, Benjamin."

"Not me?" Gary turned to Benjamin. "Why don't I get to temporal phase next time?"

"You do. There's no way I'm bringing Heidi and Iva back to this war." Benjamin turned back to the main camp. "I mean look at this place. It would be way too dangerous."

"Things change. We met father away from the camp." Hexer pointed to a temple of some sort in the distance. "Way over there."

Benjamin figured there was about the same chance Iva and Heidi would travel back in time as the Trojans winning the war. It was too dangerous. What if something went wrong? What if someone hurt the girls?

Benjamin turned as the green tent flapped open, and a man walked out. Benjamin threw up his mind blocks but brought them down when double vision took over.

"Hexer!" Andy said.

It was Hexer coming out of the tent. His hair was shorter and his face shaved, but unmistakably, this was Hexer.

"What?" the long haired, unshaven Hexer said. He had yet to turn and look at the figure.

Andy shook his head. "No, not you. This Hexer."

Hexer turned and stared.

"Surprised to see me?" the new Hexer asked.

"That's putting it mildly," the first Hexer said. "How are you here? Why are you here?"

"To bring you back—that's why," the new Hexer said. "You didn't think you'd have to stay here forever, did you?"

"Why are you me, though?" the first Hexer said.

"Some experimental transmutational temporal phasing thing," the new Hexer said. "It's kind of complicated. But essentially I'm you six months from now. Helios sent me back to get you."

"Helios?" Benjamin said. "Helios Deimos?"

"Of course," the new Hexer replied. "But let's not get into the details. It's all top secret."

"Figures," Gary said. "So there are going to be two of you from now on. Which explains how we met two Hexers last year."

The new Hexer shrugged. "Guess we'll have to wait and find out. Are you ready?"

 183

"Definitely." The first Hexer nodded. "Just get me out of this ridiculous war."

"Then let's go."

Without another word, the two Hexers stepped into the tent, the flap falling closed behind them. And by the time Benjamin walked over and opened it, the tent was empty.

Andy crossed his arms. "Never a dull moment."

Benjamin laughed. "Guess we should think about going, also. There's nothing left here now."

"But why would you think you're going anywhere?"

Benjamin looked away from the tent in time to see himself, Gary, and Andy surrounded. Ten warriors stood with swords and shields, and when Benjamin tried to move closer to his friends, one of the warriors reached out and grabbed him.

So Benjamin pulled the best trick he knew. He teleported away.

At least he tried to. But something about it didn't work—like he ended up in the same place he started. Just like back at Kronos's temple. And then he heard the laugh.

"Trying to go somewhere?"

Benjamin turned toward the voice. "You?" It was the warrior who'd almost charged them down earlier.

The warrior smiled. "Yes. Me. But allow me to introduce myself."

Andy looked at the man with a look caught between hatred and admiration. "You're Achilles."

Achilles nodded. "My fame precedes me wherever I go."

Gary nodded. "That's putting it mildly."

"Let us go," Benjamin said, and he tried to teleport again.

Achilles shook his head. "You won't be able to teleport away."

Benjamin's eyes grew wide.

Achilles smiled. "Yes, yes, I'm a telegen, too."

Gary nodded. "That helps explain why three thousand years from now, everyone knows your name."

Achilles stood straight. "They do? Ah good. Then it seems my plan is working fine."

"And what plan is that?" Andy asked.

Achilles looked around. "I'd love to discuss it with you, but perhaps we should go somewhere less...public."

Not like they'd have had a choice. The ten warriors half led, half dragged Benjamin, Andy, and Gary to some temple near the ocean. And only once they got there and Achilles shoved them in a makeshift cell, did he finally talk again.

"So what brings three little time-traveling Lemurians back to the Trojan War?" Achilles pulled up a stool outside the cell.

Benjamin stared at Achilles, but didn't say anything.

Achilles smiled. "You can't block your mind."

And Benjamin knew it was true. He'd tried, but pretty much since they'd been captured, every single thing he'd attempted had failed. "Why? What did you do?"

Achilles put his hand to his chest. "Do? I didn't do anything."

Andy narrowed his eyes at Achilles.

Achilles smiled. "I have installed telejammers around the temple here. And of course at various places around

the battlefield."

Gary's eyes opened wider than onions. "You're cheating at war?"

"It's not cheating," Achilles said. "This is war."

"But you die in this war," Andy said.

Achilles gave a dismissive flick with his hands. "So I've been told. But trust me on this." And he leaned close. "There is no way I will die in this war. I plan to live forever."

Benjamin laughed. "No one's immortal."

"Really?" Achilles said. "Because I have it on good word that immortality is possible. At least for those willing to pay the price."

Benjamin held still, not sure what to say. Could telegens really live forever? The false gods had been rumored to have unnaturally long lives.

"How?" Andy said.

Achilles smiled, and Benjamin felt shivers run up his arms. "It doesn't matter. I wouldn't want to cloud the minds of innocent Lemurians."

"Speaking of which," Benjamin said. "We're ready to go back now."

Achilles feigned confusion. "Go back where?"

"To Lemuria," Benjamin said.

"And back to our time," Gary added.

Achilles drew his sword and ran his finger along the blade. "I see. But why should I let you go?"

"Why should you keep us?" Gary looked over at Benjamin and Andy, then back at himself. "We're worthless."

Achilles laughed. "Yes, I can see that."

"We're not worthless," Andy said.

Achilles eyed him. "You're certainly not ready to fight.

But I don't think I'll let you go just yet. You may come in useful for something."

"No we won't. So unlock the door." Benjamin stood up, but he felt a crushing force slam him back to the ground.

But Achilles shook his head. "If I just let prisoners go, the other warriors would think I was weak. You invaded the camp, and I can't let you go without some sort of price being paid."

"Price?" Benjamin said. "Like what?"

Achilles looked at them. "You don't seem to have anything to trade, do you?"

Benjamin thought of the dagger telemagnifier. They couldn't really trade that. At least not if they wanted to travel back to their own time.

Achilles shook his head. "No, I don't want a temporal phasing telemagnifier." He looked around. "If you didn't notice, this is a temple to Kronos we're in right now. I can get one of those anytime I want."

"We don't have anything else." Benjamin seriously doubted Achilles would want their swords or shields based on how many he saw stashed around the place. But then he thought of the small disk he'd gotten in Geros. The life force disk. He still had it in its box, tucked under his belt. And when he thought of it, Achilles's mind froze.

Benjamin caught Achilles's face, and their eyes locked.

"Yes," Achilles said. "Now that is something we could trade."

"No," Benjamin said. Whatever reason he'd been meant to find the object in the first place, he wasn't going to just turn around and give it away a week later.

"Yes," Achilles said, and he smiled. But there was nothing humorous about his smile. "Let me give you a couple choices."

Benjamin shook his head. "I said no."

"Choice one." Achilles ignored Benjamin. "You can trade your object, and you and your two friends can time travel back immediately. You can do it from inside your cell if you want."

"I said no deal," Benjamin said, but again, Achilles ignored him.

"Or choice two," Achilles said. "I kill you and take the object anyway."

Gary looked at Benjamin. "Give it to him."

"His reasoning is pretty good," Andy said.

Benjamin turned back to Achilles. "Why do you want it so bad? What does it do?"

Achilles leaned forward again. "You mean you don't know?" And then Benjamin felt Achilles dig into his mind. "No, you don't know. But I think we should keep it that way. It's better that you don't." Achilles looked around and tapped his foot. "So what's the answer? Either way, I get the object."

Benjamin felt his mind spin. Why was the thing so important anyway? Not that it mattered. He reached to his belt and pulled out the metal box. "We can go if I give it to you?"

Achilles nodded. "The sooner the better."

Benjamin turned to Andy and Gary.

"Maybe it's why you got it in the first place," Andy said.

Now that was something to consider. Maybe the whole

reason he'd got the object at all was so he could trade it with Achilles. Otherwise, it seemed pretty random they'd have exactly what Achilles wanted more than anything else. At least that was the impression Achilles's mind was giving.

Benjamin turned back to Achilles. "Promise?"

Achilles stood and nodded. "Let it never be said I am without honor."

And so Benjamin reached the box through the bars of the cell, and Achilles grabbed it. His fingers closed over the metal, and then he looked back up at Benjamin. "Now is the time for you to go."

And the way he said it was pretty final. Like they shouldn't wait around for Achilles to change his mind. So they moved closer together in the cell, and using the short dagger telemagnifier, time traveled back to the present.

CHAPTER 22

THE FOOD OF THE GODS IS DISGUSTING

"What time is it?" Benjamin said.

It was a rhetorical question. Benjamin knew the answer even before he opened his eyes; his heads-up display told him everything. And he'd slept until ten o'clock. But with the way his head was pounding, it might have been better not to wake up at all.

"God my head hurts." Benjamin looked over at Gary's bunk bed. "And why is Gary still asleep?" He called over, "Hey, Gary, get up."

Gary didn't move.

"Come on, wake up."

Still no movement.

Benjamin stood up from his bed but sat back down when the floor started spinning under him. "Whoa."

"What's wrong?" Andy said.

Benjamin shook his head, which only made it hurt worse. "I feel like I'm gonna die."

"Maybe you're hungry." Andy hopped down from the bunk bed.

"I don't feel hungry," Benjamin said. "Just tired."

Andy walked over to Gary and began to shake him. "Come on, Gary. Get up."

Gary's eyes fluttered open. "No. I don't feel good." And

he closed his eyes again.

"Come on. This is ridiculous." Andy shook him again.

"No." Gary didn't even bother opening his eyes this time.

"What is wrong with you guys?" Andy asked. "We have Digs in an hour, and we still need to eat. Get up!"

"You go ahead and go without us." Benjamin lay back down in his bed. "I'm going to rest a while longer." And when he closed his eyes, the world disappeared around him.

When Benjamin woke it was late afternoon, and Heidi stood over him looking down. He tried to pull the covers over himself.

"He's awake," she said.

Benjamin's head felt a little better, though it still felt like someone was teleporting rocks inside it. He turned and looked over to Gary's bed. Gary looked the same as this morning—flat on his back in bed asleep.

"What are you doing here?" Benjamin asked.

"Andy told us you guys were sick," Heidi said. "We told Aurora, and she said we better check on you."

"And it's a good thing I did." Aurora pointed her finger at them. "You guys have been doing a little too much time traveling."

"We've only gone twice." Benjamin sat up in bed. The effort caused his head to swim, but he pretended to ignore it and steadied himself.

"Your chromosomes need time to realign," Aurora told him.

"I thought it would be okay," Benjamin said. "I though the TPT helped with that."

"Apparently not," Aurora said. "By the looks of Gary

over there, even with some realignment help, he won't be traveling for a good six months. Some telegens really can't handle it."

"Six months!" Benjamin said. "What about me? I can't wait six months. I don't have time for that."

"You always have time when it comes to time," Aurora said. "But I think with a little ambrosia, you'll be as good as new in a couple weeks."

Benjamin shook his head. "No, that's too long. I need to go again next Saturday."

Aurora stood up. "Not gonna happen."

"It has to happen," Benjamin said. "What if I do it anyway?"

"You might find yourself stuck back in time with no temporal chromosomes left in you," Aurora said, "Then there'd be no way—none—to get back. Once your chromosomes are gone, they don't re-grow."

"Two weeks!" Benjamin shook his head. "What do I have to do to recover?"

"You need to drink this." Aurora handed over a thick test tube with a cork in the end. It was full of some grey, chalky substance with large chunks in it—kind of like what Benjamin thought pulverized brains might look like.

"Yuck!"

"It's ambrosia, and you need to drink it all," Aurora said. "And it tastes worse than it looks."

"Wasn't ambrosia the food of the gods?" Iva asked. "Didn't it keep them immortal?"

"Exactly," Aurora said. "They all drank this. That way, they could jump around in time and look like they were immortal."

Benjamin looked at the test tube. Did he really need to drink this...stuff? He took a small taste and grimaced. "Ugh!"

"All of it," Aurora said.

Benjamin's head pounded. Not like there was any choice. Drink the brain stuff or maybe never get better. He put the tube to his mouth and drank/chewed all of the chalky substance.

"What about Gary?" Benjamin shuddered. He knew he'd be having an aftertaste from this stuff for the next month.

"We just gave him some," Aurora said. "It's starting to work, but he's still pretty beat. He'll need to sleep the rest of the day."

"Are you sure about the two weeks thing?" Benjamin gave it one final attempt. The ambrosia was working; he already felt better. His headache was fading, and the light-headedness was starting to settle.

"Two weeks. No sooner."

By Monday morning, Gary had recovered enough to get up and go to class. Skipping breakfast, he drank another test tube of ambrosia.

"This stuff tastes nasty," Gary said, swallowing it all down.

Andy laughed. "Only three more days of it."

"I don't know why I'm bothering," Gary said. "If I'm out for Troy, who knows when I'll ever need to temporally phase again."

Andy tilted his head. "You may feel up to going."

Gary shook his head. "No way. I'm not risking my extra

193

chromosome pair to go back. I'm not getting stuck back in that war."

"Then who's going?" Andy looked at Benjamin. "Just us?"

Benjamin shrugged. If he'd been doing one thing since they got back it was thinking—lots of thinking. Maybe Hexer had been right. This whole chromosome thing could be a sign.

Andy smacked his forehead with his palm. "You can't seriously be considering taking Iva or Heidi along? Please tell me you're not."

Benjamin gestured with his hands. "Well, don't you find it pretty coincidental that Hexer told us Gary wasn't going to be there and now we find out he's right?"

"Coincidental or not, you can't take girls back to that war," Andy said. "Did you even look around? What if they got kidnapped or something? What if they got killed? Achilles could get a hold of them, and I'm not sure we could trade anything to get them back."

"I don't see much choice," Benjamin said. "And Hexer didn't mention any problems."

Andy shook his head. "I totally disagree. We have two weeks. By then I'm sure you'll see there's no way they can go back to Troy."

Benjamin didn't bother saying anything. The choice was made, and he didn't even get to make it. Andy would just have to come to accepting the cold, hard truth. They'd be going back to Troy with Heidi and Iva.

The rough weekend had taken its toll on Benjamin more than he realized; it wasn't actually until telekinesis that Benjamin figured out how much the temporal phasing

had affected him. But their telekinesis teacher, The Panther, had no mercy. In fact, five minutes into the class, Benjamin felt sure somehow The Panther had found out about the time traveling.

Okay, not really, but it sure felt that way.

"Today we practice knife throwing," The Panther said. Twenty knives materialized out of nowhere, arranged in a neat pattern on the desk. "I need a victim—I mean a volunteer."

Nobody raised a hand. And then Benjamin felt his right arm begin to lift into the air. He grabbed at it with his left, trying to hold it down, but the effort was futile.

"*Stop it, Andy,*" Benjamin thought.

"*Stop what?*" Andy replied.

Benjamin found himself with his right hand straight in the air, the left hand holding it at the wrist.

Benjamin looked back to see Ryan Jordan grinning from ear to ear. That dirty, rotten snake. He would pay for this.

"Ah, Benjamin Holt, wonderful of you to volunteer." The Panther smiled.

Benjamin had no choice but to walk forward.

"I need you to stand against the far wall," The Panther said.

Benjamin walked over to the bull's-eye. He took his place and turned around. Without warning, a knife flew off the table and embedded itself in the wall to the right of Benjamin's neck. He closed his eyes tightly and didn't re-open them until he had heard nineteen more knives land. Without daring to move, he looked at the twenty gleaming daggers outlining him.

Simultaneously, they detached and floated back to the

 195

desk. Benjamin started to move away from the wall. "I need you to stay right where you are, Mr. Holt." The Panther put up his hand in a stopping motion. "Now who wants to be the first to try?"

If Ryan Jordan's arm had flown up any faster, it would have detached. Benjamin groaned and once again shut his eyes. It was just going to be one of those days. Probably for the next two weeks.

Benjamin finished up his torture in telekinesis, and he and Andy headed to eat. Since she hadn't time traveled, Heidi was as perky as normal, blond hair sparking, talking to Josh before lunch. Benjamin and Andy walked in, blowing past Suneeta Manvar as they made their way to the table where Iva and Gary already sat.

Benjamin stared when he saw Iva. If the bags under her eyes had been any darker, she'd have been a raccoon. Hadn't she gotten any sleep last night?

"Wow, what happened? You look awful," Andy said, then clapped his hand over his mouth.

Benjamin couldn't believe it; sometimes Andy really was a complete moron.

"Gee, thanks, Andy," Iva said. "That's just what I want to hear."

"I just had a talk with Magic Pan," Heidi announced as she walked up.

"I thought you were talking to Josh," Benjamin said.

Heidi smiled. "After Josh."

Benjamin ignored her smile.

"So what did he say?" Andy said.

Heidi sighed. "A whole lot of nothing. It's like he didn't have a purpose in talking to me."

"You think he knew we eavesdropped on Saturday?" Benjamin asked.

Heidi pursed her lips. "Maybe."

"Couldn't you just read his mind?" Gary asked.

"I tried, but it was blank," Heidi said. "And I mean really blank. I think he uses a telejammer."

"Aren't those illegal?" Benjamin asked.

"Yeah, they're illegal," Heidi said, then switched to telepathy. "*I think Magic Pan is actually an anarchist in disguise.*"

"*Anarchist?*" Benjamin said. "*He got the menus back online. Not to mention he was in a meeting with Helios.*"

"*Wouldn't an anarchist try to break the menu system?*" Gary asked.

"*Who broke the menu system in the first place?*" Heidi said.

"*It was broken when we got here,*" Andy said. "*Leena Teasag probably broke it for job security.*"

"*I don't think so,*" Heidi said. "*I think Magic snuck to Lemuria before the semester started and disabled the menus. Then, when it was convenient, he fixed them.*"

Andy laughed. "*That's a little farfetched.*"

"*Even if it is true, what's the big deal,*" Benjamin replied. "*It's just a prank.*"

Just then, Nick Konstantin walked into the dining hall. Iva saw him, too, and Benjamin noticed her trying to slide down in her chair.

"Hey," Andy said. "There's Nick."

Iva slunk lower.

But it was too late. Nick took one look at the table and walked over.

 197

He reached for Iva's hand and kissed the back of it. "Ah, my beautiful Ivana! There you are. I missed you in 'omeroom this morning."

"I was really tired." Iva kept her hands to her face.

"I found I could not recite the poetry without your lovely face," Nick said. "It gives me strength."

Andy groaned. Loudly.

"But I see you now, and my 'ole world is brightened," Nick continued. "But you are tired; I shall not keep you. But might I just say that you look more lovely than usual this morning, if that is even possible. Please do not neglect me tomorrow." He kissed her hand again and turned and walked away, reciting poetry as he went.

Andy rolled his eyes. "Ivana? What's that all about?"

Iva giggled. Nick had obviously flipped the right switch and turned her mood around. "Oh, it's just a nickname. He asked if he could use it to compose a poem." She looked after Nick with a dreamy look in her eyes.

"*Maybe you should compose a poem with her name in it,*" Benjamin silently suggested to Andy.

"*Whatever,*" Andy said as he pushed his chair out and stood up.

Guess it was going to be one of those days for Andy for the next two weeks, too.

 198

CHAPTER 23

GARY THROWS DOWN
THE GAUNTLET

Over the next two weeks, Benjamin checked his heads-up display constantly, making sure the clock wasn't running backwards. He didn't need any more ambrosia, and he felt fine. Only Aurora's word told him he had to wait. But her word was good; her dad time traveled all the time. If he didn't trust her, he might as well give up on time travel completely.

Not that understanding made it easier. To cope with the time, Benjamin worked out every detail of the upcoming trip. He knew where to go. He knew who was going. All that was left was picking a temple of Kronos.

"I've charted out some of the temples we can choose from," Iva said at lunch the following Saturday.

"Can't we just go back to one we've already been to?" Benjamin sat next to Heidi and flipped his menu over.

Andy shook his head and ordered a hamburger, eyeing Iva as she grimaced. "I'm not going back to Rome. I'm not lifting that wall again."

"Aurora says Kronos doesn't like the same people coming back to the same temples," Heidi said. "According to her, he loves to play games. If someone comes back, they won't find a TPT."

"And we don't want to risk that," Iva added. "After

next weekend, we have our ability tests, and then we leave Lemuria. We can't take a chance." She reached down with her fork and picked at her salad.

"So what are our choices?" Andy took an enormous bite from his hamburger.

Iva looked away, and her eyes glazed over as she checked her heads-up display. "Well, there's one in Sumeria, but it's buried underground."

Benjamin reached over and grabbed a piece of bread. "That's out. With our luck, we'd need to dig it up. What else?"

"There's Athens and Thebes in Greece; they have pretty famous temples," Iva said.

That didn't seem to meet with Andy's approval either. He took another bite and talked with his mouth full. "I don't know. All the Greek architecture has all those huge stone monuments and stuff. I'm not lifting anything else."

Iva went on. "Or we could go to South America. The Incan civilization worshipped Kronos as Viracocha, and they had a temple to him in the center of their empire."

"Hmmm. Didn't the Incans used to do human sacrifices and stuff?" Benjamin asked.

"That stopped ages ago," Iva said.

"Allegedly," Benjamin said.

"Which leaves my personal favorite," Iva said.

Benjamin knew without her saying another word that the decision was already made. She'd only been asking them as a courtesy.

"And that would be...?" Andy asked.

Iva smiled. "That would be India. There's a temple in southern India where thousands of people go every Saturday to pay their homage to Kronos."

"Or Shaneeswara as they call him," Heidi added. She flipped her menu back over and ordered a second dessert.

"With that many people around, we'll blend right in," Iva said.

"Sounds like you guys have already been talking about this," Andy said.

Heidi looked at Iva, and they both smiled. "Just a little," Iva said.

Andy scooted his chair out. "As long as I don't have to lift anything."

Heidi clapped her hands together. "Good. It's all set except for one thing."

"And what's that?" Andy asked.

"We need to get some offerings to bring to the temple."

"Offerings? Like what?" Andy said. "Human sacrifice?"

Iva glared at him. "Of course not. Shaneeswara likes iron nails and oil."

"Gee, I happened to pack a bunch of nails when I came here," Andy replied. "And we can get the oil from Leena's blubber storage cabinet."

"Ha ha, very funny," Iva said.

"So where do we get the offerings?" Benjamin asked. "Magic Pan could probably get us what we need." After all, Magic had gotten them the infrared deflector.

"Are you kidding?" Heidi said. "Did you forget he's working for the enemy?"

"We don't know that," Benjamin said. "And anyway we wouldn't have to tell him what it's for."

But Heidi shook her head. "No. Way."

"Morpheus could help us out," Iva said. "After all, it's not like nails and oil are illegal."

After lunch, they headed out into the city. It'd been weeks since they'd talked to Morpheus Midas, and Benjamin was dying to ask if he knew how the chess set had come to be at The Silver Touch in the first place.

"Just try not to be obvious," Andy said as they walked down Mu Way. "We don't want Morpheus to know we traveled back in time."

"Duh, Andy. We're not stupid," Heidi said. "Anyway, maybe I can pick something from his mind."

"Well don't probe too far," Andy said. "I don't want him to feel anything if he has some mind blocks in place."

Heidi stopped at stared at him. "Are you telling me how to do telepathy?"

Andy shrugged.

"What if Walker's in the shop?" Gary asked. "Isn't today the day they play chess?"

"That's okay," Andy replied. "In fact, that's better. We'll have two chances for success. Let's split up if he's there. Gary, you and Heidi stay with Walker, and Iva, you and I can cover Morpheus. Just get him to help you find the nails or whatever."

"What about me?" Benjamin asked.

"Just look around," Andy said. "Act like you're looking for something."

"What?" Benjamin asked.

"Who cares," Andy said.

When Benjamin walked into The Silver Touch, he saw Morpheus just sitting back down to the Ammolite chess board, across from Walker Pan.

"Hello." Morpheus stood back up. "I've been wondering when I would see you again."

"Hi, Morpheus," Benjamin said. "Long time, huh?"

Morpheus nodded. "I was wondering if you'd ever come back."

"We've been busy." Andy moved away from the chess board, toward the other side of the store. Iva and Morpheus followed him.

"Busy?" Walker turned to Gary, Heidi, and Benjamin. "What could five teenagers be busy with? Certainly not school."

"Oh, you know, there's lectures on Tuesdays and Thursdays, Digs on Sundays." Heidi listed the days off on her fingers.

"Ah, yes, youth. It takes so long to realize there is always more than enough time," Walker said.

Benjamin exchanged a quick glance with Heidi. What did Walker mean by that? But if Heidi detected anything, she certainly wasn't giving it away.

Benjamin decided to hang around a bit longer with Gary and Heidi. He didn't trust Walker any farther than the chess table, but he did control his suspicions way better than Gary.

Gary leaned over the board. "So, have you been cheating at any chess lately?"

Walker sighed. "Will you ever let me live down the Bangkok Chess Open last year?"

"I doubt it," Gary said. "I don't have much use for cheaters."

"I'm actually a decent chess player," Walker said. "I had to resist the urge to go back again this year and play."

"I guess it would get boring if you always knew who was going to win," Gary replied.

Walker crossed his arms. "I don't always know who's going to win. Even if there is a high probability of victory."

Gary flicked his eyes upward. "Sounds pretty challenging."

"You act like you're pretty good," Walker said.

"That's because I am pretty good." Gary held his ground, not giving Walker an inch. "And I don't cheat."

Walker raised an eyebrow. "I'm willing to bet you're not as good as me."

Gary leaned forward. "Why don't you put your money where your mouth is?"

"Is that a challenge?"

"You can call it what you like," Gary said.

"Be here tomorrow at four," Walker said. "We'll see who's better."

"What's the use?" Gary said. "You'll just cheat."

"Morpheus has some telejammers in the back we can use," Walker said. "That way, neither of us can cheat."

Benjamin walked away. It looked like Gary had it under control. Keep Walker occupied with bickering—good strategy. He decided to make a play on asking Morpheus about the history of the store. Walking over, he pulled out his Geodine. "Hey, Morpheus, how old is this Geodine?"

Morpheus took it and squinted. "Oh, this particular one is only about a hundred years old. But some of them in here go back for centuries."

"Really?" Benjamin asked. "When were they invented?"

"Funny you should ask." Morpheus handed it back. "It was actually one of my own ancestors who came up with the idea for a Geodine inside a small globe about a thousand years ago."

Benjamin glanced over to Gary and Heidi who still seemed occupied by Walker. "You don't say."

"I do." Morpheus nodded. "His name was Minnolo Midas, and he worked in this very same shop."

Benjamin tossed the Geodine up and caught it. "So, he just came up with the idea one day?"

"That's right," Morpheus said. "The story goes that he was working late one night trying to transmute a golf ball into silver when, out of nowhere, it occurred to him—what if a Geodine was the size of a golf ball? And looked like a globe. It would be perfect, compact, portable."

"Your ancestor must have been very smart," Andy said.

Morpheus smiled. "Yes, very smart indeed. It runs in the family."

"So this was the same shop a thousand years ago?" Benjamin asked. Like he didn't know the answer.

Morpheus nodded. "It's been in the family for ages."

"What do you still have from back then?" Andy asked.

Morpheus went behind the counter. "I keep some of my favorites back here." He proudly held up a silver object. "This is the very golf ball Minnolo Midas transmuted into silver."

They oohed and ahhed appropriately, and Morpheus returned the golf ball to its resting spot. He walked back around the counter and over to another display case. "This is the oldest object in the shop. It's over two thousand years old." He proudly held up a long purple item.

"What is it?" Iva asked.

Morpheus looked at the object like it was the first time he'd really seen it. He scratched his head. "Well, actually, I

don't know." He replaced the purple thing into the display case.

"What about the chess set?" Benjamin motioned across the room. "How long have you had that?"

"Oh, my, how could I forget?" Morpheus replied. "We've had that over a millennia, too. It's older than the golf ball. That's why I was so upset when Walker bought it last year. I would have done almost anything to keep it, but business is business. Now I have it again, even if it's not mine. I'm still working on a way to buy it back from him."

"You could play him in chess and make a bet," Andy said.

"What if he won?" Morpheus lowered his voice. "Walker is very cunning."

Benjamin tried to keep his mouth from hanging open. "Isn't Walker your friend?"

"Of course. But that doesn't mean he'd just hand over a priceless Ammolite chess set."

"Gary could play him in chess for it," Benjamin said. "Tomorrow."

Morpheus's eyes flickered with hope. "Not a bad suggestion." He leaned close. "Do you think Gary could win?"

"If you have a couple telejammers, I'd bet my credit account on it," Benjamin said.

Morpheus looked toward his illegal basement stash. What else was down there anyway?

"Telejammers? I'll see what I can do." Morpheus cleared his throat. "I may have some connections."

"So who are your connections?" Andy asked.

"Friends and acquaintances," Morpheus answered.

"When you're a salesman of oddities for a living, you deal with many interesting telegens."

They left the Silver Touch with plans to return the following day. Gary had the chess challenge against Walker Pan, and they had to return anyway to pick up the nails. Heidi and Iva were sure they could get oil from Leena Teasag. Benjamin figured she must take baths in it. And luckily to pass the time, they had Arch Digs in some top secret place the next day before the match.

"Where are we?" Andy looked around. He'd teleported himself and Iva to the provided coordinates.

Benjamin pushed Andy and his teleportation from his mind. Andy had been able to teleport for a week now and wanted to do it everywhere. Not that it bothered Benjamin.

Okay, it did kind of bother him. A lot. Was Andy destined to be better than him at everything?

Gary studied their surroundings. "Given the present location of the sun and the stars, I'd say we're in Northern Africa."

Heidi squinted up at the sky. "How can you see the stars?"

Good question. It was broad daylight on Sunday afternoon in the middle of a desert.

"I can always see the stars," Gary said. "They're up there all the time, even when they aren't very bright."

"You're right about the location." Jack materialized in front of their eyes.

"What are you doing here?" Benjamin reached out to swat at the Nogical who ducked and moved out of the way.

"I'm joining you guys for Digs of course," Jack said. "I love Egypt."

They walked over to join Sci Omega and the rest of the students who had already arrived.

"Benjamin, where are you?"

Benjamin jumped as the voice and image came from his heads-up display. It was Nathan Nyx.

"What?" he asked.

"Where are you? Your father was looking for you, and we scanned Lemuria but couldn't find you," Nathan said.

"I'm in Egypt," Benjamin said.

"You're not supposed to leave Lemuria," Nathan said. "You know that. Your father is not going to be happy when I tell him this."

Benjamin felt his blood start to boil. "For your information, I'm here for a class, with a teacher."

"What teacher?"

"What does it matter?" Benjamin asked. Jack who was sitting on Benjamin's shoulder must have been able to see or hear part of the conversation somehow and now listened with his small head cocked to one side.

"You shouldn't be leaving Lemuria, even with a teacher," Nathan said. "What if something happened to you?"

"What if?" Benjamin said.

But Nathan never got the chance to reply. Instead his image vanished, and the conversation abruptly ended.

"Did you hear that?" Benjamin asked Jack.

"Yup."

"What just happened?" Benjamin asked.

"I telejammed the signal," Jack replied.

"Why?"

208

"*Because that guy's annoying,*" Jack said. "*I don't like how he always gives you advice. That's weird.*"

"*But he works for my dad,*" Benjamin said. "*He's just doing what he's told.*"

"*Maybe,*" Jack said, but didn't look convinced.

"*Won't he just try to call back?*" Benjamin asked.

"*He'll try,*" Jack said. "*But the signal's jammed. No more calls from Nathan on this line.*"

Egypt lived up to Benjamin's expectations, but keeping his mind focused proved to be a bit of a challenge. Exiting the secret city underneath the Sphinx, they teleported back to Lemuria. The day was far from over, so they headed for The Silver Touch. Though Gary sucked up every bit of knowledge he could from Egypt, Benjamin could tell his friend was preoccupied and knew it was because of the upcoming chess match. Walker had agreed to the challenge. If Gary won, Morpheus got the chess set back. If Gary lost, Walker got...well, anything he wanted from The Silver Touch.

They decided to wait for Gary outside on a bench. It had been a long day—a long summer—so far, and Benjamin just wanted to relax. Plus no need to add any distractions.

"Well, I'm going back in to watch," Jack declared, blinking out of existence. Benjamin saw him reappear inside the shop.

"Couldn't he have just levitated or walked or something?" Andy asked. "Why does he always teleport everywhere?"

"Why do you always teleport now that you can?" Benjamin snapped, and then hoped Andy didn't realize it. Apparently Andy didn't.

"You know, come to think of it, I don't think I've ever seen Jack walk," Heidi said.

"Maybe he can't," Iva said.

"*I most certainly can walk,*" Jack replied in their minds.

"*I thought you were watching the chess game,*" Andy said.

"*That doesn't mean you should start talking about me,*" Jack said.

"*So why do you teleport everywhere?*" Andy asked.

"*Because I can,*" Jack said.

"*Sounds like a good reason to me,*" Andy said.

They waited forever. Benjamin even had time to take a nap. Sure, he'd woken himself up after having some horrible nightmare that involved Heidi and Josh, and, well, not him. Not that he cared. He'd just slept enough. Still he prayed his mind block would hold. The last thing he wanted was Heidi thinking he was having dreams about her.

"So how's the match?" Benjamin asked Heidi.

Heidi sat still for a moment before answering. "Gary and Walker are on their third game. The first two ended in stalemate."

"*Calm down, Morpheus,*" she added telepathically. And then they decided to go in and watch the rest.

"*I don't think I've ever seen Gary sweat before,*" Heidi said as they walked up to the chess board.

"So who's winning?" Andy asked.

Walker, playing black, had a bishop and his king on the board. Gary, playing the white, had a knight and his king.

Gary picked up his knight and moved it. "That's checkmate," he announced. Standing up, he unclipped something

invisible from his right ear lobe and placed it on the table where it became visible.

Walker stared at the board. Without standing, he unclipped an identical device from his ear and set it down next to Gary's.

"Good game," Gary said to Walker, extending his hand.

Not that Walker shook it. His face had turned red, and it looked like smoke might curl out of his ears at any time. "Good game for you. I bet you think you're pretty clever pulling off that checkmate."

Gary tried to suppress a smile. "I've been playing that checkmate in my head for years. But I've never had the chance to use it. At least not until today."

Walker stood up, still not smiling. "Well I'm glad I could be of service." Benjamin thought Walker might try to vaporize Gary right there on the spot, but he finally shook Gary's hand.

"I'll be putting these away now." Morpheus scooped the two telejammers up off the table. "I wouldn't want anyone to find them."

"Yes, take them off *your* chess board," Walker said.

Benjamin noticed Morpheus didn't look Walker in the eye. "You're always welcome to come play on it."

Walker said nothing, just ran his hand over the black king that still sat in checkmate.

"So do you have our stuff?" Andy asked.

"Ah, yes. Nails." Morpheus pulled them out from under the counter. "As requested."

"That's a strange request." Walker set the king down and walked over to the counter. "What do five teenagers

 211

need with nails in Lemuria?"

"It's for a project at school," Benjamin said.

"Actually a project at our school back in Virginia," Andy said. "We're supposed to build something, and we were trying to get it done ahead of time."

"That's very proactive of you." Walker looked to Morpheus. "I'm afraid I won't be able to make our game next Saturday. Something unexpected has come up."

Morpheus inclined his head. "Perhaps we can re-schedule?"

"Perhaps, but if I don't show up for a couple weeks, don't worry. I'll be fine. Gary—I wish I could say it was a pleasure. Maybe some time in the future I'll have the op-portunity for revenge."

"Whenever you're ready," Gary said. And he smiled.

CHAPTER 24

IVA GETS IN A CAT FIGHT

Just when Benjamin was convinced time really was moving backwards, Saturday finally rolled around. It had been settled with pretty much no debate. Benjamin would travel with Andy, Heidi, and Iva.

The Deimos Diner wasn't crowded, and Aurora met them early for breakfast sporting bright yellow hair. "How soon until you leave?" she asked, tapping her matching yellow fingernails on the table.

"Half an hour," Benjamin said, but he found he couldn't eat—his jittery nerves kept stomping on his empty stomach.

"So what are you planning on doing?" Aurora asked Gary.

Gary didn't hesitate. "I'm heading to one of the Ruling Hall libraries."

"Which one?"

"The science library. I hear they have some great information on genetic engineering locked away."

"Do you want some company?" she asked.

Gary's eyes opened wide, and he dropped his menu. Not that Benjamin could blame him. No one ever volunteered to go to the library with Gary.

Aurora continued. "It's just that I don't have any plans for today, so we might as well wait around together."

"I'll be busy doing research," Gary said.

 213

Was he seriously trying to talk her out of it?

Aurora took a long sip of her Amoeba juice before answering. "No problem. I have some of my own research I can do on genetic engineering."

Benjamin had never seen Gary look at anyone like he looked at Aurora at that moment. He figured Gary might buy her a box of chocolates next.

"So what are we going to do with your brother Cory when we get back?" Heidi had ordered her own Amoeba juice but hadn't taken a sip—either because she was also nervous or because of the awful taste. Or both. "Do we just sign him up for summer school?"

"I'm not sure," Benjamin said. "I guess he can live with me back in Virginia during the school year."

"Maybe he'll have to stay in Lemuria," Andy said. "I can't imagine an ancient Greek warrior going to high school with us."

"Let's just get him and get back," Iva said. "We already have enough to worry about with our ability tests next week."

Heidi shook her head. "And I haven't had any time to practice. I think I'm a little better in telekinesis than I was at the start of the summer."

"You're a lot better," Benjamin said. "I hate to say it, but Andy really has helped." And truly, he did hate to say it.

Heidi smiled and her hair curled up at the ends. "You think so?"

Benjamin nodded. "And probably it won't be long before you can teleport."

"What about me?" Gary asked. "You think I'll be able to teleport? And what about Iva?"

 214

Iva smiled but it didn't reach her eyes. "I already know I'll be able to."

"How?" Gary asked.

"I've seen it in the future."

"Have you seen me teleport in the future?" Gary asked.

Iva shook her head. "No. But that doesn't mean you can't," she quickly added.

"We probably need to get going." Benjamin paid using his credit account, and they left, heading for the park off Mu Way.

"Are we ready?" Iva asked.

Benjamin noticed she was chewing on her hair. "Is everything okay?"

"It's fine. Why do you ask?"

"You look a little preoccupied," he said.

Iva took the hair out of her mouth. "I'm just excited. That's all."

"Let's go then," Andy said. "We'll be back in no time. Get it—no time."

Gary laughed. "Yeah, I get it. See you guys in no time."

The first thing Benjamin noticed when he arrived in India was the heat. With the three silky layers of Indian clothes on that Aurora had insisted he wear, it was unbearable. He put his hand to his collar, unsuccessfully trying to loosen it, and felt sweat springing up everywhere.

"Ugh, how does anyone stand this?" Andy asked once he and Iva arrived.

Iva settled herself. "Try to control the heat, Andy. Decide how much you want to get through your skin. Don't you remember Mr. Hermes going over that in science?"

"Vaguely," Andy said.

They walked toward the main road. Well, not actually a road. It was like a hard packed dirt pathway. And it was mobbed with people.

After the heat, the next thing Benjamin noticed was that this temple thing was more of a social event than a religious gathering. Nobody was worshiping; nobody was praying; they were just standing around flashing gold jewelry and gossiping.

Iva stopped walking and looked around. "I don't sense the TPT."

"Maybe it's not here yet." Andy groaned. "Could be that Kronos wants to play some sort of game again. Like making me lift another heavy door."

Iva shook her head. "I don't think so. A telekinetic challenge here in the middle of all these people?"

"You haven't met Kronos," Andy said. "He's a bit extreme."

"Or maybe he'll make me watch time in the Temporal Orb." Benjamin remembered the images that had flashed by. Even though two weeks had passed, they still haunted him. He saw them even when he closed his eyes at night. And the worst thing was he had no idea which ones would be true and which wouldn't be.

They walked toward the temple, following the massive flow of people. Once they reached the buildings, Heidi led them to the back of a line of worshippers waiting to offer their goods and pay their respects to Shaneeswara. Benjamin had never seen so many nails or so much oil in his life. Not even in Leena Teasag's hair.

"Hey, isn't that Suneeta and Julie?" Benjamin pointed toward a temple.

"It most certainly is." Heidi put her hands on her hips. "They aren't supposed to be outside of Lemuria."

"Duh. Neither are we," Benjamin said.

"Try not to let them see us," Iva said.

But it was too late. Suneeta and Julie had spotted them in line and were weaving their way over.

"Ah, so I see we are not the only ones sneaking out of Lemuria," Suneeta said. "Though I would not have thought you all were capable of actually getting out of the capital city."

"That's nice," Heidi said. "What are you two doing here?"

"I came to pray to his holiness, the Lord Shaneeswara, to have the evil eye removed from me. And you?" Suneeta asked. "What are you doing here?"

"We came for the same reason," Andy said. "Removal of the evil eye."

"Really?" Julie asked.

And then she did something Benjamin would have never thought possible. Julie was just always so…nice. She lunged forward, grabbed Iva's hair, and started pulling.

"You're trying to steal Ryan from me, aren't you?" Julie snarled at Iva.

Benjamin stepped back involuntarily; Julie had gone crazy.

Iva winced and grabbed her hair, trying to get it out of Julie's hands. "What are you talking about?"

"Don't act like you don't know!" Julie shouted. "I've seen the way he looks at you."

This was going downhill fast. People all around were backing up and staring. And Benjamin had no idea what to

say. He'd honestly never in his life been in this type of situation—thank God—and couldn't even imagine what he should do. He looked to Andy who shrugged and stepped backwards.

"Stop it!" Heidi said.

"This is most disrespectful," Suneeta said. "The Lord Shaneeswara will be most unhappy to have such behavior at his temple."

"Julie, stop it," Iva said. "I don't have the least bit of interest in Ryan."

Julie hesitated. Iva took the opportunity and pried Julie's hands off her hair. Julie sunk to the ground. "I just want so badly for Ryan and me to be happy forever. I'm so in love with him."

Benjamin stared. Had Julie really just said what he'd thought she said? She must've. Andy's mouth hung open with disbelief. Girls were nuts.

"Julie thought the Lord Krishna could help her, so I allowed her to come along with me." Suneeta nodded her head to the temple from where they'd come. "Lord Krishna has the larger temple just over there."

Julie glared at Iva as Iva rubbed her head and tried to ignore her. Iva took two steps back. She was now almost right behind Andy.

"So you come here often?" Heidi asked.

"No," Suneeta said. "But this year is special. There is much preparation for the major event next year."

"What major event?" Andy asked.

"You remember, Andy." Iva nudged him. "The one we were talking about earlier. The reason we decided to come pay our respects this year."

"Oh, that event," Andy said. "Maybe you should tell Suneeta what event it is so we can see if it's the same one."

"You know," Iva said. "Next year is when the planet of Saturn transitions into the zodiac sign of Taurus."

"Right," Andy said. "And that's why we're here."

"So who knows you left Lemuria?" Iva asked.

"Only Magic Pan," Suneeta said. "He was able to get us a teleporter ticket out."

"Did he ask for anything in return?" Heidi asked.

"No, nothing at all. Only wanted us to tell him about our trip when we were done," Suneeta said. "Now if there is nothing else, we had better get in line."

"Why don't we cut ahead of you guys?" Julie stepped directly in front of Iva.

"That would be inappropriate and rude," Suneeta said. "The Lord Shaneeswara would not look favorably on that. The Lord Shaneeswara will show his wrath on those who are rude at his temple. The evil eye would descend upon them. And the Lord Krishna will torment them with constant mischief."

Julie jumped out of line and plastered the fakest smile Benjamin had ever seen in his life on her face. Iva raised an eyebrow in reply.

"Oh, we don't want any wrath or evil eyes." Julie whipped around. "It was nice seeing you guys. See you back at school."

"Right. See ya," Benjamin said.

Benjamin waited until they'd left and established themselves far back in line. *"Does anyone else think it's odd they showed up here the same day we did?"*

"And that Magic Pan helped them?" Heidi added.

 219

"*I'm sure it's just a coincidence,*" Andy said.

"*I don't believe in coincidence,*" Iva said.

"*You're just upset because she pulled your hair and accused you of stealing her boyfriend,*" Andy said. "*So do you want to steal him?*"

Iva didn't reply.

"*Maybe the Lord Shaneeswara somehow arranged it,*" Benjamin said. "*He's sneaky enough to do something like that.*"

"*Are you suggesting that Kronos managed to get Julie and Suneeta to come visit the same time as us, and that Magic Pan was also involved?*" Andy asked.

"*I'm not sure what I'm suggesting,*" Benjamin said. "*All I know is that the odds are pretty small that we'd run into them in India today.*"

They'd almost reached the temple; only about five people were in line ahead of them. Benjamin scanned the crowd, looking for his holiness, the Lord Shaneeswara, a.k.a. Kronos. He knew Kronos would make an appearance; he just didn't know when.

"So here's the plan," Iva said. "We walk into the temple, walk up to the altar, and place the offerings there. Then we step back and pray for a little bit. If nothing happens, we leave the temple and start looking around outside."

"Can you sense anything yet?" Heidi asked.

Iva shook her head. "No, nothing."

"You didn't ask me if I could sense anything," Benjamin said. "Last time I found the telemagnifier, and Iva wasn't even around."

"Oh," Heidi said in her best patronizing voice. "Well, do you sense anything?"

"No," Benjamin said. "But I'll let you know if I do."

Whomp. Benjamin felt it like a weight being dropped on top of him. He staggered before regaining his composure.

"I felt it, too," Iva said before he spoke. "The TPT is in the house."

Benjamin could sense the familiar presence. "And with it is the Lord Shaneeswara."

CHAPTER 25

BORROWING A
SACRED LINGAM

When Benjamin stepped into the large temple, it was empty. Empty except for two telegens he recognized right away.

"Ananya?" Even though Benjamin hadn't seen her in a year, he would have recognized her dark Indian features anywhere. Ananya was a perfect mixture of composure, intelligence, and beauty. She was even prettier than Iva. Not to mention she ruled Xanadu where Benjamin had found the second key of Shambhala last summer.

"Benjamin, do not come any closer." Ananya's fifty golden bracelets jingled on her arms as she motioned that the four students should remain where they were.

"What's wrong?" Heidi asked.

"It seems the 'Lord Shaneeswara' and I have somewhat of a disagreement," Ananya replied.

"There's no disagreement."

Benjamin turned his head in the direction of the voice. This time Kronos was young again, maybe around twenty. Possibly even younger than the first time they'd seen him at the ruins in Tunisia.

"Yes, there is," Ananya said. "This is not the TPT they should use."

"It is the only TPT I'm providing today. Anywhere. In

the whole world." Kronos's reply left no doubt it was final.

"What's wrong with the TPT?" Heidi asked.

"Aside from it being an inappropriate object for a tele-magnifier, I foresee trouble with it," Ananya said. "This TPT will not bring all four of you back safely."

Benjamin froze. It had never occurred to him that someone might not return safely from the past. It was a simple matter of getting the TPT, using it to time travel to the past, and then using it to return to the present.

"Who won't it bring back?" he asked. Was it him? Would he be stuck in the past forever? Was it Heidi?

"I can't tell you that," Ananya said. "Only that you should not use it. You should go back to school immediately and try again next week."

"We're not going to wait any longer," Benjamin said. "I've been waiting long enough."

Kronos laughed. "You can't stop the power of time. Don't you know anything?"

"What's that supposed to mean?" Andy asked.

"That means that time does as time wants, and no one can stop what will happen. Time flows and stops for none in its path." And Kronos crossed his arms and smiled.

"Those are nothing but worthless words," Ananya said. "Traveling across the world and time does not make you all powerful. And time won't stop for you either. Even your destiny cannot be changed."

"We'll just wait and see about that, now won't we?" Kronos answered her. "You may think I can't do anything about my son burying me underground in the future, but I'm working on it. I have a plan. Anyway, if 'destiny' can be believed, it says I eat my children and a rock I think is one

of my kids. Who'd be dumb enough to do that? And then I puke up the rock and Zeus traps me in the bowels of the Earth."

"The Navel of the World exists, Kronos. You cannot change it." Ananya turned back to Benjamin. "You must not use this telemagnifier. It is tainted."

Benjamin shook his head. "I have to use it, Ananya. I need to find my brother."

"Are you willing to risk yourself and your friends to do so?" she asked.

"I don't have to. I'll figure out a way we can all come back."

"No, you won't." Her face remained expressionless.

But it didn't deter Benjamin. He would travel back in time today. He would find his brother Cory. And then all five of them would use the TPT—this TPT—to return to this time.

"Your decisions are your own," Ananya said. "Just know the cost of them. Do not say I didn't warn you. There may be no options but destiny."

"There are always options," Benjamin said. "They just have to be found."

"Great!" Kronos clapped his hands together, grinning.

Boy, he really was young.

"So you want the TPT?" he asked.

Benjamin nodded his head.

"Excellent. It's yours to have. After I get my offerings of course."

"Oh, I almost forgot." Andy fumbled with the bag containing the nails. He moved forward at the same time as Iva; they each placed their bags by the altar where stacks

of oil and nails were already heaped high. "What do you do with nails and oil anyway?" Andy asked.

"The uses are endless. The Lord Shaneeswara must keep his secrets though." Kronos waved his hand toward the altar in approval. "The TPT is now yours. Though everyone else outside is going to wonder where the lingam went."

If Ananya's whole demeanor wasn't above it, Benjamin was sure she would've rolled her eyes.

"What's a lingam?" Benjamin walked forward to the altar. But he knew when he saw it. The emerald green object lay on the altar, resting in a bowl. Without pause, he reached out for the object and grabbed it.

Kronos laughed again. "Oh, it's just one of the famous objects of worship in the Hindu religion. I'll probably have to put a new one here, or the masses may think I've shown my wrath by taking away their lingam."

"More likely they'll just think we stole it," Andy said.

"That's why we'll use it here, inside the temple." Benjamin turned back to Ananya as his friends gathered around. "Will I see you again?"

"Yes, if time can be trusted." She cast a long glance at Kronos. And then she leaned close to Benjamin and grabbed his hand. He felt her put something—cold like metal—into the palm of his hand, and then she pressed his hand closed. "You know what you need to do with this," she said. "And don't touch it." And then, without another word, she teleported away.

Benjamin looked down at his hand, but kept it closed. Whatever she'd given him, she hadn't wanted anyone to see. He looked over at Kronos who hadn't seemed to notice.

 225

"Can time be trusted?" Andy asked.

"Only time will tell." Kronos laughed and then teleported away, also.

Benjamin, Andy, Heidi, and Iva were left in the temple. "Let's just be careful." Benjamin shoved whatever Ananya had given him into his pocket. Once they got out of here, he'd figure out what it was. "We're all going to return as long as we all stick together back in Troy. Don't leave the temple we arrive in, and don't talk to anyone besides Hexer and Cory. Understand?"

They nodded their heads in agreement.

"Okay, are we all ready? Reach out and hold onto the lingam."

The world started to bend, their shadows shrunk, Benjamin's body crunched and imploded, and they phased through time.

 226

CHAPTER 26

BENJAMIN TELLS THE ENEMY EVERYTHING

"We met Hexer over there last time," Benjamin told Heidi and Iva once the world had settled. "You see those tents on the outskirts of the camp?" He pointed out through the columns of the temple toward the war.

"Is that really the Spartan camp?" Heidi's eyes were wide, but with curiosity, not fear.

"Yeah, I know," Benjamin said. "It's kind of hard to believe."

"This is nothing like Lemuria a thousand years ago," she said.

Andy chuckled. "Wouldn't it really be Lemuria two thousand years from now?"

"You know what I mean."

"Maybe we should look around," Iva said.

Benjamin shook his head. "No, don't wander. We need to stick together like glue."

"And whatever you do, don't lose the TPT," Heidi added.

"It's fine. I have it in my pocket," Benjamin said.

Benjamin had to admit it. Ananya's warning did have his stomach in knots. Would someone be left behind? But how could anything go wrong? It seemed so straightforward.

Iva went first, leading them out of the inner temple. She walked around the corner and stopped dead in her

tracks. Andy ran into the back of her.

"Why'd ya stop?" Andy followed her gaze to the side of the temple where two figures sat lounging against the wall. "Oh."

"Hey, Hexer!" Benjamin said. "Looks like you were right."

Hexer sat on the grass with another man, probably over twenty years old, but stood when he saw them. "Hello, strangers," he said. "Do we know each other?"

"Of course we do," Andy said. "We just saw you again a couple weeks ago."

Hexer shook his head. "Were you fighting in the war? I don't remember seeing you."

"Hexer wouldn't know us yet," Benjamin said.

"This is the first time Hexer meets us," Iva added.

"Isn't it your first time meeting me?" Hexer asked.

"No, actually it's me and Andy's third time and their second time." Benjamin motioned to Heidi and Iva.

Hexer narrowed his eyes. "And how exactly is that possible."

"*Because we're from Lemuria,*" Benjamin replied silently.

"What are you doing here?" Hexer asked, and Benjamin noticed his hand went to his sword.

"Don't worry," Iva said. "We're friends."

"Yeah. We came back to get my brother," Benjamin said. "You said he'd be here, but I don't see him."

"We're the only ones here." Hexer motioned to the man next to him.

"Hi," the man said. "My name is Koriakos, but everyone calls me Cory."

Benjamin felt his mouth fall open, and he didn't even

 228

try to stop it. He had no idea how to respond. This man, who called himself Cory, was easily as old as Joey Duncan. At least ten years older than Benjamin.

"But...but...how is that possible?" Benjamin asked. "We're the same age."

Cory laughed. "We don't look the same age. And I'm pretty sure I don't have a brother. Do I?" he asked Hexer.

Hexer shook his head. "Not that I know of."

"That's because you couldn't be told," Benjamin said. "None of our guardians could be told."

That did it. Hexer pulled his sword out so Benjamin could see the glint of metal. "How do you know I'm a guardian? Nobody knows that."

Benjamin tried to ignore the sword. Wouldn't Hexer have mentioned if this had come to blows? "Helios knows. And I know," Benjamin said.

"And we obviously mistimed something, Benjamin, because your twin brother is probably ten years older than you," Andy said.

"Twins?" Cory said. "I have a twin brother?"

"Actually we're two of triplets. We have another brother out there somewhere," Benjamin said.

"Maybe we should just start from the beginning," Iva said. "There's a lot of things that need explained."

"Where does the story begin?" Cory asked.

"How about three thousand years from now minus fifteen years," Heidi suggested.

Benjamin told Hexer and Cory everything he could think of. He relayed his discovery of the world of Lemuria, the finding of the Emerald Tablet, and the prophecy. He told of Kenias Burton, his own guardian who had turned against him and tried to bring down the shields. He told of his increasing powers, of Helios and Selene, and of the three keys and their power to destroy the shields. Hexer and Cory sat rapt, not daring to interrupt. When Benjamin finished, the questions began.

Cory bunched up his forehead. "So just to clarify, we're really two of triplets, and our mother is dead."

Benjamin nodded his head.

"So where is our other brother?" Cory asked.

"That's what we need to find out," Benjamin said. "But as long as we stick together, the shields should stay up. The prophecy said two of the three would be needed to bring down the shields."

"What about our father?" Cory asked. "Where is he?"

"Helios thinks he's in Atlantis hiding," Benjamin said.

"And Helios is right, though he's not hiding," a voice said. They all turned as a figure stepped from behind a column. "And thank you for the wonderful story, Benjamin," the familiar voice said. "Your father would be pleased if he were here to listen to it himself."

"Nathan?" Benjamin asked. "What are you doing here?" This guy turned up everywhere. Even three thousand years in the past. Talk about extreme.

"Keeping an eye on you," Nathan Nyx said. "Just like I'm supposed to. Just like your father wanted me to."

A thousand loose pieces came together in Benjamin's mind and clicked. His father wondering if he took something from Wondersky City. His father giving him a special line of credit. His father telling him someone was spying on him. His real father would never mind his business like that.

"You liar!" Benjamin said. "You've been deceiving me and my dad this whole time. You don't really work for my dad."

"Of course I do, Benjamin," Nathan said. "I work for both of your dads. I think you father—your biological father—will be happy with all the information you've managed to collect. And I've never lied to you. I resent that statement."

"You deliberately misled me. And probably my dad also."

"You interpreted my remarks how you wanted to," Nathan said. "But I'm afraid with all the information you've collected, I can't allow you to travel back to the present. You would cause way too much damage."

Andy took a step forward. "You can't stop us, Nathan."

"You've misjudged me," Nathan said. "A common mistake. I'm a more powerful telegen than any of you could ever dream of being. Just be good little children and wait here in the past. We'll come back and get you when we're ready to bring down the shields."

"Mr. Burton couldn't bring them down last year, and you won't be able to do it either," Benjamin said.

"Kenias Burton was a fool," Nathan said. "Convincing him to join our cause couldn't have been easier. He was a spineless, powerless puppet. The only reason we even let him join us was because we figured the child he guarded must have been one of the three. He played his part perfectly—every predictable bit of it."

Had Mr. Burton really been a puppet, used as they wanted to use Benjamin himself? Benjamin felt himself actually feeling sorry for Mr. Burton, the man who had

tried to convince him to destroy the barrier strength shields. Yet he knew this was a ridiculous thought. Mr. Burton had tried to destroy everything, and had very nearly succeeded.

Benjamin realized this whole thing was a race. He had to get back to Lemuria before Nathan. "Nathan, I'd love to stay and chat, but we're going back now." He reached down to his pocket for the TPT. And stopped.

"I can't let any of you return just now." Nathan smiled when he saw the shocked look on Benjamin's face. "Oh, were you looking for something in your pocket? Something shiny and green that's looks something like this?" He held up the emerald green lingam telemagnifier. With a laugh, he dropped it to the floor where it shattered. Picking up his foot, he ground the individual pieces of the lingam into the hard stone beneath.

CHAPTER 27

ACHILLES IS OUT

Benjamin watched as their ticket back to the present was pulverized before his eyes. But before he could say anything, Nathan Nyx vanished, leaving nothing but the emerald dust on the stone floor.

"Where did he go?" Andy asked.

Heidi threw her arms up. "He teleported away. And with him our way back."

Hexer stood staring at the spot where Nathan had been, his hand still on his sword. "Who was that man?"

"He works for my dad," Benjamin said. "We met him earlier this year when we were working at his office."

"Our dad?" Cory asked.

"No. My dad," Benjamin said. "The one I've lived with my entire life."

Cory put his hands to his forehead. "So who lives in Atlantis?"

"Our biological father," Benjamin said.

"Nathan was a double agent." Andy gritted his teeth. "He was playing both sides."

"I can't believe my dad trusted him," Benjamin said. "Remember he was the number one guy at the office?"

"Yeah, I remember." Andy glanced around at the war grounds. "You know this has been really fun and everything, but what are we supposed to do now? We're stuck

here three thousand years in the past."

"And now there's six of us to time travel back to normal time," Benjamin said.

"Is this abnormal time?" Cory asked.

Benjamin looked off in the distance at the Trojan War. He could see the fighting and hear the sounds of battle. "We're in the middle of *The Iliad*. That's abnormal."

"*The Iliad*?" Cory said.

"Yeah," Andy said. "I think if we waited around here long enough, we'd see the Cyclops."

"Oh, no, he actually lives on his own island in the middle of the Aegean Sea," Cory said.

"You're kidding, right?" Heidi asked.

Cory shook his head. "No, not kidding. We teleported over to see him one time. Hexer says he's just a genetic engineering experiment gone bad."

"Wouldn't Gary like to see that?" Benjamin looked down at the dust from the lingam TPT and sighed. "Do you think the dust will have time traveling effects?"

In answer, the wind picked up and blew the majority of the green powder away.

Iva shook her head. "We need another way."

Andy looked at her in challenge. "Do you have any suggestions?"

"Sure," Iva said. "We find a new place of worship for Kronos."

"Of course." Benjamin hit his forehead with his palm. "That's so easy."

"Too easy," Heidi said.

"Why?" Benjamin asked.

"Can you tell me where there's a temple of Kronos

now?" she asked. "Can you tell me what day is Saturday?"

"Saturday?" Cory said.

Which Benjamin took as a bad sign. But maybe Kronos wasn't so concerned with days of the week back in this time. An idea sprang to Benjamin's mind. "I'm not sure on the day, but as far as the temple goes—"

"No way," Andy said.

"I know no way," Benjamin said. "I'm just saying—it is a temple of Kronos."

"What?" Iva asked.

"They're talking about Achilles hideout," Hexer said. "It's a temple to Kronos."

"And you don't think Achilles would let us in to look for a TPT?" Heidi asked.

Cory actually started laughing.

Heidi looked at him like he was nuts. "What's so funny? What if we asked nicely?"

"Maybe after he made you his concubine," Cory said. "Have you ever met Achilles?"

She shook her head no.

"He kidnapped us last time." Benjamin's thoughts went to the exchange they'd made. "He's a telegen, and I don't think he's from Lemuria." And then his mind flew to what Ananya had given him back in India. The life force disk. He reached into his pocket and pulled out the metal box, and when he opened it, he saw the golden disk he'd traded with Achilles.

"What's that?" Cory leaned closer.

Benjamin shrugged. "Something Achilles wants pretty bad."

"So we're going to give it to him?" Hexer asked.

Benjamin shook his head even as his mind melded around the idea forming there. "No. But before we leave, I need to teleport to Geros and hide it there."

"So Achilles is out," Andy said. "What does that leave?"

Heidi looked back toward the battle. "Are there any other temples around?"

"I can think of one," Iva said.

They all turned to face her.

"And that is...?" Andy said.

"The Navel of the World."

"Delphi?" Hexer said.

Iva nodded. "Delphi. The City of the Oracles. In Greece."

Benjamin smiled. "Of course. And that's so close. We can teleport over there and use the Navel."

Heidi bit her lower lip. "And we better go soon." In the distance, the sounds of war had increased, matching the darkening sky.

Benjamin looked at Hexer and Cory. "Can you both teleport?"

Cory nodded.

Hexer shook his head. "I'm not going with you."

Cory turned quickly to his guardian. "What do you mean? You can teleport. You have to go."

But Hexer sighed. "No, Cory. This is where we part ways."

"But why?"

"You heard Benjamin and Andy. They see me here in a few weeks. If I leave now, that'll never happen. And if that never happens, then maybe they'll never find out when they really need to return to get you." Hexer put his hand

 236

on Cory's shoulder. "It's time for us to separate. You have been the best son I could have ever asked for."

The blood drained from Cory's face. "But they could be wrong. Or things may still happen as they should even if you return with us now."

Hexer shook his head. "I'm not willing to take that chance. Someone will come for me, and I'll return to the future. You're more than able to venture out on your own." And then Hexer embraced Cory in a strong hug, compelling Benjamin and his friends to remain silent—nobody wanting to break up the moment. Benjamin wondered how long it would be before Hexer and Cory would see each other again—if ever.

"Thank you for everything." Cory's voice quivered just the smallest amount as he spoke. "You have been like a father to me."

"And you a son." Hexer backed off from the embrace. "Now, you need to get going. We can't risk anything going wrong."

Cory's ashen face pained Benjamin. He thought of how he would feel if he were to never see his parents again.

Hexer stepped back a few paces. "I'll make it easy for you and just walk away." He turned and began to move. "Until we meet again." Quickening his pace, he never looked back.

CHAPTER 28

CORY LEARNS ABOUT THE TROJAN HORSE

Cory watched Hexer until he reached the tents at the far boundary of the camp. "Does he return safely? Will he really get out of this horrible war?"

Benjamin nodded. "Yeah. We watched Hexer teleport away."

Cory sighed with relief. "He's the only father I've ever known. My parents were killed when I was a baby."

"That's what Hexer told us a couple weeks ago," Andy said.

"I hate to be the one to put a damper on things, but we need to get out of here," Heidi said. "I don't want to meet Achilles."

Apparently she'd taken the concubine threat to heart.

Cory pulled his eyes away from the direction Hexer had gone. "You're right. We need to go. With as crazy as everything is around this war, even this temple's not sacred any more. Do you guys know the way to Delphi?"

Iva nodded. "We went on an archaeological dig a while back."

"Really?" Cory said. "Delphi isn't an active oracle city in your time?"

Iva actually laughed. "Not hardly. It's been gone for over two thousand years."

"Yeah, humans don't really put much credibility in oracles anymore." Andy managed to avoid the glare Iva shot him.

Cory looked like he'd missed a punch line. "So how do people know their futures?"

"They don't," Heidi said. "Have you been to Delphi?"

"Once about ten years ago," Cory said. "The Spartan army was fighting Athens, and we were pretty close. Hexer insisted we teleport over and visit."

"Did the oracles read your future?" Iva asked.

"Sort of," Cory said, "but it's the weirdest thing. I can't remember what they said."

Iva pursed her lips. "They must've placed a block on your mind."

"Why?" Benjamin asked. Had the oracles seen something about the triplets or the keys of Shambhala in Cory's future?

"I don't know," Iva said. "But it may be important."

"Then we need to get the mind block removed," Benjamin said. "Let's go. But I'll meet you guys there. I need to go to Geros first."

Geros took a good two hours, what with having to sneak into the Ruling Hall, travel down the lift tube, and figure out how to get the picture to store the life force disk. That was going to be the hard part until he conveniently ran into a Nogical named Lulu who claimed to know Jack. Lulu claimed Jack had sent her from the future, and before Benjamin had time to ask any more about it, she'd taken the disk, hidden it in the picture, and was just about to teleport away when Benjamin stopped her.

 239

"Wait!" Benjamin said.

Lulu put her hands on her little hips. "What?"

"I need one more thing."

She narrowed her eyes and tried to look put-upon. Benjamin almost laughed, but didn't want to make her mad. He really did need her help.

"What else could you possibly need?" Lulu said. "I've already missed lunch to come back here."

"I need you to make a record for me."

"A record?" Lulu said. And then her eyes lit up. "Oh, yeah. A record. Jack mentioned that."

Benjamin smiled. "So you'll do it?"

Lulu started up the tube in the Ruling Hall. "No."

Benjamin started after her. "But I really—"

Lulu stopped moving and turned back to face him. "Jack already did it. I was supposed to tell you that."

"So why didn't you?" Benjamin asked, and they started up the tube again.

"I forgot," Lulu said. "Anyway, have a nice time in Delphi." Then she laughed and teleported away, leaving Benjamin there in the tube in the Ruling Hall of ancient Geros.

By the time Benjamin finally teleported to Delphi, Iva looked like she'd claw his eyes out if they didn't go into the city immediately.

And not surprising, as soon as they did enter the city border, Iva walked away from the group and closed her eyes. They walked over to join her. And then Benjamin felt his mouth fall open. Though he'd seen the vision of Delphi in the past—the vision in which he'd seen Iva—he wasn't

 240

expecting this. Delphi was a bustling metropolis. And then he caught sight of it—right where he knew it would be. The Navel of the World.

Behind it sat a blindfolded woman—no scratch that— a blindfolded girl. She couldn't have been any older than they were.

"I sense a familiar presence," Iva said at last, not yet opening her eyes.

"Kronos?" Andy guessed.

Iva shook her head and opened her eyes. "No, not yet. Though he could still show up before this is done. No, it's someone else."

"Nathan?" Benjamin asked, gritting his teeth.

"Not evil. Not like Nathan Nyx." Iva took a deep breath and looked down to the oracle girl. "And as for a TPT, there's only one thing in this entire place that has any power at all."

"The Navel of the World," Heidi said.

"Exactly. It's bursting with telenergetic power." Iva looked like she might burst with excitement when she said it.

Cory narrowed his eyes. "We need to be careful. Delphi is not as it may seem. And getting to the Navel may not be a simple matter."

"Why don't we split up and look around?" Andy said.

Iva nodded "That's a good idea. But I don't think any of us should go near the oracle. Or near the Navel of the World. Not just yet."

"Iva, Heidi, and I will go look down the hill," Andy said.

Benjamin almost objected. Why did Andy want to be paired off with Iva and Heidi? But then he stopped himself.

He hardly knew Cory—his brother—and it might be nice to have a few minutes alone with him.

"Just use telepathy to contact us if you need to," Heidi said.

They split up, and Benjamin and Cory started walking.

Delphi was a city. This might seem kind of obvious, but Benjamin had just never thought about it before. It was in fact a large city. Seeing the ancient world in a ruined state had tainted his perspective.

"The colors on everything are so bright." Benjamin tried to make conversation with his ten-years-older-than-him twin brother.

Cory laughed and put a hand on his shoulder. "Did you expect them to be dull?"

"When we visited here a while back, there was no color. Just plain white stone," Benjamin said. "But that's how all the archaeological sites are."

Cory glanced over at the nearest building—bright gold and blue. "So the buildings never get repainted?"

"Actually, most of the buildings are falling down," Benjamin said.

"How come people don't take better care of it?" Cory asked.

"Lots of reasons," Benjamin said. "War—that's a big one."

"Yes, war." Cory shook his head. "It should be averted at all costs. You know the war has been going on for ten years now. Sometimes I think it will never end."

"It will," Benjamin said. "In fact, it must end pretty soon. It only lasts about ten years."

"Do the Spartans win?" Cory stopped walking and

looked at Benjamin.

"Yeah, they destroy Troy and either enslave or kill everyone."

Cory sighed. "It's brutal business, war. So much death and destruction. And all caused by telegens."

"Have you actually met any of them?" Benjamin asked. "The false gods or goddesses?"

"I've met Athena," Cory said. "And I've seen Aphrodite."

"What were they like?" Benjamin asked.

"Aphrodite was beautiful." Cory's eyes glassed over. "But Athena was the one who made the lasting impression. And not just her brilliance; she was kind and loving and caring."

Benjamin laughed. "It almost sounds like you were in love with her."

Cory shook his head and the dreamy look in his eyes started to fade. "I wasn't the one in love with her. That was Hexer."

"Hexer and Athena were in love?"

"From the first moment they met."

"So what happened?" It's not that romance was so interesting to Benjamin. But they were talking ancient gods here.

"Responsibility got in the way," Cory said. "I think I was the reason Hexer and Athena never married. For years they saw each other, on and off. She was like a mother to me. But thanks to the war, I don't think Hexer has seen Athena in over five years."

"Wow. I never would have guessed," Benjamin said.

"Hexer doesn't talk about himself very much," Cory

 243

said. "He rarely mentions his parents or his youth. I know he never knew his father and saw very little of his mother." Cory shifted.

Benjamin figured maybe the conversation reminded him he might never see Hexer again.

"You mentioned the Spartans win the war," Cory said. Benjamin nodded.

"Do you know how?" Cory asked.

"You've never heard the story of the Trojan Horse!" Benjamin said. "Of course not."

"A horse from Troy causes the war to be won?"

"No. A great deception from Sparta wins the war," Benjamin said. "The Spartans pretend to give up. They move all their ships away from port. They pack up their camps. And they build a giant wooden horse which they leave outside the city walls as a gift before leaving."

"The Spartans give the Trojans a gift?" Cory asked.

"Uh huh. So the Trojans wake up to find this giant horse outside the wall and the whole Spartan army gone. They open the gates and wheel the horse inside. Then, later that night, there's a big party. The Trojans eat and drink until they pass out."

"Sounds just like the Trojans. They're a worthless bunch." Cory shook his head. "So then what happened? Did they forget to lock the city gates?"

"No. Once the Trojans pass out, a secret door on the side of the horse opens, and ten Spartan warriors climb out. They unlock the gates and set the city on fire."

"Amazing," Cory said. "I'm impressed that we actually came up with that. I wonder whose idea it is."

"A warrior named Odysseus," Benjamin said. "Have

you heard of him?"

"Are you kidding? Everyone's heard of Odysseus. If people aren't talking about Achilles, they're talking about Odysseus. He can't stand the war. He just wants to get home."

"Yeah, but it takes him ten years even after the war is over to get home," Benjamin said.

Cory shook his head. "I'm just happy to be getting out of there." But then he stopped walking.

"What is it?" Benjamin asked and then followed Cory's gaze.

It was Ananya, dressed in a green silk sari, sitting on the ground. Chaos, her tiny monkey, clung to the long dark braid hanging over her shoulder.

Benjamin stared at the woman he had seen only hours before in present day India.

"Ananya!"

Benjamin looked as he and Cory said the name at exactly the same time.

"You know each other?" he asked Cory.

"You know each other?" Cory asked in return.

"I see you two have been reunited." Anaya stood up, and Chaos jumped to her shoulder and screeched.

"What are you doing back here?" Benjamin tried to get a grasp on what was going on—unsuccessfully.

Ananya smiled. "Time is not the same in the world of Xanadu as it is for the rest of the Earth."

"What does that mean? I just saw you in India a few hours ago," Benjamin replied.

"Did you? Then I will have that to look forward to. What am I doing in India?"

"You were in the temple of Kronos—I mean Shaneeswara—trying to warn us not to use the TPT there to travel back to now," Benjamin said.

Ananya laughed. "So I guess you didn't listen?"

Benjamin shook his head. "No, we didn't listen, and now we're stuck."

"Ah, yes—we. Where are Heidi, Andy, and Iva now?"

"They're trying to find a way to use The Navel of the World," Cory said.

"It will be nearly impossible," Ananya said.

"Why?" Benjamin asked. "I thought Kronos likes when people use his telemagnifiers."

"You forget. This is not a temple of Kronos. This is a city founded by Apollo, who maintains control with an iron fist. And Apollo and Kronos don't always see eye to eye."

"But the Navel of the World is here," Benjamin said. "How come Apollo lets that stay?"

"You forget what the Navel actually is," Ananya said.

"The Navel of the World is the stone Kronos' wife fed to him in place of Zeus. It caused him to throw up the children he'd eaten," Cory said. "And Apollo is none other than one of the sons of Zeus."

"So Apollo is Kronos's grandson?" Benjamin asked.

"Yes, though there is no love lost between the two," Ananya said. "The Navel represents a victory over Kronos."

"But it's a telemagnifier," Benjamin said. "I can sense its power."

"It is a very powerful telemagnifier—especially for temporal phasing," Ananya said, "for it was once inside Kronos."

"So can't we just sneak over and use it to time travel back to our time?" Benjamin asked.

"It's not that easy," Ananya said. "None but the oracles are allowed near the Navel. And Apollo keeps a tight rein on them."

"So what do we do?" Cory asked. "From what Benjamin has been telling me, we really need to get back to his time. And Nathan Nyx could show up at any time."

"You're right. But I believe I have a plan. Let's find your friends, and then I'll explain it." Ananya didn't wait for a reply. She walked toward a small temple with an altar in the center, and when she got there, she stopped. "We'll wait here until they arrive."

CHAPTER 29

Ananya Calls in a Favor

In less than five minutes, Heidi, Iva, and Andy crested the hill. Heidi ran up to Ananya and embraced her. "It's you. It's really you."

"Yes, it's me," Ananya said. "Benjamin tells me I saw you a few hours ago, though I have yet to experience that moment in time."

"You were in a temple arguing with Kronos," Heidi said. "And then you vanished."

"But now I'm here, and I have an idea how to get the five of you back to the present," Ananya said. "Follow me inside the temple."

They walked in, single file, through the small entrance then circled around the altar in the center.

"This is a temple to Apollo," Iva stated it more than asked it.

Ananya nodded her head. "Yes, though not nearly as popular as those closer to the oracle. I come here when I need to talk directly to his holiness." She gave a sideways grin as she said it.

"Does he listen?" Andy asked.

"To me? Always. Apollo has had need to seek refuge in Xanadu from time to time. Let's just say Apollo owes me a favor or two." Chaos jumped to the altar and perched in the center, and Ananya placed her hands palm down on the altar. "Apollo, would you please do me the courtesy of a visit? There's something I need to speak with you about."

And then they waited less than a minute.

"Ah, lovely Ananya. To what do I owe this pleasure?"

Benjamin turned to see a handsome, though familiar, man with shining golden hair walking toward them and the temple. The sun glinted off his bronzed skin and blond hair, creating a glowing aura around him. Benjamin heard a sharp intake of breath and turned to see both Heidi and Iva staring. Benjamin couldn't place where he'd seen the man before, but he knew this wasn't the first time they'd met.

"Apollo." Ananya moved her lips into a flicker of a smile. "You're looking well."

"The sun will do that to you," Apollo said. "Did you know it's the most plentiful source of energy anywhere near our small little planet?"

"I believe you mentioned that to me once or twice before," Ananya said. "Apollo, I'd like you to meet a few of my friends."

She introduced them with first names only. Did Cory even have a last name? And then it dawned on Benjamin where he'd met Apollo before.

"You were in Xanadu," Benjamin said.

Apollo flashed his gleaming smile and laughed. "Many times."

"I knew I'd met you before." Benjamin turned to Heidi. "Remember?"

Heidi nodded. "But I had no idea you were a god when we met before." Her eyes were still a bit glazed over which kind of irked Benjamin.

"For me that time hasn't come," Apollo said. "Though

 249

now I will anxiously await it." He spread his arms wide. "Friends of Ananya are friends of mine. Welcome to Delphi. How do you like my city?"

"It's the loveliest place I've ever been." Iva could hardly take her eyes off the man.

Thought it pained him, Benjamin had to admit that Apollo was a perfect specimen. His physique looked chiseled, each muscle sized just right. His golden hair topped his head like a crown. And his teeth shone as his smile lit up the world around him.

"Would the young ladies like a tour?" Apollo extended each arm; it wasn't a request.

Benjamin felt a strong urge to say, "No, the young ladies would not like a tour," but held back when he saw the look on Ananya's face. And then he felt Andy's rage in the Alliance bond. Andy was furious. And jealous.

"Nathan could show up at any time," Andy said.

Apollo turned to look at Andy. "Nathan Nyx? Oh, I don't think so."

How can you be so sure?" Andy said.

Apollo laughed and walked closer to Iva and Heidi. "Nathan Nyx is banned from Delphi. If he comes here I will kill him myself."

Andy opened his mouth to say something else, but Ananya shot him a glance to silence him. And so Heidi and Iva walked over and each interlaced an arm with Apollo.

"I won't take long," Apollo said. "But I must extend proper courtesy to my beautiful young guests. When I return, we can speak." Leaving no room for argument, Apollo turned, with Heidi on his left arm and Iva on his right, and walked away from the temple.

Benjamin looked to Ananya.

She sighed. "Though he does owe me favors, we need his help, so I dare not dispute. At least not just yet. Apollo likes to feel he is king of Delphi—which I suppose he is. They shouldn't be gone longer than an hour or two."

"An hour or two!" Andy said.

"Delphi is a large city," Ananya said. "And Apollo knows I need something. He will give it to me. But he'll also make me wait."

Benjamin shrugged and sat down. Now seemed like as good a time as any. He formed a mental image of the disk he'd traded with Achilles in his mind.

"There's something you need to give me when we're in India," he said to Ananya, and he shared the image with her.

Ananya sucked in her breath. "That's not possible."

Benjamin looked at her. "Why not?"

"Do you even know what that is?" she asked.

"Not really," Benjamin said. "I mean I know it's a life force disk."

"It's dangerous," Ananya said. "You should not own one."

"It's not for me," Benjamin said. "I need it to trade with Achilles."

But Ananya shook her head. "Even if I wanted to give you one, I'm not sure where I'd get it. They're rumored to be made in the workshop of Hephaestus."

"Ananya gave it to you?" Andy said. "When?"

"Back when we were in the temple," Benjamin said. "And now it's hidden safely in Geros." He looked back to Ananya. "But if you don't give it to me, then I'll never be able to hide it and find it and trade for our freedom."

 251

"And Achilles could kill us," Andy said.

Ananya shook her head slowly back and forth. "I'll see what I can do. It may involve calling in more favors, and I'm not making any promises."

Benjamin smiled. "It'll work. It has to. Otherwise we'd never be here right now."

By the time Benjamin heard laughter four hours later, he'd run out of things to say. After unsuccessfully trying to pry information from Ananya about the life force disk, they'd spent the time asking everything they could think of, then catching up, and then just sitting there saying nothing. Four hours is a long time to spend with anyone, even a brother you've just met.

Heidi and Iva were arm in arm with Apollo when they crested the hill, but they didn't have the Indian saris on they'd started in. Now they had on golden togas which tied around their necks and showed plenty of leg above the knee with golden sandals that laced around their legs and reached all the way up to those knees. Benjamin tried to force himself to look away, but his eyes kept taking control and roving back over to Iva and Heidi. He couldn't believe girls in ancient Greece had worn stuff so short.

"What was wrong with your other clothes?" Andy asked in a super calm voice though Benjamin was sure he could hear Andy's heart beating. Or maybe it was his own heart; he couldn't be sure.

The girls giggled.

Andy frowned.

"They were soaked," Heidi said. "We fell in the fountain down on the lower level of the city."

"Well, not quite fell in," Iva said. "Apollo pushed us in."

"Really, Apollo, isn't that a bit childish, even for you?" Ananya said. "Pushing young ladies into fountains?"

"Ah, but you see it was all in good fun," Apollo said. "We were enjoying ourselves, making wishes in the fountain when, the next thing I knew, somebody splashed me."

"I didn't do it," Heidi said.

"Neither did I," Iva said.

"As I wasn't sure which of the ladies had splashed me, I pushed them both in. But then I couldn't let them run around in soaking wet saris, now could I?"

Ananya sighed. "No, I suppose not."

"And you just happen to have spare clothes?" Andy said.

Apollo chuckled. "In a city full of female oracles there's never a shortage of clothing. But I must apologize for taking so long. The time somehow just, oh, you know. It just got away from us."

"There's so much to see," Heidi said. "You guys should have come along."

"I don't think we were actually invited," Benjamin said.

Apollo feigned shock. "Oh, my, did I forget to invite you? I've been a rude host, I'm afraid. Would the gentlemen like to go on a tour?"

"And get dunked in the water?" Andy said. "No thanks."

"Shall we eat then?" Whatever his true intentions, Apollo played the perfect host. Too perfect. He was obviously stalling.

"Enough games, Apollo." Ananya no longer smiled at the golden god. "You know why we're here."

Apollo sighed. "Ah, yes. I know why you are here. And the lovely ladies have been so kind in helping me to understand your plight. It seems the five of you have a problem."

Anger flared up inside Benjamin. What had Heidi and Iva told Apollo? Everything? Taking a deep breath, he forced his face to be calm.

"Thanks to the trickery of your grandfather Kronos, your guests are currently confined to this time," Ananya said.

"And is there something wrong with this time?" Apollo motioned around with his head. "You would all be more than welcome to stay forever in my city."

And it was about here that Benjamin noticed Iva dropped her arm from Apollo's. She looked at Heidi, something passed between them, and they both walked over to join their friends.

"I'm afraid that's out of the question," Ananya said before Benjamin could speak.

"But why not?" Apollo asked. "And Cory could happily return to fighting in the war. In fact, Cory, you could work for me. I have a debt to pay. I need someone to assassinate Achilles."

If Cory was shocked by the request he didn't show it. But his face did darken. "I'm no assassin. If you have a vendetta against Achilles, it's yours to pay. I want no part in that war."

"But why? Fighting over women, land, and power. Isn't that what life is all about?" Apollo said.

"Not my life," Cory said. "My destiny lies in the future. And that's where I need to go. With Benjamin."

"So true. So true." Apollo clucked his tongue. "But

 254

what could I possibly do to help?"

"You can allow the Navel of the World to be used to temporally phase all five of them back to their own time." Ananya wasn't asking.

"Yes, I suppose I could do that," Apollo said. "But why should I?"

"Because you care for Kronos even less than I do," Ananya said. "It's his fault they're stuck back here at all."

"I thought it was the fault of Nathan Nyx," Apollo said. "Who as I mentioned before is banned from Delphi."

"Why?" Benjamin asked.

"It has to do with the visit he paid to Delphi just a couple weeks ago," Apollo said.

Benjamin's mouth dropped open. "He came to see you? Why?"

"Why does anyone come to Delphi? To get their future told of course." Apollo sighed. "Yet the quality of oracles I am finding just isn't measuring up. He, like so many others, was disappointed."

"Was it untrue?" Iva said. "I mean, was the oracle wrong?"

"That moment has not come to pass yet," Apollo said.

"So the oracle wasn't wrong." Iva narrowed her eyes. "Why was he disappointed then?"

"I would like the oracles who serve me to be able to give more than one possible future," Apollo said. "Too many times all they deliver is bad news. Aside from not creating many return customers, it causes very bad press outside of Delphi."

"Maybe they are telling all they see," Iva said.

"Perhaps," Apollo said. "But that isn't good enough."

And then Benjamin looked at Iva. She still stared at Apollo, but her eyes had gone from moonstruck to intense. Benjamin felt like at any moment, she'd begin to challenge his control of the oracles. Heidi must've noticed, too, because she shuddered, just a bit, and moved closer to Benjamin.

"Regardless," Apollo went on, "threatening my oracles with death is not acceptable."

"Death?" Heidi said.

Apollo nodded. "Nathan Nyx has a bit of an evil side, it seems."

That was putting it mildly.

"We aren't here to discuss the abilities of oracles," Cory said. "We're here so we can time travel."

"Yes, Apollo," Ananya said. "Cory is right. We are here because they need your help to get home."

"Ananya. Ananya. Why is it I have such a hard time saying no to you?" Apollo brushed something off the golden hair on his arm.

"Because you owe me plenty of favors?" Ananya said.

"Yes, there is that," Apollo said. "But I can't just let them use the Navel and leave Delphi."

"Why not?" Andy asked.

"Why that wouldn't be right." Apollo pretended to look sad. "I would be getting nothing in return."

"And what is it you want in return?" Ananya asked.

But then Apollo's fake sad look vanished. "I want her," he pointed directly at Iva, "to remain here in Delphi."

Benjamin heard Heidi suck in a deep breath. He turned to look at Iva and saw the color drain from her face.

"Out of the question." Andy took a step forward, mov-

ing so Iva was behind him.

"Iva has important responsibilities back in the future," Ananya said. "That's just not possible."

"No way," Benjamin said. Why had he brought Iva back in the first place?

"Yes way," Apollo said.

Heidi stepped forward. "Iva can't stay here. She has things to do."

Apollo pursed his lips together. "Nothing that can't wait. I mean this is time we're talking about here. I'll send her back at some point."

"No," Andy said.

Benjamin glanced at Iva. She'd been silent this whole time.

"Then I'm sorry to say the Navel of the World is off limits." Apollo crossed his arms. "Either Iva Marinina stays with me here in Delphi, or you all stay with me here in Delphi."

"I'll stay." Iva's face had drained of every bit of blood, but she held it steady.

Andy shook his head. "No, you won't."

"I would only ask for, oh, let's say, a year." The golden smile began to creep back onto Apollo's face.

"I'll stay for a year," Iva said again.

Andy whirled on her. "Iva, you are not staying here in Delphi. There's no way."

"Andy, you heard Apollo. If I don't stay, then Benjamin and Cory can't get back. And they need to. That's what's most important. There's no other choice."

"I would of course need you to serve me as an oracle," Apollo said.

 257

Iva nodded. "I know."

"You can't stay," Heidi said. "We need you."

"You need me to stay here," Iva said. "It's the only way."

"Iva, come to your senses," Andy said. "Listen to yourself. You are not living in Delphi for a year to be an oracle."

Benjamin turned to Iva. "You don't have to do this. We could find another way."

"No, Benjamin," Iva said. "There isn't going to be another way."

"Wonderful," Apollo said, clasping his hands together. "Iva Marinina will stay with me here in Delphi for one year, and the sooner the rest of you leave, the better."

Benjamin looked at Iva and saw it in her face. There was to be no changing her mind. She was going to stay.

"So it's all settled?" Apollo beamed. "Then I believe we can head down to the Navel of the World."

"It's not quite settled," Andy said.

Benjamin turned quickly to look at his friend, knowing before Andy opened his mouth, what he was going to say.

"What part of it isn't settled?" Apollo asked. "Iva's made her own decision to stay. What else could there be?"

Andy looked Apollo directly in the eyes. "I'm staying, too."

CHAPTER 30

PHASE OF THE NAVEL

"Absolutely out of the question," Apollo said.

"I stay, or there's no deal," Andy said.

"Andy!" Iva said.

Andy turned to her. "You're not staying alone. That's all there is to it. If you stay, then I stay."

Benjamin watched Apollo closely, unsure what the Greek god would do. Apollo looked at Ananya who raised an eyebrow in return.

"So what's your answer to that, Apollo?" Ananya asked, and Benjamin saw the smile she hid.

Apollo looked from Ananya to Iva to Andy, then back to Ananya. "Delphi is not accustomed to male residents."

Andy crossed his arms. "I guess you'll just have to become accustomed to it."

Apollo glanced once again at Iva. And then Benjamin knew. Apollo would agree. He didn't want to risk losing Iva. "Fine. But there will be no special privileges made for you. And you cannot—and I repeat—cannot interfere with her work as an oracle. Iva will serve for a year as the high oracle of Delphi."

"High oracle!" Iva said. "I'm not qualified for that."

"You are more than qualified to be high oracle of Delphi," Ananya said.

"When will Iva and Andy return to our time?"

259

Benjamin asked.

Apollo waved dismissively. "They will return when they return. You cannot expect me to be bothered with such petty details. And now if there is nothing else—which I certainly hope there is not—I suggest we head down to the Navel of the World."

Apollo took the lead, not waiting for anyone to join him. Ananya joined Iva and Heidi, and Benjamin, Andy, and Cory took up the rear.

"Are you really gonna stay?" Benjamin asked Andy.

Andy let out a half-hearted laugh. "Yeah, I am."

"But you don't know anything about this time," Benjamin said. "What if you get into trouble?"

"How much trouble could I get into?" Andy asked.

"I can't imagine my time is much different than yours," Cory said. "And I think it is a very courageous offer you are making."

"Yeah, I agree," Benjamin said, and he felt a weird sense of pride for Andy well up in him. "I have to admit, I am surprised."

Andy shrugged. "I just don't think Iva should stay back here alone. And if no one else is around, what's to say Apollo doesn't just keep her here forever?"

"That's a good point," Benjamin said. "But with her busy being the high oracle of Delphi, what are you going to do for a year?"

"I haven't quite figured that out yet," Andy said. "But I'd have to guess there'd be plenty to explore, even just inside the city. And with the way all this time travel stuff works and all, we'll probably get back to Lemuria a couple minutes after you guys."

"Yeah, that's true," Benjamin said. "And a year older." Talk about weird.

The crowd was gone when they reached the bottom of the hill. Visiting hours were over and the sun had sunk low on the horizon. The blindfolded oracle still sat upon the dais in front of the Navel of the World.

Apollo walked directly over to her and stopped. "Leave us now."

The girl quickly rose and hurried away from the area. Even with her blindfold intact, she didn't stumble. Benjamin could sense her fear as she walked away. Would Iva feel the same fear in the year to come? Benjamin didn't know what he could do for her now. The decision had been made, and he needed to get back to Lemuria as soon as possible.

"Do you speak to all your oracles so?" Ananya asked Apollo.

"Only those who displease me," Apollo said. "Which seem to be all of them these days." He walked directly to the Navel and placed his hand palm down on top of its intricately carved surface. It sprang to life, light emanating from a seam around the center of the stone. "Quickly now. You three must gather round. If you need to say goodbye, then I suggest you do so immediately. The Navel of the World acts quickly. There will be no time for goodbyes once you touch the stone."

Benjamin turned first to Iva. *"I'm not sure what to say, Iva. Thank you for doing this for me. For me and for Cory."*

"There's nothing to thank me about. You know as well as I do that this was my destiny. You saw me here in Delphi. Remember?"

 261

Benjamin immediately remembered the vision. How could he have forgotten? He *had* seen Iva. He nodded. *"I remember. Just be careful. I don't trust Apollo."*

"I will. I promise. Plus I'll have Andy here to take care of me. I'll see you before you know it."

He next turned to Andy. *"Seriously. Try not to get in trouble. And take good care of Iva."*

"It's the only reason I'm staying," Andy said.

When Benjamin turned to Ananya she smiled at him. *"So we say goodbye again, Benjamin Holt, but once again, not for the last time."* He noticed Chaos, her monkey, still sat on her shoulder.

"When will I see you next?" he asked.

"I cannot say," Ananya said. *"I can only say that it will come to pass."*

"Will you be able to stay here and help Iva and Andy?"

"No. The path they have chosen is their own to tread. And they will do fine. I will, however, come back in a year to make sure Apollo keeps his end of the deal. Try to stay away from Kronos. He is only trouble."

"Thank you for everything," Benjamin said. *"I'll look forward to the next time we meet."*

"As will I, Benjamin Holt."

"Is everyone ready?" Apollo asked, not waiting for a reply. "Place both hands on the Navel as quickly as you can."

Benjamin didn't hesitate; he did exactly as Apollo instructed. The Navel of the World flared out, casting light the entire way across the dais. In his mind, Benjamin felt the presence of Cory and Heidi. And the crunching began. But no sooner had it started that it stopped, and the light

from the Navel began to dim.

Benjamin looked up across the Navel to the new presence he felt there.

"Nathan."

Nathan smiled. "Benjamin. Did you really think you were going somewhere?"

Benjamin pushed his hand down harder on the Navel, hoping that might help, but it remained lifeless.

"I'm telejamming it," Nathan said in answer to Benjamin's unvoiced thoughts.

Near him, Benjamin saw Apollo step forward. "Get out of my city. You are not welcome here."

Nathan turned to Apollo. "This has nothing to do with you. I suggest you stay out of it."

"In my city, everything has to do with me," Apollo said. "You have been banned from ever setting foot in here again."

Nathan laughed. "Your ban won't keep the oracle from dying. How dare she tell me such a future?"

Iva stepped forward. "The oracle wouldn't lie."

Nathan turned his head slowly to look at Iva. Benjamin willed her to silence. Why had she drawn attention to herself?

"Now what do we have here, Apollo? A new oracle?" His eyebrows went up. "A new high oracle?"

Iva glared at him, even as Andy stepped in front of her. "Leave her alone, Nathan." And then Andy lunged for Nathan.

Nathan lifted a hand off the Navel and extended it, trying to push Andy aside with an invisible force. But Andy's telekinetic strength didn't fail him. He stopped in

his tracks and put up his own hand, and there they fought pushing one against the other.

Under his own hands, Benjamin felt the power of the Navel flare. With Nathan distracted, there was a chance he'd take his other hand off it, and Benjamin, Cory, and Heidi could use it to get out of here.

"I think when I'm done killing the oracle who gave me such a horrible future, I'll kill your new high oracle, Apollo. What would you do then?"

Iva. He was talking about killing Iva.

"I would kill you, of course," Apollo said, and energy sizzled through the air.

"*We can't let Nathan stay back here,*" Benjamin said to Cory and Heidi in his mind.

"*I know,*" Cory said.

"*But what can we do?*" Heidi said. "*He's telejamming the power of the Navel.*"

"*But if he stays he'll kill Iva,*" Benjamin said.

"*If there was only some way to stop the telejamming,*" Cory said.

Benjamin wracked his brain, going through everything he'd learned in telejamming this summer. With as strong as Nathan was, there was no way Benjamin would have the power in his own mind to stop it. And then he remembered at the start of summer when he'd joined minds with Iva. In addition to sharing each other's thoughts, their powers had been combined.

"*Yes, Benjamin,*" Heidi said in his mind. She'd apparently followed along with his line of thought. "*I think it will work.*"

"*What?*" Cory said.

"*We combine minds,*" Benjamin said. "*We combine minds and fight Nathan together.*"

Outside of their minds, the electricity cracked in the air. Benjamin felt the battle between Andy and Nathan, between Apollo and Nathan. And felt Nathan's still unwavering hold over the power of the Navel. But if this was going to work, Benjamin needed to force everything else from his mind. To focus only on Cory and Heidi and the hold Nathan's mind had on the Navel.

He reached out with his thoughts and found Heidi and Cory there. And within seconds he'd been able to join with Cory's mind. But as soon as he tried to grab for Heidi's also, the link severed. So he tried again, first grabbing Cory's mind, and then trying for Heidi's also. And again it fell away. The energy from Apollo sizzled around him, but still Nathan fought it.

"*Heidi, I can't form a link with you,*" Benjamin said.

"*I know,*" Heidi said. "*You and Cory will have to do it on your own.*"

"*No,*" Benjamin said. "*We need your telepathic strength.*"

"*No you don't,*" Heidi said.

Cory shook his head. "*We're not strong enough.*"

"*Together you will be,*" Heidi said. "*Remember your twin brothers, Benjamin? Remember the Deimos twins?*"

Immediately Benjamin knew she was right. Derrick and Douglas were off the charts when it came to telekinesis And Helios and Selene Deimos ruled an entire world. He and Cory should be able to defeat Nathan Nyx. He grabbed back hold of Cory's mind and linked with it again. And then using every bit of telekinetic combined forces they could muster, they started pushing on Nathan's mind.

 265

Outside of Benjamin's mind, the battle stopped. Nathan's other hand flew back onto the Navel. Benjamin and Cory pushed harder on his mind, and under their fingers, it sprang to life. The crunching sounds began again, and this time they didn't stop. Then, before Nathan had time to attempt to stop them, Benjamin, Heidi, Cory, and Nathan began to phase away.

Benjamin waited until his shadow disappeared, and then he knew he needed to act. He couldn't leave Nathan behind to kill Iva and possibly Andy also. And he couldn't bring him back and have to fight him anew.

"*Cory...*"

"*I know,*" Cory's thoughts returned to Benjamin.

And within a split second, using their linked minds, Benjamin and Cory telekinetically pushed Nathan's hands from the Navel of the World, right in the middle of the temporal phasing. And Nathan disappeared.

The crunching grew so loud, Benjamin thought his eardrums might burst. But a few seconds later, the noise diminished, and Benjamin felt his body uncrunch and again felt grass beneath his feet. It was dark, and the journey was over. There were here. Somewhere. Somewhen. And Nathan was not with them.

A quick glance around told him exactly where they'd ended up.

"Delphi," Heidi said.

"I can't believe Apollo let this happen." Cory's jaw dropped open as he looked around at the ruins.

"Frankly, after meeting Apollo, I can't either," Benjamin said. "It makes me wonder why."

"That was close," Heidi said.

266

"Too close," Cory said.

Heidi bit her lip. "Do you think Iva will be all right?"

Benjamin squeezed his eyes shut and tried to force the horrible image he had there from his mind. "I hope so. But it's out of our control."

"Andy is there with her," Cory said. "And Apollo will also protect her."

Heidi nodded. "Yeah, I know. But who knows where Nathan ended up."

"Not to mention he could find a way back at any time," Cory said.

Benjamin laughed. "Maybe he got stuck back in the crusades. Maybe he'll get executed."

Heidi smiled. "That would be nice. But pretty unlikely."

"His power was strong," Cory said. "Stronger than Achilles."

"Who is stronger than Achilles?"

Benjamin felt the familiar thoughts in his mind just as he heard the voice. His muscles relaxed as he saw Helios Deimos striding toward them.

"Nathan Nyx. The man who worked for my dad in Wondersky City."

"Do we need to worry about him?" Helios asked.

Quickly, they explained to Helios what had happened with Nathan, both before the trip back and the unfortunate encounters with him in the past. Helios listened the whole time, only interrupting once or twice with a question.

"We need to put out alerts," Helios said. "He does not sound like the type who will let himself be confined." He looked away, outward, and Benjamin felt a solid mind block go up around Helios. Within moments Helios again

 267

returned to the conversation. "Selene is setting up global alerts for Nathan Nyx. And she is notifying your father of the situation."

"My father as in my dad in Virginia?" Benjamin asked. It was a weird question, but after all the confusion Nathan had caused, he just wanted to be sure.

"Yes, your father in Virginia. The father who raised you." Helios turned his attention to Cory. "I see you are a couple members short but have gained a new ally along the way."

With all three of them filling in the gaps, Helios learned the story of the retrieval of Cory, the trip to Delphi, and the ensuing deal made with Apollo there.

"So he's causing trouble even three thousand years ago."

Heidi sighed and her eyes got a glazy look. "He seemed so nice at first."

"That's because he wanted something," Helios said. "He must have been able to sense Iva's telegnostic abilities miles away. Even years away."

"He said Iva was going to be the high oracle of Delphi," Heidi said.

"And I believe she will be remembered as one of the best," Helios said. "History would confirm that a female of unknown origin sat upon the high seat in Delphi years ago and prophesied for all the world to hear."

"You mean we can read about Iva in history?" Benjamin knew as soon as he told Gary, Gary would run to the nearest library to research it.

Helios nodded. "But as much as I would enjoy being able to stay and catch up, I'm afraid I must be on with my business."

"And we probably should get back to school," Benjamin said, wondering at the same time he said it if Cory would go to school; he was just so old.

"Yes, but only the two of you," Helios said, pointing at Benjamin and Heidi.

Benjamin glanced over at his new-found brother. "I figured Cory could just come back with me."

"I have other plans for Cory," Helios said. "Though in the future your combined powers may be required, for now Cory will have other obligations. Obligations which do not involve learning telekinesis at summer school."

Benjamin's heart started to pound. "But we just met. I thought we could spend a little time getting to know each other."

"I understand," Helios said. "Though it is not to be. You, too, Benjamin, have other duties."

Benjamin shook his head. What was Helios thinking? It wasn't fair that Cory would be taken away so soon. "Where will Cory be going?"

"A secret assignment," Helios said. "I'm afraid I cannot share the nature of the assignment with even you."

Apparently the secret assignment thing surprised Cory. "What will I do? I'm from three thousand years ago."

"Yeah. That's a good point," Benjamin said. "A lot of things have changed in three thousand years."

"And many things have remained the same," Helios said. "You will do just fine, Cory. But to be safe, you'll be working with someone else."

"Who?" Benjamin asked.

Helios shook his head. "Sorry, Benjamin. That's

classified information."

"When will Benjamin and I see each other next?" Cory asked.

"I have no idea." Helios took a few steps back, away from Benjamin, Heidi, and Cory. "And now, Cory, if you will please join me."

Cory looked at Benjamin, and Benjamin could see the sense of loss in his eyes. But he noticed those same eyes held no fear. Cory's eyes were those of a trained warrior. Trained his whole life. Cory would take the assignment ahead of him and tackle it with all that he could. Benjamin fought against the lump he felt in his throat and forced a smile onto his face.

"Come back safely, okay?" Benjamin said.

"I'll come back safely, and I'll come back soon," Cory said. "You just find our other brother and be waiting for me." He embraced Benjamin first and then turned to Heidi. "I'm glad you didn't become a concubine for Achilles."

Heidi laughed. "Me too."

Cory moved away from Heidi and Benjamin, stepping over to where Helios waited. And then Helios grabbed Cory's wrist, and they teleported away.

 270

CHAPTER 31

AMBROSIA IS STILL GROSS

A whole minute went by before Benjamin or Heidi said anything. Benjamin sank to the ground, sitting on a ruined column. Heidi sat beside him and intertwined her hand with his. And even with all that had happened, with the Trojan War, and Delphi, and Cory being gone, it felt so right sitting there in the dark, listening to the world around them. Benjamin looked down at his hand, realizing for the first time that Heidi had grabbed it. She looked down at it, too, and gave it a squeeze.

And then, finally, Heidi broke the silence. "It's pretty quiet around here at night."

"Yeah, pretty quiet," Benjamin said.

"Do you think we'll see him again soon?" she asked.

"Yeah, I do," Benjamin said. "I mean, I hope so."

"I'm sorry he's gone."

"I am, too," Benjamin said. "But whatever it is Helios has planned for him must be important for Cory to be taken away so suddenly."

Heidi shrugged. "Maybe Helios didn't want Cory to get too comfortable in his new surroundings."

"Maybe not," Benjamin said.

They sat longer, saying nothing. Again Heidi broke the silence.

"So I guess that just leaves you and me."

271

"Yeah, you and me," Benjamin said, unsure what she expected him to say.

"And of course Gary," Heidi said.

"Oh, Gary! Wow, I forgot." Benjamin jumped up, shaking his head, and letting go of her hand. "We better get back. Do you want to try to teleport?"

Heidi stood up and laughed. "No, not yet. Let's just get back to Lemuria, through the barrier shield. Maybe tomorrow I can give it a whirl."

"Okay then." Benjamin moved close to Heidi and took her hand in his without saying a word. She looked at him, and he smiled back. And then they teleported away from Delphi.

The second they arrived at the park, Benjamin stumbled and fell to the ground.

"No more time traveling for you." Aurora rushed over and knelt beside him.

"I'm fine." He attempted to wave her off. "It's just the teleportation and everything I think."

"Whatever it is, that's the last of it." Aurora crammed some ambrosia at him.

He involuntarily shuddered, but then took a big swallow, almost gagging on a couple chunks that stuck in his throat. But he forced them down. Yuck! It was worse than it had been two weeks ago.

"Have you guys been waiting here the whole time?" Heidi asked.

"Only for the last few hours." Gary looked around the dark grassy area. "Where are Andy and Iva?"

"And where is your brother?" Aurora asked. "Didn't

you find him?"

Benjamin stood up and moved to a nearby bench. Guiding himself to a sitting position, he took his time waiting for the ambrosia to clear his head. "No, we found him. And we got him back safely."

"So where is he?" Gary asked.

"Helios took him in Delphi," Benjamin said.

"Delphi? What were you doing there?" Aurora asked.

"Finding a way to travel back," Heidi said.

"So where are Andy and Iva?" Gary asked.

"Still back in Delphi," Heidi said. "It was part of the deal Apollo made with us so we could use the Navel of the World."

"Apollo!" Aurora almost spat the name. "Does my dad have stories to tell about him."

"What kind of deal?" Gary said.

"He only let us use the Navel of the World—which is, by the way, an incredibly strong telemagnifier—if Iva agreed to stay for a year," Benjamin said.

"Serving as high oracle of Delphi," Heidi added.

"Ugh! Wait until my dad hears about this," Aurora said. "He's gonna be furious."

"You can't tell him," Benjamin said.

"I know," Aurora said. "But he'll find out anyway. My dad finds out everything to do with temporal phasing. Remember he's an agent for DOPOT."

Benjamin tried to remember what that stood for, but it hurt his head just to think about it.

"So when are they getting back?" Gary asked. "I mean shouldn't they be arriving any time?"

"Apollo wouldn't specify a time," Heidi said.

"It could be now. It could be four days from now," Aurora said. "With Apollo, there are no guarantees."

"So I guess we just wait," Benjamin said.

"Wait and get ready for our ability tests," Gary added.

But the following day no one felt like practicing. Heidi, Benjamin, and Gary sat around a table in the dining hall eating breakfast.

"I don't care how I do on my tests," Heidi said. "Not even telekinesis."

"Yeah, me neither," Gary said.

"But that is precisely the time when you need to practice the hardest," Suneeta said, walking over to their table with Julie in tow. "You already spent yesterday goofing around."

"Not really goofing around," Benjamin said.

"Then why did you lock the doors to the temple when you entered?" Suneeta asked.

"We didn't lock the doors. It was just an accident," Heidi said.

Julie leaned in close so no one else would hear. "Hey, you guys. Can we just forget the fact that you saw me in India yesterday?" She motioned with her head over to the table where Ryan and Jonathan sat. "I don't want you-know-who to find out."

Suneeta put on her best disgusted look. "Must we call him you-know-who? It is not like it is a secret."

"Shhhh!" Julie said.

"Julie, your secret is safe with us," Benjamin looked to Heidi. "Right, Heidi?"

"Right."

 274

"And you'll pass it on to Iva and Andy when you see them. Right?" Julie's eyes were as wide as apples.

"Where are Iva and Andy anyway?" Suneeta asked.

"Iva wanted to get some extra telegnostic practice in," Heidi said quickly which was a totally impressive non-lie.

"You all should learn from her example. By the way, have you seen Magic Pan? I can't find him anywhere." Suneeta turned and left, trailed by Julie.

"So what are we going to do today instead of practicing?" Heidi asked.

"Who cares?" Jack said, appearing on the table. "Let's just get out and walk around the city a little." He made a show out of walking on the table, but stopped suddenly. "Hey. Where are Andy and Iva?"

"Popular question," Gary said.

"Yeah, why don't we tell you the whole story once we get outside," Benjamin said.

They started relaying the story to Jack, but he stopped them. "Okay, okay, I can see it in your mind. So they're stuck in Delphi. Right?"

"Hopefully not stuck," Heidi said. "We're expecting them any minute."

"I wouldn't hold my breath if I were you," Jack said. "It could be weeks or even months."

"Great," Benjamin said. "The outlook just keeps getting better and better."

"So what's your brother like?" Jack asked. "Does he look like you? Does he act like you?"

"I guess he kind of looks like me except older. As for how he acts..." Benjamin shrugged. "Kind of like an adult."

 275

"That's because he is," Heidi said. "So what are we going to do today?"

"Let's just wander around the city," Benjamin said.

They walked around for a couple hours, but somehow managed to pass the park four times. "Why do we keep ending up back here?" Jack asked.

"I don't know," Benjamin said. "I guess I keep thinking that Andy and Iva might show up."

"So what kind of assignment did Helios take Cory away for?" Jack asked.

"He wouldn't say," Heidi said. "I tried to pick it from his mind, but I think he can put up stronger mind blocks than even you."

"Not better than me," Jack said.

"I don't know," Heidi said. "It was pretty strong."

"No matter how hard any of you telegens try, you can't have a stronger mind block than even the weakest Nogical," Jack said. "It all comes down to genetics. Right, Gary?"

"It's true," Gary said. "The telenergetic strength in Nogical DNA is off the scales. We learned about it in Genetic Engineering."

"So I have a question," Heidi said. "Why was Apollo roaming free three thousand years ago? I thought all Atlantian gods were rounded up and imprisoned within the barrier shield like ten thousand years ago or something." ·

"Yeah, that's true," Jack said. "But you're forgetting about the forbidden doors."

"Of course," Heidi said. "Like the one we saw in Delphi."

"Right," Jack said. "Lemuria closes them whenever

they're found, but they turn up everywhere."

"Which lets lots of false gods come into the world," Gary said.

Jack nodded.

"So there are still more forbidden doorways out there?" Heidi said.

Jack nodded. "Lots."

"Wow. Hard to believe that Lemuria is such an advanced civilization, but things still manage to slip by it," Benjamin said.

"You have to remember Atlantis is equally advanced," Jack said. "So it all kind of balances out."

CHAPTER 32

THE FUTURE IS AHEAD.
THE PAST IS BEHIND.

It wasn't the next day, or even the day after that Iva and Andy finally came back. It was, in fact, the following Saturday, well after the ability tests were over. With Jack's encouragement, Benjamin managed to drag himself through.

"So what do you think will happen to Iva and Andy?" Benjamin asked. "Are they gonna flunk everything?"

Heidi shook her head. "I checked with Proteus. They'll advance one level in each subject."

"You mean if I didn't even go to these tests I would have done the exact same?" Gary asked.

"You only got one level in each subject?" Benjamin said. "Me, too."

"Hey, me three," Heidi said. "I'm just happy to get out of level two telekinesis."

"Do you think we really have to keep taking telekinesis?" Gary asked.

"Of course you do." Benjamin's stomach growled. "Anyone else ready for lunch?"

They headed to the dining hall, but when they walked in, Benjamin felt dread in the pit of his empty stomach.

"What happened to the menus?" he asked. "Please, just please, tell me Leena Teasag isn't working."

278

"I'm afraid it's true," Magic Pan said, already ahead of them in line. "This morning after breakfast, the menu system again went off line."

"How very coincidental," Heidi said.

"Yeah, last day of school and we have to eat strained spinach," Gary added.

"I am sure I'll be able to figure out the problem by next year," Magic said.

"Yes, I'm sure you will," Benjamin said, looking at Heidi.

She smirked and nodded her head, but said nothing.

They sat at a table near the back—just the three of them. Benjamin looked out across the cafeteria. "You think he's going to get that kind of attention once he gets back to Russia?" He motioned toward Nick Konstantin who, as always, was surrounded by a throng of girls.

"Probably," Heidi said. "There's just something special about Nick."

Benjamin laughed. "Don't let Andy hear you say that."

But Heidi didn't hear his reply. She'd stopped eating and dropped her fork. Standing up, she stared across the cafeteria to the door. Benjamin followed her gaze.

Iva and Andy stood at the entryway, holding hands. Benjamin rubbed his eyes to make sure. Yes, they were holding hands. Slowly, the entire dining hall grew silent and stared at the couple.

They did look older. Andy's hair was long, reaching well past his neck. And his shoulders, once about the same size as Benjamin's, looked about twice as wide. And Iva looked years more mature—not just the one year she'd been gone. Her calm eyes looked through the students.

Benjamin heard a large clattering sound and turned

to see Ryan Jordan staring wide eyed at Iva. His plate was in pieces at his feet. Julie glared at Iva and grabbed Ryan's arm like she thought it would run away. Jonathan was also watching Iva, but it wasn't with the same puppy-dog face as Ryan. He looked annoyed. But then, why shouldn't he be? His number one competitor in telegnosis had just come back from nowhere.

All at once, Andy must have noticed the entire dining hall watching them. He looked down at his left hand and quickly released Iva's own hand from his. Benjamin felt Iva's hurt through the Alliance bond. Was Andy stupid? Still? Even after a year alone with Iva?

Iva spotted them and started walking over, ignoring the rest of the tables, and Andy followed close behind. Heidi didn't wait for Iva to reach the table. She ran over to her friend and hugged her. "What took you guys so long?"

"We were starting to think you'd never come back," Benjamin said.

"Sometimes it felt like the year would never be over," Andy said. "But Apollo was good for his word, with a little encouragement from Ananya, of course."

Heidi bit her lip. "So how was it? Was it horrible?"

"No, it wasn't horrible," Iva said. "I would never want to stay there, but I'm glad I've had the experience." She laughed. "And I'm glad the experience is behind me."

"You guys missed your ability tests," Gary said. "We got our results this morning."

"I don't feel like I missed any kind of testing," Iva said. "I've been tested constantly for the last year. Working for Apollo is challenging, to say the least."

"Well, your time with Apollo is behind you," Heidi

said. "That's what's important."

"Let's hope," Iva said.

"So what did we miss?" Andy asked.

"Who cares," Heidi said. "We want to hear all about Delphi."

"Not yet," Iva said. "We just got back, and I'm tired. And I'm not quite ready to talk about it."

Benjamin noticed Iva and Andy still remained close, even though they weren't holding hands. What had happened for the last year in Delphi? Were Andy and Iva dating? He'd make sure to ask Andy about it once they returned to Virginia tomorrow morning.

"Ivana?"

They all turned in the direction of the speaker. Nick Konstantin stood a few feet away.

"Hi, Nick." Iva smiled at him.

He beamed back in return. "Iva, where 'ave you been? I 'ave missed you more than words describe."

"You didn't look like you missed her." Andy pretty much snarled his reply. "How'd you disentangle yourself from all those girls?"

"Ah, the girls." Nick waved his hand dismissively. "They are but diversion from Iva, of course."

"Of course they are," Andy said.

Iva ignored Andy. "I'm fine, Nick. I just had to go on a trip. But now I'm back, and everything's normal again."

Nick clapped his hands together in front of him. "I am so 'appy to 'ear that. Would I be asking too much if I requested permission to keep in touch with you over the next year?"

Okay, Benjamin had to give Nick some credit. That

281

took nerve. He wasn't going to give up on Iva so easily.

"Yes," Andy said. "It would be asking too much."

"Andy!" Iva said. "That's rude. That would be fine, Nick. I'd love to hear from you."

"Can I keep in touch with you too, Iva?" Andy asked.

Iva cast him a glance that would have flash-frozen water.

"Then I shall look forward to it." Nick delicately lifted her hand to his mouth and kissed the back of it.

Iva smiled in return.

Andy stared at her like she'd lost her mind. "You're not seriously going to talk to him over the year, are you?" he asked once Nick had walked away.

"Why not?" Iva said. "He just wants to be my friend."

"Friend! Give me a break. He wants to be your boy-friend."

"Don't act so jealous, Andy," Iva said.

"I'm not jealous. I just think it's ridiculous that you would keep in touch with him," Andy said.

"And why shouldn't I?" Iva asked. "You're the one that obviously doesn't want anyone to see us holding hands."

"I don't care if anyone sees us," Andy said.

"They why'd you let go of my hand?" Iva asked.

"I didn't."

"Yes. You did."

"Hey, you guys. I hate to break this up, but why don't we talk about this later," Benjamin said. "People are staring."

Whatever conversation Andy and Iva had later, it didn't include Benjamin. And he decided against asking Andy about it. Instead, he packed his bags and went to sleep, thinking about his trip home.

The atrium was packed when they arrived after breakfast.

"I hope you have a wonderful year," Proteus said. "And we'll see you back here again next summer. Make sure you plan out your schedules before you get back."

"I planned mine out last night," Gary said.

"That figures," Andy said.

Benjamin looked around. "Hey, where's Heidi?"

Andy didn't even hesitate. "Over there." He pointed across the atrium. Heidi rested against a column, talking with Josh. Benjamin watched as Josh leaned over and kissed her on the lips before walking away. Heidi placed her hand to her mouth—just for a second—and her hair turned platinum blond.

"You think they'll be talking on the telecom this coming year?" Andy asked.

"Who?" Benjamin asked, pretending he hadn't seen. Had Josh really just kissed Heidi?

"Yeah, whatever dude," Andy said. "You can act all you want. But now you have something to think about for the whole year."

"I'll be busy thinking about Cory and whatever mission Helios sent him on." Benjamin tried to shove the image of Josh kissing Heidi out of his mind. "Plus I need to figure out how to find my other brother."

Gary perked up. "I've been doing a lot of research, and I have some fantastic ideas."

"Great! Let's make sure we get together," Benjamin said.

"Are you guys making plans without us?" Heidi asked.

"It seemed like you were already making plans of your own," Benjamin said before he could stop himself. Now why had he gone and said that?

Heidi rolled her eyes, but didn't deny it. "Just make

sure to include me."

"I learned some pretty good telegnostic techniques I think could help," Iva said. "How about I give you a call in a couple weeks, and we can talk about it."

Benjamin nodded his reply. He was next in line for the teleporter, and with each step, he was more ready to get home. Derrick and Douglas would be waiting to levitate cars with him, and Becca could probably already sense his impending arrival.

"I think we'll be able to get together a lot this year," Benjamin said. "After the fiasco with Nathan Nyx, I don't think my dad will make me work in his office again."

Andy laughed. "Good thing. I couldn't take a repeat of that."

"Did they find Nathan yet?" Heidi asked.

"No," Benjamin said. "I talked with Helios early this morning, and he said there was still no sign of him."

"I guess I don't have to tell you to be careful," Iva said. "Nathan is dangerous and not out of our futures."

Iva—always the bearer of good news.

"Okay," Benjamin said. "I'll be waiting for your call."

"Better yet, let's plan on meeting somewhere fun," Heidi said. "How about Egypt?"

"Sounds like a plan," Benjamin said.

"Let's meet by the Sphinx," Gary said.

"Egypt? Two weeks? Sounds great," Benjamin said.

"It's your turn, Benjamin Holt," the old man with the colossal ears operating the teleporter announced. "Step right up. Your future awaits you."

Benjamin laughed. "I hope it's only my future that awaits me this year."

Acknowledgements

To Riley for giving me the gift of time to write and for convincing me to buy a new computer.

To Zachary for inventing the Nogical. Keep the ideas coming! And make sure you tell me first.

To Lola for reminding me to never give up...and for convincing me I can hold a scorpion!

To The Far Flung Writers, the most amazing critique group in the world...you guys rock!

To The Class of 2k8 for an amazing debut year.

To the awesome Austin writing community...long live the kumquat!

To the blogging world...yes, it is possible to have true friends via the Internet.

To Madeline for seeing the potential in me and *The Emerald Tablet*.

To my parents and sister for helping make me the person I am today!

To my extended family and friends who all supported me beyond belief. I owe you guys big time!

In fact, I'm pretty sure I owe everyone big time. I couldn't have done it without you all.

Thank you!

5-12-12